G&B Detective Agency
Where the Hell is Angie?

By R. L. Link

A Max Mosbey and Skip Murray
G&B Detective Agency Novel

G&B Detective Agency
Where the Hell is Angie?

ISBN-13: 978-1724630360
ISBN-10: 1724630369

G&B Detective Agency
Where the Hell is Angie?

Prologue

In one corner of the briefing room a plainclothes officer used a plastic ruler to push a transceiver, a microphone and an antenna down into the cast that the young man wore on his leg. Beside the officer, another sat conferring with the young man, giving him instructions. A uniformed sergeant walked up to the podium and addressed the others in the room who were sitting around looking bored. A patrol lieutenant was leaning on the back wall next to the door that stood open.

"Gentlemen," the sergeant addressed them. "And lady," he continued. "Listen up. Okay, as soon as Officer Mosbey gets Charles wired for sound, I'll have him come up here and give you the rundown on what's going down tonight. Officers Mosbey and Murray will be heading up this operation, so pay attention."

The sergeant looked over at Max, who was giving the cast one last inspection.

"Before he gets up here," the sergeant went back to addressing the room, "this is a joint operation with the County Attorney's Office, the Sheriff's Office, the DCI and the Ames Police Department's Special Operations Unit. I got two uniforms from Special Ops working this, and I got two on-duty officers. We want this all to go down quick and smooth so that my people can get back on the street."

Max had walked up beside the sergeant and was looking at the officers and agents sitting in the room. Many of them were there for no other reason than to represent their agencies. Others were critical to the success of the operation. The sergeant introduced Max and stepped aside. Max took his place behind the podium.

"Okay, I'll try to make this briefing brief," Max began. "Over there is Charles, county attorney's office intern and college football player, third string, I believe. You can easily identify him by the cast on his leg from an unfortunate accident that he suffered on the practice field a few weeks ago."

Everyone laughed at Charles's expense.

"Okay," Max addressed them again. "This will be a basic prostitution bust. County attorney's office got the information during a plea bargaining deal that there is a prostitution ring being run in the two-story house at Cherry and Lincolnway."

Everybody laughed again at the mention of the whore house on Cherry Street.

"So we are going to take Charles over there to Cherry Street because he is a little depressed about being out for the season. Not that he was playing much anyways. But Charles needs a little cheering up."

Everyone laughed again. Max was feeling like he was on a roll. He was quite the comedian.

"These girls have been around the block. They've been busted before, and they are going to make sure that no one coming through the door is wired. As you all know, or maybe some of you don't know, in these operations the girls like to take the 'client,'" Max made air quotes with his fingers, "into a room and get him stripped down before they start talking money. At the very least, they will feel him up pretty good before they commit themselves. So we are going to have to get a little creative tonight. What we are going to do is that two of us are going in, Charles and his Uncle Bob." Max waited a moment. "That's me, I'm Uncle Bob. Uncle Bob is treating

Charles to a blowjob, and he is the man with the money. That way the girls are going to have to talk money right up front with Uncle Bob. Charles isn't going anywhere until Uncle Bob has a deal. So that is the setup. Any questions on what's going on here?"

Max waited for a moment, but no one said anything.

"Charles and I will be inside. Skip and Deputy Carlisle will be in the van parked across the street behind that old restaurant, on the recorder and listening in." Max was absently pointing toward a satellite map projected on a screen behind him. "Sarah and Frank," Max nodded toward a female and a male officer sitting on one side of the room. "You guys will be staged in an unmarked car down at the south end of Cherry Street. The rest of you will be staged in the UPS parking lot east of there. The code will be "we're good to go." When she takes Charles back in the room and asks him to drop 'em, he is going to give the code. If he forgets the code, he is going to scream, "Help."

They all laughed again.

"When Skip and Carlisle get the word, they will send the signal and everyone will converge on the front door. I don't know if they will lock it when we go in or not. A lot of times they do. I'm going to try to keep it unlocked, but we will have to see. But uniformed officers, just try the knob before you decide to hit it with the battering ram, please. Last thing we want is the door to come flying off the hinges and hurting someone. Also, uniformed officers, don't come in screaming and yelling. We're not trained by TV here, this is not *Cops*. Come in, order everyone on the ground, and leave it at that. Get the front room secured fast and keep moving, because you two need to take control of any male suspects on the premises. There will be at least two pimps in there, maybe more, and we probably won't know where they are at. The girls probably won't be a problem. I should be able to control them and Skip will come in after the uniforms to assist me. The pimps could be another matter. There will be two more uniforms in the alley covering the back door in case anyone tries to go out that way. They are shift units, so we don't want to tie them up any longer than we have to."

Max looked toward the lieutenant, hoping that he was convinced that his two officers would be back on the street in no time. The lieutenant stood expressionless. Max looked around the room at the faces looking back at him.

"That's it," Max said. "We cannot even imagine or plan for everything that could happen. Stay aware of your surroundings. Communicate, don't yell. This should be pretty routine, and let's hope that it is. One other thing," Max continued. "The tape runs from the minute Charles and I walk out of here until the whole thing is over. So remember that. Everything that goes down is on tape."

Max paused again. "These are prostitutes," he held up his hand. "They're selling sex. That's it. Take it easy on the prostitutes. They don't get slammed around, they don't get guns waved in their faces. Let's try to do this with as little theatrics as possible."

No one responded. "Let's do it," Skip said from his chair where he had been listening to Max speak.

Max and Charles parked a few blocks away to give the rest of the circus enough time to get set up. When Max heard a couple of clicks over the portable radio that sat on the floorboards beneath his feet, he and Charles started moving again. Max reached down and clicked the transmission button on the radio twice.

"We don't want any radio traffic if we can help it." Max was making small talk with Charles, who was starting to fidget. "We just use clicks. We don't want anyone with a scanner getting wind of what we're doing."

Max parked in front of the house at Cherry and Lincolnway and turned to Charles. "You good to go?"

"I think so." Charles took a deep breath.

"Listen, this is going to be easy for you," Max reassured him again. "Just like we talked about. You're just some dumb kid. That shouldn't be too hard for you, right? Just act natural. I'll do all the talking; you just stand there and grin like you're about to get a blowjob. All you got to do is say 'we're good to go,' or 'help.' Either one will do, but you need to make that call. Let her go as far as you can without doing the dirty. It is up to you when you give the signal."

Max got out of the car. Charles followed. The two walked up to the front door and knocked. A young buxom blonde woman in a pink negligee opened the door enough to peek out. When she saw the two men standing expectantly on the front stoop, she smiled and opened the door to let them pass.

"How are you boys tonight?" she asked.

'Doin' good, doin' good," Max bellowed. "You open for business? I got me a young man here that needs a little lovin.'"

"That we are," the young woman replied. "So what do you two have in mind for tonight?" The woman slid up against Max and started running her hands up and down his chest, the sides of his body and around his waist.

"Well, lookie here," Max said in a low tone, winking at the woman, letting her search his body for a wire. "This here is my nephew, Chuck. He hurt himself playing football." Max pointed toward Charles's cast. Another woman dressed in a negligee walked into the room. She was taller and thinner than the first woman, with darker hair. She sidled up to Charles, smiled up at him and started running her hands over his body. Charles wiggled nervously.

"Here's the deal," Max continued. "Charles hurt himself playing college football and his fancy cheerleader girlfriend doesn't want to hop in the sack with him, because she says his cast there bruises her legs. And she's too damned good to give him a blowjob, so he's startin' to get a little clogged up." Max grinned at the two girls. "So, one of you ladies want to clean his pipes?"

"I think that we can take care of that for Chuck," the first woman remarked.

"So what's it gonna cost ol' Uncle Bob to get Chuck a blowjob?" Max looked over at Charles, who had calmed down a bit and was standing with a wide unnatural grin on his face. "That's what you want, right? Ain't that what you was saying on the way over here, you wanted a blowjob?"

Charles nodded and turned his grin toward the skinny girl who was standing next to him with her arm around his waist.

The first girl, who had been the one talking so far, looked over at the other girl, who shrugged her shoulders. "So we talking about both of you? Because we can give you a deal."

"What's your name, honey?" Max asked.

"I'm Peaches, and she's Cream," the girl replied, tipping her head toward the other girl.

"Well, Peaches," Max went on. "I'm a happily married man, but Chuck here isn't. He isn't happy or married," Max added. "So I think just him is fine."

Peaches smiled at Max. "You got a hundred bucks? And he can take his pick of either of us."

Max took out his billfold and fished a crisp hundred-dollar bill out of it. "I keep this in there just for emergencies." Max handed it to Peaches.

She looked over at Charles. "Which one of us gets the honors? You two look like you're already getting to know each other," she smiled.

The other girl was already pulling Charles toward the hall. Charles followed along, limping on the cast. Max plopped down on the couch. Peaches walked over and locked the door, then sat down on the couch beside him, snuggling up close, putting her head on his shoulder and her hand on his knee.

"Why did you lock the door?" Max asked her, feigning concern. "I wish you wouldn't lock it. That makes me nervous."

"Don't worry, I just don't want anyone coming in and disturbing us," she said. "What do you think, Uncle Bob? Don't you think you could use a little loving?" She moved her hand up his leg.

"Oh, I don't think so," Max let her keep moving her hand. "You are one tempting young lady, but you know, I better not."

Peaches stopped her hand just shy of his crotch. "You sure, Bob? We could make deal: Chucky for a hundred bucks and you get one for half price?"

Max had quit listening to Peaches and was concentrating on the hallway, listening to see if he could hear what was going on in the back bedroom. He thought it was about time for Charles to give the code.

"What's wrong, honey?" Peaches was asking him. "What are you thinking about? Don't worry about Chuck, he is in good hands."

Max was looking at the door, expecting the officers outside to come through it at any moment.

"You want me to unlock the door?" Peaches asked as she got to her feet. "If it is bothering you that much, I can unlock it for you."

"No," Max said, taking her hand. "Stay away from the door."

Peaches turned to Max with a questioning look.

"Come and sit down," Max said.

Just as Peaches turned back toward the door, it burst open, pieces of splintered door frame flying across the room. Peaches jumped back as Max jumped up off the couch. As Peaches fell backwards and Max caught her in his arms, the two uniformed officers came through the door. Skip was standing just outside the door with a battering ram in his hands.

"Get down on the ground and keep your hands out where we can see them," Sarah, the female officer, ordered Peaches.

Peaches turned to Max with a confused look on her face.

"On the ground," a second officer ordered.

Peaches glanced over at Max with an apologetic look. "Just do what they tell you, it will be okay."

"I know it will be okay," Max reassured her as she was getting down on the floor, motioning him to do the same. It still hadn't registered with her that Max was with them.

Skip came into the room and looked toward the hall. "You know which room Charles is in?" he asked Max as he handed him his Smith and Wesson two-inch thirty-eight special and his badge.

"Nope," Max replied. "Back there somewhere."

Skip moved toward the hallway. Sarah and the other officer had already gone that direction toward a ruckus that could be heard. Max clipped his badge on his belt and sat back down on the couch, his pistol in his hand. He looked down at Peaches on the floor then at the gun in his hand. "What the heck am I supposed to do with this?" He smiled at her. Peaches buried her face in the dirty carpet and began to sob.

Max was standing on the porch with Sarah and Peaches. Sarah was new to Special Ops. She was good, though, and she caught on quickly. Peaches had quit crying and was standing next to the two police officers with her hands cuffed behind her back. Milton pulled up on the street in front of the house. Max took Peaches by the arm and helped her down the steps to the sidewalk. "Careful," he cautioned her. "Don't fall."

Peaches didn't answer.

"Hey, Milton, how's it goin'?" Max said.

"Looks like everything went smoothly," Milton commented. "I was stuck out back."

"Went well," Max agreed. "Milton, this is Peaches; Peaches, this is Milton. He's gonna give you a lift down to the station." Max put Peaches into the back seat of Milton's car. "We're going to book you on two counts of soliciting for prostitution. You'll see the judge in the morning if you don't make bail."

"What happened to Yarnez and Garth?" Peaches asked.

"That the guys in the back?" Max asked, knowing that they were. "They got arrested, too," Max informed her. "Everybody got arrested. They're already down at the station."

"I won't make bail, then," Peaches said in a resigned tone.

"You'll be okay," Max reassured her. "You'll get to talk to the judge in the morning and maybe he will let you go on your own recog. It will all work out eventually." Max shut the door and slapped the top of the car. Milton pulled away.

"You think that she'll get out on her own recog?" Sarah asked absently.

"No, I don't think she will," Max replied. "I just said that."

Chapter 1

Monday

Max drove into the parking lot at the G&B Detective Agency and parked his car. Monica's car was already there, parked in her reserved space directly in front of the door. Max could see her daughter Essie peering out the window of the agency at him while he got out of the car, licking the condensation that had collected on the cold glass, then smearing it with her hands. Max started to turn toward the street and walk across to Filo's Coffee Shop to get his morning cup of joe, but then turned back for no reason and walked into the office building instead.

"Hey there, Essie," Max exclaimed. "Are you washing the windows for us?"

Essie hugged his leg. He reached down and tousled her hair.

"What are you up to so early today?" Max asked Monica. "I thought this was spring break. Why aren't you home sleeping in?"

"I'm waiting for you and Skip," Monica answered with a bit of urgency in her voice. "I got something that I need to run by you two."

"Where is Skip?" Max asked. Skip was usually in the office early.

"I don't know," Monica replied with the same urgency. "Leave it to Skip to be late the one day that I need to talk to you two about something."

"Want to tell me about it, or do we want to wait for Skip?" Max asked.

"Well, I'd rather just wait until you are both here. I don't want to go over it twice, and it might not be anything, anyway," she answered.

Max didn't reply. Essie was still hanging on to his leg, wiping her nose on his pant leg. "Why do kids do that?" Max laughed.

"They're just gross," Monica remarked. "She's taken to licking everything for some reason I don't know."

"Hey, wanna go over to Filo's with me and I'll get you a blueberry muffin?" Max asked Essie.

"Can I have chocolate?" Essie replied.

"Sure," said Max, "You can have whatever you want. You're buying." Max turned to Monica. "I'll take her across the street and I'll keep an eye out for Skip." Monica just nodded her head and busied herself with some mail on her desk.

Max took Essie's coat from one of the chairs across from Monica's desk that served as the waiting area and helped Essie into it, then he took her hand and led her out the door. She tried to shake loose and run, but Max held on.

"Slow down, little lady," Max said to her as she led the way.

At the street Max stopped and instructed Essie to look both ways before crossing. When she had done so, he let her pull him across the street and into the Filo's parking lot.

"Heads up," he instructed Essie. "First rule of survival, be aware of your surroundings. Don't be looking down at the ground for pennies. You'll get run over."

He and Essie did an exaggerated scan of the parking lot while they walked across it. It was something that they did every time that Max took Essie to Filo's.

Once inside, Max ordered his morning cup of coffee, a hot chocolate for Essie, and she decided that she wanted a chocolate chip cookie for breakfast instead of a muffin. Max got a blueberry muffin for himself. The two sat down by the window. It didn't take the barista more than a few minutes to bring the order to their table.

"Thanks," Max said as the barista put the plates and mugs that he had juggled across the floor on the table in front of Essie and Max. "So how's business been? Got any plans for spring break?"

"Just working," the barista answered. "It's slow in here, you know, with all the students gone. I'm just trying to get in some hours and make a little money for next semester."

"Gonna work through the summer?" Max asked.

"Planning on it."

A customer came through the door, and the barista turned and made his way back to the counter. Max looked out the window and saw Skip's car pull into the parking lot and park next to his.

"Eat up," Max said to Essie. "We need to get back over to the office and see what your mommy is up to."

Essie was slow to eat her cookie and drink her hot chocolate. Max downed his muffin and coffee in short order.

"Let's eat up," he urged her. Essie was fiddling around with a ribbon sewn to her blouse and wasn't listening to Max. "Here, honey," Max took her cookie and put it in a napkin. "Let's just take your cookie with us and go back to the office." Essie looked up. Max was getting out of his chair and pulling Essie's coat off the back of hers.

"Come on," he said. "Get your arms in here and we'll go back to the office."

Essie climbed off the chair and did as Max asked. The two went outside and hurriedly walked toward the building across the street. Max made sure, though, to take enough time to scan the parking lot as they crossed, and to look both ways when they crossed the street. When they got through the door, Monica was at her desk and Skip was in his office. Max helped Essie out of her coat and gave her the cookie. She immediately ran to the conference room that did double duty as a playroom.

Skip started to come up front when he heard the two come in, dodging Essie in the hallway, and sat down in one of the chairs across from Monica's desk. Max already occupied the other.

"So what's the deal?" Skip asked.

Monica collected her thoughts for a moment. "Do you happen to remember Angie Williamson? She used to dance at the Ladybug a lot."

Neither Max nor Skip answered her.

"Blonde girl, used to have a biker boyfriend who sat at the bar all night while she danced? Skip used to talk to him all the time."

"Okay," Max said. "I remember her. Stopped them one night and she had his pistol on her. She put it in her purse when they got stopped. She took the CCW charge so he wouldn't get possession of a firearm by a felon. You remember them?" Max turned toward Skip.

"Yeah, I remember them now," Skip remarked. "So what about her?"

"Last night I got a call from her. Probably ten-thirty. All she said was, 'Monica, this is Angie, can you guys help me?' That's it, nothing more."

"That's it? She didn't say what she needed you to help with?" Max asked.

"She didn't say 'Monica, can you help me,'" Monica replied. "She said, 'can you guys help me?' You guys."

"She talking about G&B?" Skip asked.

"I don't know," Monica answered. "But who else is 'you guys'?"

"Does she know that you work for us? Does she know your circumstances now? Is that why you think she's talking about us?" Skip asked.

"Yes," Monica answered. "I ran into her a couple of times over the years. I'm pretty sure that I told her what I'm doing. I mean, 'what are you doing?' 'oh, I'm working for that detective agency that those two cops that won the Powerball started, and I'm back in college.' That's what I tell everyone who asks me what I've been doing."

"You got a callback number?" Max asked.

"Yes," Monica answered.

"Did you try to call it back?" Max asked.

"Yes," Monica replied. "I tried several times, and I don't get an answer. It also tells me that the mailbox hasn't been set up."

"Did you google the number?" Skip asked her.

"I did," Monica answered. "It says it's a Council Bluffs area code, and nothing more. I even paid one of those internet sites that traces numbers, and got nothing."

"So what are you thinking?" Skip asked.

"I'm thinking that we need to investigate a little bit and see if we can find her and see what she needs help with," Monica responded.

"In other words, we got a new case?" Skip gave Monica a questioning look.

"I'll pay the two hundred bucks myself," Monica said. "That's what we get, right?"

Max looked at Skip. "Isn't she supposed to screen these and tell people we don't take any cases?"

"I thought that is what we paid her for," Skip replied.

The two looked up at Monica and saw that she was irritated with them. Ignoring their banter, she continued. "So what's the plan?" she asked. "Let's get started."

"Let me go get my notebook so that I can write stuff down, you dig through the trash for a scrap piece of garbage for Max to take notes on, and we'll get whatever we can find on her, and go from there." Skip left for his office, and Monica dug into her desk looking for a pencil and a tablet for Max to write on.

Skip returned and took a seat. He looked up at Monica, who also had a notebook and was poised to take notes.

"So first of all," Skip began, "what is Angie's full name? Or at least what is her last name?"

"Angie Williamson," Monica answered. "She also went by Angie Grubber, her biker boyfriend was Winston Grubber and she used his last name sometimes. I don't think that they ever got married, but she used it anyway."

"Okay," said Skip. "So Winston Grubber is, or was her boyfriend, I guess. Didn't he go to federal prison for auto theft and taking stolen property across state lines?" He looked at Max.

"Sure did," Max replied. "Then he died a couple of years ago. Cancer or something. Anyway, I heard that he was sick, and then I heard that he died."

"He had a brother," Skip remarked.

"Yeah, Gonad," Max replied. "I can't remember his real name. It will come to me."

"I can't remember, either," Skip remarked. "How about family?" Skip asked Monica. "You know if Angie has any family?"

"No," said Monica, "she never mentioned family."

"Okay," Skip said to Monica. "First thing you do is get on the internet and look around for relatives. Go to Iowa Courts Online, you might get some names there, if they ever got arrested for anything. Any Williamson or Grubber that you come across that lives around here, put them on a list, and we'll run them down."

"Do you know where she was living?" Skip asked.

"At one time she and Grubber were living over in Fraser with some other bikers," Monica answered.

"Not surprising," Max said. "So Grubber, was he a Sons or was he a Hell Fighter?"

"Hell Fighter," Skip answered.

"How do the Sons let the Hell Fighters operate on their turf?" Max asked.

"Farm team," Skip remarked. "Hell Fighters are wannabes. Sons are big league."

"Maybe," Max said, "but it never appeared to me that Grubber was second fiddle. He ran some pretty serious shit."

"I think that he was running the show. I think that the Sons put him in there to ride herd. Truth be known, maybe he was both," Skip observed.

Skip turned to Monica. "Call that number again, and let's see what happens."

Monica put her phone on speaker and called the number again. It rang six times, rolled over to voicemail, then informed them that the voice mailbox had not been set up.

"Same thing," Monica said.

"You have another number for Angie?" Skip asked. "From back in the day?"

Monica looked in her contacts. After a moment she tapped the screen and the phone rang. "Good thinking,

Skip, I didn't think of that," Monica remarked. After three rings, someone picked up and a man answered.

"Hello."

"Hello," Skip replied. "Is Angie there?"

"You got a wrong number."

"Sorry, this is the number I have for Angie Williamson. You got any idea what her number is?"

"I don't know Angie Williamson," the man's voice answered. "I got this number two years ago. I don't know her. I've gotten a couple of people calling for her, but I have no idea who she is."

"Okay," Skip said. "Sorry again. I'll take it out of my contacts."

The man ended the call. Monica shrugged her shoulders.

"Don't delete that number," Skip said. "Just because he says that it's his new number and he doesn't know Angie, that don't mean he's telling the truth. Let's just keep that number handy."

"Byron," Max blurted. "Byron Grubber. He was the brother. And he got kicked out of his own brother's club. The Boone cops used to write parking tickets on him all the time and he wouldn't pay them. Then when they got a couple that had gone to warrant, they would sit back and wait for him to go into the clubhouse, then they would kick the door in and arrest him on parking warrants. Old Snake Eyes told him if it happened one more time, he was out, and it did."

"Snake Eyes," Skip remarked. "That's right, they called Grubber Snake Eyes. I wonder if Gonad is still around? He would be a good one to talk to right off the bat."

"Monica," Max said, turning toward her desk. "Call Milton and see if he can get a last known address from records on Byron Grubber."

"I'm not calling Milton and asking him to do something against the rules," she shot back, absently turning the engagement ring on her left hand.

"This here arrangement between you two is not working," Max observed.

"It is working fine," Monica retorted.

Max pulled his phone out of his pocket, pulled up Milton's number and pushed call. The phone rang twice.

"Hey," Milton answered.

"You wanna do a favor for me and Monica?" Max asked. "I need a last known address on Byron Grubber."

"Byron Grubber, Snake Eyes Grubber's little brother?" asked Milton.

"That would be the one," Max replied.

"Last time I talked to him he was living in Fraser," Milton said.

"I could use an address," Max said. "We need to pay him a little visit."

"Well, why don't you just go over there and drive around town and read the names on the mailboxes until you find his? There can't be over a dozen or so people living over there."

"You aren't going to help me?" Max asked.

Milton didn't answer.

"We're working a case for your fiancée, you know," Max informed him.

"I know," Milton replied.

"Okay," Max said, and ended the call. "Why does he have a burr up his ass?" Max asked.

"He just doesn't like being used all of the time," Monica replied. "I told him that if he is getting a wife and a kid to support, he can't keep going out and passing information to you two like that, especially NCIC information."

"So you are undermining your own case?" Max remarked.

"No, I just don't think that you need to compromise Milton all the time," she responded.

"Let's just move on," Skip broke in. "Let's just drive over there this afternoon and look around. Let's just see what is over there."

Max shrugged his shoulders. "Might as well, we got nothing else to go on, and it looks like it's going to be a nice day. You're driving," Max added hastily.

"Monica," Skip addressed her, "You get on the internet and come up with anything you can on Snake Eyes, Byron and Angie. And anyone connected to them in any way. Important thing here is relatives. If we can come up with any relatives for Angie, that is big."

Monica nodded her head affirmative and started the search.

"What do you need to do?" Skip asked Max.

"Nothin'," Max replied. "Get my pistol and my camera, and I'm ready."

"Let's do it then," Skip said. "We'll find some local café or somewhere to eat over there. We can ask around and see if anybody knows anything. Maybe we get lucky."

"Sounds like a good place to start," Max agreed.

Chapter 2

Monday

Skip was driving, which surprised Max, considering that Skip never liked to drive. They were westbound toward Boone on US Highway 30 in his brand new Audi, which probably had something to do with his willingness to drive. Skip had caught the new car bug last fall when he and Max went looking for a car to replace the yellow Mustang that Allan Proctor had destroyed with his tractor and end loader during the lonelyfarmer.com case, which is what Max had taken to calling it. Unlike Max, who bought the replacement that very day, Skip took his time to buy the Audi. He had gone off to Hawaii for a couple of months, and had returned at the end of February. He bought the Audi shortly after he got back.

"Beautiful day," Max commented as they rounded the curves at the United Community School that sat out in an open field halfway between Ames and Boone. The new car was rock solid.

"It is that," Skip replied. "Do you know how to get to Fraser?"

"I think that you have to go through Boone," Max answered. "I used to go there to fish on the Des Moines River years ago, when I was a kid, but I don't think that I know the way off of the top of my head anymore."

Skip grunted his reply.

"I'll do this GPS thing on my phone," Max suggested.

"Here, let me try this," Skip said, pushing buttons on his steering wheel.

"Say a command," a woman's voice with a decidedly British accent came through the speakers in the dash.

"What's with the English accent all the time?" Max exclaimed. "They got the same thing at the airports."

"I didn't understand the command," the woman's voice came over the speakers again, "please repeat."

"Destination," Skip said in a loud and even voice before Max could say anything else.

"Did you say 'destination'?" The woman's voice asked. "If you said 'destination,' please say 'yes.' If not, please say 'no.'"

"Yes," Skip and Max said at the same time.

"I'm sorry, I did not understand the response," the woman's voice said. "Please repeat your command."

Skip gave Max a stern look.

"Here," Max said, "I'll just do it manually on the screen." Max was studying the screen, trying to figure it out.

"I did not understand the command," the woman's voice said as Max was poking at different points on the screen.

"Eat shit," Max said out loud.

"I did not understand the command," the woman's voice responded.

Max pushed on the screen with his index finger where it said "Navigation."

"You cannot manually operate the navigation feature while the vehicle is in motion," the woman's voice said. "Please pull over and stop, or use voice commands to operate the navigation feature."

Max pulled out his phone. "Just let me do it on my phone," Max said, pushing the button at the top of the phone to activate the screen. There were three map apps on his phone. He picked one and brought it up.

"Turn right at that four-way stop up ahead," Max instructed Skip.

"Then what?" Skip asked.

"I don't know," Max replied. "I haven't even got this thing to work yet. I just know that you have to turn there and go up the main drag and over the railroad tracks."

"Whatever," Skip replied.

While Skip pulled up to the stop sign and turned right, Max was working on his phone.

"In two point seven miles, turn left," a woman's voice with a decidedly British accent ordered them.

"There you go," Max said with satisfaction. "Modern technology, same woman with the English accent."

Skip followed directions through town, and then west on a blacktop county highway that curved north.

"In one mile, turn right at the intersection," the woman's voice instructed them.

"Are you sure of this?" Skip asked, scanning the countryside. "I don't even see anything that looks like the Des Moines River. Isn't Fraser on the Des Moines River?"

"Do phones lie?" Max responded.

Skip kept driving until they suddenly came to a steep descent into the river valley below.

"There you go," Max remarked.

"Wow," said Skip. "That's something."

They drove down the incline until they reached the bottom and crossed a bridge over the river. Max looked upstream.

"That dam up there is Fraser," Max informed Skip. "That's where we used to fish."

"Turn left at the next intersection," the woman's voice said.

"Turn left up here," Max instructed Skip. "I know my way around from here."

"Turn off the GPS then," Skip said with a bit of irritation in his voice.

Max did as Skip told him to. Skip drove into town. It was almost like time had not moved in Fraser since its heyday when coal mining was Fraser's main industry. There were slag piles rising above the trees in a couple of places. Skip and Max drove through the streets calling out the names on the mailboxes as they passed them, Max reading the ones on the right, Skip on the left.

"Used to be a bar over there," Max remembered out loud as they passed the ruins of a building built into the side of a hill. There was a house above it. "We used to go in there and buy beer under age," Max said, thinking back. "Guy over there had a yard full of old DeSotos. I wonder where they all went."

"We're going out of town already," Skip observed.

They drove out of town on a gravel road that was more like a driveway than a street, and Skip was wondering if he had missed a turn. Skip spotted a driveway ahead where he could turn around. As they approached it, they saw an acreage with a new ranch house, garage and machine shed. There was a Boone County deputy sheriff's car parked in front of the garage, and a man was out laying up landscaping stones along the driveway.

"Duffy," Max read the name on the mailbox. "You know him?"

"Don't think so," Skip replied as he pulled in and drove up the driveway toward the man, who had stopped working and was watching them.

Skip rolled down his window as he reached the man. "Deputy Duffy, how's it going? Max Mosbey and Skip Murray, we retired from the APD; I don't know if you remember us."

The man leaned on the car and looked through the window at the two. "You're the guys that won the Powerball jackpot," he exclaimed. "Sure, I remember you. I was on the Tri County Drug Task Force. You guys came in and gave us a hand on a couple of drug busts."

"Yep," Max replied through the window. "That's us."

"So you guys started a detective agency, I hear," Duffy remarked.

"Yes, we did, G&B Detective Agency," Skip said, digging a business card out of his billfold and handing it to Duffy through the window. "Nice place," he said. "Looks new."

"Built it last summer," Duffy said with some pride in his voice. "Didn't get the landscaping done, though."

"Place like this is a lifelong project," Skip reflected. "Anyway, seems like I've been working on mine for a lifetime."

"I think that I'm learning that," Duffy laughed. "I got thirty acres here to keep me busy. That, a wife, three horses, two kids and a dog." Duffy paused for a moment while the two detectives chuckled with him. "What brings you to Fraser?" he asked.

"We're looking for Byron Grubber," Skip replied. "Actually, we are looking for his brother's old girlfriend, Angie Williamson, and we are looking for him to see if he knows where she's at."

"Wow," said Duffy, "I haven't seen any of those guys for a while. They're long gone. There was a big rift between the Hell Fighters and the Sons after the big bust. The Sons blamed the Hell Fighters for bringing the heat down on them. Which was valid, I guess, as the undercover agents went in through the Hell Fighters. But whoever was left after the big federal bust moved out of town. Some of them quit the gang and moved over to Pilot

Mound, some of them left and relocated with other chapters. Grubber might be over in Pilot Mound. I haven't seen him for over a year, though. He was one of the last ones to leave Fraser. Of course, he wasn't in either gang by the time the bust went down, so he sort of stayed dry during the whole thing. Lucky him. And I haven't seen Angie since Snake Eyes went to prison. She just sort of disappeared along with everyone else."

Max and Skip digested what Duffy had told them. "Sounds like you got a pretty good handle on it," Skip observed.

"I was on the task force when they busted those guys. We were helping the feds," Duffy explained.

"Ever get any backlash around here from that?" Max asked.

"No," Duffy said. "Nothing."

"That's good," Max said.

"We'll get out of your hair and let you get back to work," Skip piped up. "If you wouldn't mind asking around while you're out and about, we would really appreciate it. Anything that might be remotely connected with her," Skip trailed off. "You got our number there."

"I'll do that," Duffy replied. "Good to see you guys."

Skip reached out the window and shook hands with Duffy, then backed out of the drive and onto the road and toward town.

"Nice guy," Max said.

"Yep," Skip agreed. "Real agreeable, too. I think it is good that we ran into him."

"Pilot Mound?" Max asked.

"Plug it into your phone," Skip replied. "I got no idea how to get there."

"Go straight," the woman's voice on the phone instructed. "In six-tenths of a mile, turn left."

"Already punched it in," Max said.

Skip followed the directions on Max's phone, which took them to the small town of Pilot Mound, slightly larger and a bit more prosperous than Fraser. As they were approaching the city limits, they met two Harley Davidson motorcycles leaving town. As they passed, Max swiveled in his seat to get a better look at them. Skip was doing the same thorough his rearview mirror.

"Patched?" Skip asked.

"Don't see anything," Max replied. Max watched them disappear in the distance. "Who knows?" he said absently. "Kind of cold out for a motorcycle ride."

"One thing about Harley riders," Skip observed. "They like to ride their Harleys. It wouldn't surprise me if they are just some guys out for a ride."

Skip drove down the main drag through town. They both scanned the side streets as they went, looking for anything that might help them connect the dots. It was like a ghost town. Nothing was moving. Skip got to the end of town and circled the block to go back the way they had come. As he was doing so, he saw a man standing in front of his house watching them drive by.

"Check it out to the right," Skip said.

Max looked over and saw the man. Skip stopped the car and backed up while Max rolled down his window. Skip stopped the car in front of the man's house.

"Sir," Max called out. "I'm trying to locate someone who we were told might live here. Could you help us out?"

The man walked closer to the car where they could talk.

"Who you looking for?" the man asked.

"Actually, two people," Max replied. "We're looking for a guy named Byron Grubber, and a woman by the name of Angie Williamson, or maybe Angie Grubber."

The man stood for a moment looking like he was thinking about whether he was going to answer the question, ask a question, or if he was just going to say that he didn't know anyone named Byron Grubber or Angie Williamson and walk back up to his house.

"That Grubber guy used to live here. I don't know of the woman," the man finally answered.

"So he doesn't live here anymore?" Max asked, hoping for a little more from the man.

"He moved to Ogden," the man replied. "But I see him in the bar once in a while."

"The bar in Ogden?" Max asked.

"No, the bar here in town," the man answered.

"There's a bar here in Pilot Mound?" Skip asked through Max's window.

"Yep, right back down the street. I see him there once in a while."

"You know what he drives?" Skip asked. Max was leaning back against the seat so that Skip could talk to the man.

"An old beat-to-hell Harley during the summer," the man said. "Whatever piece of shit he can find that runs, in the winter."

"Thanks," Max called out to the man as Skip put the car in gear and drove ahead to go around the block. "We must have drove right by it," Max said to Skip.

Skip drove back the way they had come. They spotted the bar right away this time. There was one old blue Saturn and a broken-down Ford pickup truck with a flat tire sitting out front.

"Let's check it out," Skip said as he pulled in and parked next to the pickup.

The two detectives got out of the car and Skip locked the door. They had to walk around behind the truck to reach the entrance to the bar. Skip walked in first and Max followed. It was dark inside; most of the light came from the neon bar signs that hung on the wall. There was a pool table on one side of the room, a half dozen tables on the other. A man was sitting at the bar with a glass of beer in front of him, talking to the bartender. As soon as the two entered, they recognized Grubber. He had not changed.

Grubber turned toward the two as they came in. He had a look of confused recognition on his face. He gave them a guarded smile as the two approached.

"What's up?" he asked.

Max took up a bar stool on one side of him, Skip took the one on the other side. Grubber was facing Max. He was a little nervous with Skip sitting behind him. He turned toward Skip, and realized that he could no longer see Max, and that made him more nervous. He turned back toward Max.

"Byron Grubber," Max said, getting the man's attention. "Long time no see. How they hangin'?"

"What are you guys doing here?" Grubber asked. "I heard you guys won the lottery and quit the police or something."

"We did," Max said. "What we're doing here is looking for you," he went on. "You and Angie Williamson."

"I ain't seen Angie for a long time," Grubber replied. "Why you lookin' for me?"

"We're looking for you, because we're looking for Angie," Max reiterated. "Where's she at?"

The bartender was standing on the other side of the bar listening. Grubber gave him a glance. "I said I ain't seen her," he replied to Max with some half-hearted insolence in his voice.

"Well you seen her sometime, she was your brother's old lady. When was the last time you seen her?" Max asked, turning the inflection and syntax in his voice to match Grubber's.

"I don't remember," Grubber replied, looking toward the bartender again, as if he was looking for some help.

"You guys need a drink?" the bartender asked.

"You got Miller Lite?" Max asked, looking at the handles on the taps behind the bar. "I'll take a glass of Miller Lite."

"Me, too," Skip chimed in.

The bartender walked away to get the beers. Max turned his attention back to Grubber.

"You guys are putting me in a dangerous situation here," Grubber said, lowering his voice. "Just talking to the cops, I mean."

"We aren't cops," Max replied. "We're private detectives."

"I don't care what you are," Grubber said impatiently. "You're asking questions that I shouldn't be answering."

The bartender was pulling the last glass of beer.

"So where do you want to talk?" Max asked. "Because we aren't going to just go away without some answers."

"Maybe we go out in the parking lot and talk," Skip suggested from behind. Grubber turned around.

"I ain't going out in the parking lot with you two. I've seen you guys operate. I don't want my ass kicked."

"We aren't going to kick your ass," Max responded. "We don't go around kicking people's asses. We've never gone around just kicking people's asses. We just want to ask you some questions and get some answers. We're not kicking your ass."

"Yeah, well, that's not what people say," Grubber said.

"What do they say, that we go around kicking people's asses?" Max asked.

"Well, that's what they used to say," Grubber replied.

The bartender returned with the beers and placed one in front of each of the two detectives. "Wanna start a tab?" he asked.

"We'll pay up," Skip replied. "He paid for his yet?" Skip nodded toward Grubber.

"Nope," the bartender answered.

"I'll pay his, too," Skip said to the bartender, handing him his G&B Visa card.

The bartender took it and went to the cash register at the end of the bar.

"Okay, where can we go to talk?" Max asked Grubber.

Grubber thought for a moment. "Hows about Temple's in Ogden?"

"When?" Max pressed.

"Tomorrow, maybe around six?" Grubber suggested.

"How about in an hour?" Max replied.

Grubber shrugged his shoulders. "I guess."

Grubber downed his beer, got up and left. Max moved over and took his chair next to Skip, facing the bar, drinking their beers. The bartender returned with the receipt and waited for Skip to sign it.

"You guys are going to get ol' Byron a beat down if you keep it up," the bartender commented.

"How's that?" Skip asked.

"Some of the Hell Fighters are still around, and they blame Byron for everything that happened. Even though he didn't have anything to do with anything, they blame him for everything."

"Why?" Skip asked. "What did he do? I didn't even think he was in the club anymore when they all got busted."

"He talks too much," the bartender answered. "It don't make any difference to them. They just got used to blaming him for whatever happened. When his brother was still alive, they sort of laid off him, but after Snake Eyes died, they blamed him for everything. He's convenient."

"So do you know anything about Snake Eyes's old girlfriend, Angie?" Skip asked, considering that the bartender had started the conversation.

"No," the bartender answered. "I think that she left with the Hell Fighters. She danced here for a while—Snake Eyes would bring her in to dance for tips—but after those guys all got busted things around here sort of died out. I wasn't making enough money to pay my bills, and I wasn't getting enough customers in here for the girls to make any money dancing for tips. Besides, most of the girls belonged to the bikers and when they all left they took the girls with them."

"So you don't have any idea where she went?" Max asked again.

"No idea," the bartender answered. "Honestly, the bikers ran that part of the business. I sold the beer, that was where I made my money. The bikers brought the dancers in. I didn't pay them. We had a back room there, and some of the girls would take customers back there for a little one-on-one. Either that, or out in the parking lot.

But I never had much dealings with them. I was discouraged from getting too friendly with them. I just sold beer. I do know that every dollar they made, they gave to the bikers."

"Interesting," Max said.

"Yep," the bartender said. "Anyway, most of them took off and went elsewhere. The only bikers we get through here these days is the guys who buy the biker look with the bonus dollars they get when they buy their new Harleys."

"You said most took off. Are any Hell Fighters still around?" Max asked.

"Not but a handful, and they ain't Hell Fighters anymore. They are just losers who didn't have anyplace else to go. Haven't seen one in here for a long, long time."

Max and Skip thanked the bartender for the beer and the info, then left the bar.

"Talkative sort," Max observed as they walked outside.

"Those kind worry me," Skip replied. "Never know if they are legit or if they're just feeding you crap."

"Probably a little bit of both," Max replied.

Chapter 3

Monday

Skip pulled into the parking lot at Temple's Burgers and Beers in Ogden. "Burgers and beers," Max read. "That's pretty creative, don't you think so?"

Skip couldn't decide if Max was being sarcastic or if he was serious.

"Burgers and beers," Max repeated. "My two favorite foods. It sort of rolls off the tongue: 'burgers and beers.'"

Skip decided that Max was serious. He parked beside Byron's Saturn and the two got out. Max surveyed the surroundings, something he did out of habit. There were two other cars and a pickup parked in front of the bar. They walked through the door and spotted Byron sitting at a table in the farthest corner, away from the bar. He had a beer on the table in front of him. Max and Skip took seats at the table. Max looked over at the bartender, who looked like was hoping that Max would just come up to the bar and order. Max just smiled at him. Finally the bartender left the bar and walked over to the table.

"What do you need?" he asked the table in general.

"I'll take a Miller Lite," Max said.

"Make it two," Skip said.

Max was looking at the menu posted on the wall behind the bar. "What time is it?" Max looked at his watch. "Eleven-thirty. You want to do lunch as long as we're here?" he asked Skip.

"Might as well," Skip answered.

"I'll take a cheeseburger and fries," Max told the bartender. "You want something?" Max asked Byron. "I'm buying."

"I'll take a burger and fries," Byron answered.

"Same here," Skip added.

The bartender did not reply. He turned, walked back to the bar and through a door that went into the kitchen behind the bar. They could see him putting the hamburger patties on the stove. They heard hot grease sizzling from the frozen french fries that he poured into the fryer.

Skip turned to Byron. "Okay, Byron, we are looking for Angie. She's not been heard from for a while and her friend hired us to find her. So bottom line, whatever you have that will help us do that would be greatly appreciated."

Byron hesitated.

"Don't think about it, just give us what you got," Skip urged him. "And we'll get out of your hair."

Byron took a deep breath and let it out, then began. "When my brother went to prison, he gave Angie to a biker named Billy the Kid. You gotta understand that my brother took good care of Angie because he really liked her. And when she was with my brother he would give her some money and take her shopping once in a while, and he would make sure that she took care of herself. Like he would make her eat right and go to the dentist. But Billy had another girl, and she was his girlfriend, kind of, and she didn't like Angie being around him. But my brother was still the president of the club even if he was in the slammer, and there were still enough members around that Billy didn't want it getting back to him that he wasn't treating Angie good, so he made sure that at least she wasn't complaining to anyone about him."

Byron quit talking when the bartender brought Skip and Max their drinks. As soon as he left, Byron continued. "But then my brother got sick, real sick. He'd been holding the club together from his jail cell, but then when he got sick there wasn't anybody to take over, so everyone just drifted away. And when that happened, Billy got real mean with Angie. He'd beat the hell out of her for stupid stuff, and then she would have to go out and dance. She'd have big ugly bruises, maybe a black eye or a swelled-up lip, and she wouldn't get much for tips lookin' that way, and then he'd knock her around for that. It just kept getting worse, and I went over there to take her away, but he and his buddies threatened to throw me down an abandoned coal shaft if I didn't make myself scarce. So I just left without her."

The bartender brought their burgers and put them on the table. Then he went back to the bar and returned with a bottle of ketchup, a bottle of mustard and a handful of napkins, and put them in the middle of the table. "Anything else?" he asked.

"No, I think that we're good," Max replied. The bartender went back to the bar. A few more patrons were coming in to drink their lunch. The bartender was starting to get busy.

"Holy shit," Max remarked after he had swallowed his first bite. "How the hell does that happen? I mean, why didn't she call the cops? Why didn't she just leave?"

"'Cause that's the way it is," Byron said. "No one leaves. Once you are a part of it, you never leave."

Byron stopped for a moment, a somber look on his face. "Worst thing that can happen to you is they kick you out. If they kick you out you got nothing. Better to take the abuse and have something than to get kicked out and have nothing." Byron sat in silence, lost in his own thoughts.

"That's sad," Max remarked.

"Yes, it is," Byron replied. "But people don't understand how it is."

Byron perked up a little and continued. "So the Sons left right after everyone got arrested. There was just too much heat and they didn't know who they could trust anymore, so they just left. And what was left of the Hell Fighters hung on until my brother died and then they left too, and when they did, Billy took Angie with him."

"Where did Billy go?" Skip asked.

"Oelwein," Byron answered. "At least that's where I heard he went. I didn't go looking for him to ask him how he was doing. But that's what I heard. And I also heard that he sold Angie to someone."

"Sold her?" Skip asked.

"Yeah," Byron said. "I mean, you don't sell her like you do a car, you sell her to someone and they take responsibility for her."

"That is slavery," Max exclaimed.

"Not really," Byron said. "Girls like Angie come into the club knowing that they are giving themselves to the club. They can leave if they want, but they don't want to. They want to stay. Belonging is everything. They want to belong."

Max snorted in disbelief. "I can't fucking believe it."

Byron shrugged his shoulders.

"You keep calling it a club," Skip said. "But actually it is a gang, it is a criminal gang. Motorcycle clubs go for a supper run on Wednesday nights; gangs run dope, steal cars and sell women."

Byron just shrugged his shoulders again.

"You have any idea where Angie went from there?" Skip asked.

"No idea," Byron responded. "No idea. I never heard from her again after Billy left with her. Anything after that I heard from some of the guys when they were coming back through."

"How long ago we talking?" Skip asked.

"Maybe three years ago," Byron answered.

"Does this Billy the Kid have a real name?" Skip asked.

"He does, but I don't know it. No one goes by their real name. I've known a lot of these guys for ten or fifteen years and I don't know their real names. That's how they protect themselves. If no one uses their real name then no one can rat on them. If someone turns into an informant, or if some LEO spy gets into the club, they don't know who anyone is. They just got their club names. I don't think anyone ever knew what Billy's real name was. He came from another chapter. He showed up Billy the Kid, and everyone called him that.

Max was finishing his lunch; Skip and Byron had hardly touched theirs.

"Eat up, boys," Max said.

The two started eating their food. It had gotten cold and neither seemed to have an appetite for it. After a few bites, Byron put both hands on the table, bracing himself to get up.

"You guys done with me now?" he asked. "Because I'm ready to leave."

"I got nothing more for you," Skip said.

"Thanks for the info," Max added.

"You guys got this?" Byron asked, glancing down at his half eaten burger and fries.

"We got it," Skip answered.

Byron stood up and left the bar. Max watched Skip try to eat his cold plate of food. After a minute Max waved at the bartender for the bill, but the bartender was busy talking to one of the customers at the now full bar. Max got up and went to the end of the bar to pay, leaving Skip to his meal.

When Max had paid, the two detectives left the building and got into Skip's car. Skip waited for a car to go by, backed out into the street and turned toward US Highway 30.

"You know, you hear about this shit, but it isn't real until you talk to someone like Grubber, and then you realize that it is." Max said.

"You mean about the women being property of the motorcycle gang?" Skip asked.

"Exactly. I mean, we walked those strip bars every weekend, and every weekend ol' Snake Eyes was sitting there at the bar, and we just assumed Angie was his girlfriend just like everyone else's girlfriend. But she wasn't. She belonged to him. He owned her. And Byron is acting like it's all good. Like all there is in life is to be the property of a motorcycle gang. And woe is the day when that that comes to an end."

"Yep," Skip replied. "No accounting for people."

"It kind of burns me up that we never saw it," Max said.

"What would you have done about it?" Skip asked.

"I don't know," Max said. "I would help them get out. I would have promised to protect them."

"But you heard him," Skip replied. "They don't want to get out. They are willing to put up with it, because they belong. They want to belong."

"They're brainwashed," Max said. "It is like a cult. They're brainwashed."

"Yep," Skip said. "We're all brainwashed in our own way."

"So you are defending it?" Max asked.

"Nope," Skip replied. "I'm just saying that we all are trapped in our lives in one way or another."

"You're getting a little morose," Max observed.

"I guess that I am," Skip replied.

Max sat in silence, looking out across the fields as they made their way back toward Ames. Remnants of snowdrifts clung to the fencerows. Max had not seen fencerows in a long time. Leave it to Boone County to still have fencerows. Farmers in the rest of the state had gotten rid of fencerows years ago so that they could plant an extra row of corn and beans, but Boone County still had fencerows.

"Fencerows," Max remarked to Skip. "When is the last time you saw fencerows out in the fields?"

"This morning," Skip answered. "There's a fencerow in the field across from my place."

"You always gotta do that," Max complained.

"What?" Skip asked.

"Prove me wrong," Max replied.

"So don't ask me when was the last time I saw a fencerow," Skip said.

Max didn't say anything back. The two bickered all the time. It didn't bother Max. In fact, if Skip wasn't jerking his chain Max started to worry. He and Skip had been friends for a long time. They were comfortable with each other.

"So I'm thinking that we need to hunt down this Billy the Kid," Skip broke the silence. "And I'm thinking that if he left Fraser, or Pilot Mound or wherever, and went to Oelwein, then we head to Oelwein tomorrow and ask around about Billy the Kid."

"Sounds like a plan," Max agreed.

Skip was pulling off of Highway 30. He took the exit, turned left and headed toward the offices of G&B Detective Agency. As he drove down the street toward the entrance to the parking lot, the two could see Monica's car parked in her reserved space. Milton's patrol car was parked next to it.

"They spend a lot of time together at the office," Max remarked.

"Well, Monica has her mom living with her, maybe they need somewhere to get away," Skip replied.

"Well, Milton has his own place and no one is living with him, so they could go there," Max said.

"Maybe they like the office," Skip said. "They can do what they want."

Skip parked his car and the two detectives went in. Milton was sprawled out on one of the easy chairs just inside the door reading a *Car and Driver* magazine. Monica was at her desk, studying. She looked up as they came in. Max slapped Milton's leg that was dangling over the arm of the chair.

"That's my place," he said.

Milton gave Max an annoyed look, but stood up, giving the chair up to him. Skip took the other chair.

"What do you do?" Max asked Milton. "You just hang out here all day with Monica when you're supposed to be working?"

"I'm on lunch break," Milton replied defensively.

"I don't see any lunch," Max observed.

"I already ate in the car," Milton explained. "I'm leaving, anyway," he said, walking toward the door. "You're sure in a pissy mood," he said over his shoulder.

"See ya," Monica called to him, puckering her lips when he turned back toward her.

Milton walked back to the desk and gave Monica a little kiss on the lips.

"Monica," Skip said as Milton went out the door. "I got a couple of questions."

"Shoot," Monica replied.

"So we talked to Snake Eyes's brother and he was telling us how Angie belonged to Snake Eyes. That she was his property, not his girlfriend. You know anything about that?"

Monica collected her thoughts. "She was both," Monica sighed. "With Snake Eyes and Angie, she was both. They were a couple. It wasn't like that with everyone, though. And sometimes Snake Eyes would bring another girl with him and Angie, but most of the times it was just Angie. There was never any doubt that she was his and there was hell to pay if she got him riled up. So she was careful not to do that. But they had it worked out and she always seemed reasonably happy with the arrangement. But I danced with plenty of girls who belonged to bikers, and sometimes it was terrible. Some of those guys treated the girls worse than they treated their dogs."

"Monica, how did you stay out of it?" Skip asked. "I mean, didn't they make a move on you?"

"Yeah," Monica replied, "and it wasn't just bikers, there were plenty of gangbangers out there who tried to put some pressure on me, but I had a couple of things going for me. First of all, I had my mom and Essie. I had a home to go to. Second, I had a future. I knew that I wanted to go back to school. Those girls that get tied up with the bikers and the gangbangers and the pimps, they got nothing else. But it all starts out pretty subtle. They find a girl who doesn't have anyone or anything and they give her something in her life. Maybe not what we would call a happy and caring environment to grow in, but something just the same, and that is more than some of them have ever had. So they fall into it. And after a while they think that their life is normal. That there isn't anything better."

"That's interesting," Skip remarked. "You've given this a lot of thought."

"Actually, I have," Monica nodded. "Because I want to be a psychologist and I want to help women like Angie. I've seen what happens to them when they are no longer of any value to the gang, and it is heartbreaking. I got opportunities and I've got a future. They don't have that. Everyone deserves a future."

Max and Skip sat in silence for a moment.

"Did you ever hear of some biker named Billy the Kid?" Max asked.

Monica thought about it. "I think so," she said in a hesitant voice. "You've got to understand that I stayed close to home. I didn't make the circuit. But there were some girls that made the rounds and I kind of remember hearing about this Billy the Kid. But this was Snake Eyes territory around here, and that was never contested."

"Did you dance for tips?" Max asked. "Or did you get paid to dance?"

"I got paid each night and then I split my tips with the bartender," Monica answered.

"So did Angie have the same deal?" Max asked.

"No, she danced for tips, and she would take it out to the parking lot for a little extra money between sets," Monica replied.

"And Snake Eyes never challenged that arrangement?" Skip asked. "You getting paid by the bar, I mean?"

"Nope," Monica replied.

"Why?" Skip asked.

"Don't know, it never came up," Monica said. "My friend was dancing there and I needed some money. So she introduced me to the bartender. I went to work the next weekend. Fifty a night in cash, and I split the tips with the bartender. Most nights he came out ahead. The nights that there weren't very many customers, I knew that I would at least walk out with fifty bucks. I never questioned it. But my friend that got me started at the Ladybug took off to Milwaukee with some guy shortly after, and I stayed there dancing until you guys came in and offered me the job at G&B. I don't think Snake Eyes and I ever even had a conversation. He might say hi. He did try to bring in more dancers one time to squeeze me out, but it just didn't work. I think that the other dancers were more than he could handle. And Angie didn't like it. As screwed up as those two were, Angie was Snake Eyes's woman."

"Interesting," Max said.

"You know something?" Monica went on. "I think that I've always had confidence in myself. I think that people recognized that and left me alone. I think that there are plenty of girls out there that are vulnerable. Predators know how to spot those girls. They know how to get into their heads and control them. That's what they do. There was no doubting that, psychologically, Snake Eyes owned Angie."

The two detectives sat digesting what Monica had told them.

"What's up with Billy the Kid?" Monica asked. "Does anyone else feel goofy calling these guys 'Snake Eyes' and 'Billy the Kid'?"

Skip and Max both laughed.

"After Snake Eyes went to prison, Angie evidently got handed off to Billy the Kid," Skip explained. "And yes, it feels stupid to call him Billy the Kid, except that is the only name we have for him right now. But Billy the Kid took off with her to Oelwein, maybe, and then we think that he might have sold her to someone else. So we need to find Billy the Kid."

Monica sat for a moment. "I'll get on the internet and start looking. I don't know for what, but I'll keep looking."

"I'm going to call around and see if anyone knows someone on the Oelwein Police Department," Max said. "Maybe Carlisle knows a deputy down there. There's got to be someone we can connect with in the law enforcement community over there that knows Billy the Kid."

"Let's meet here tomorrow first thing and regroup. Then we road trip down to Oelwein to ask around," Skip said.

"Sounds like a plan," Max said.

Chapter 4

Monday

Max drove home in his Camaro. He pulled up the driveway and parked, leaving it outside instead of putting it in the garage. He walked in the front door. The house was quiet. Max walked down the stairs to Gloria's office, but she wasn't there. He looked at her calendar on her desk. Max wondered if she kept it there just for him. She had often told him that they could link up their calendars on their phones, but when they did, it just confused him. So he kept hers hidden and forgotten. The calendar on the desk showed that she was doing an after-work wine tasting for a local realty agency. He wondered how late that would go. Gloria enjoyed living the wine life. She liked doing wine tastings and Max was happy that she was happy doing it.

Max took his phone from his pocket and sat down at Gloria's desk. He went through his contacts, found Carlisle's number and pushed the call button. It rang three times.

"Hey Max, what's up?"

"Got a question for you," Max replied. "You know anyone on the Fayette County Sheriff's?"

There was silence on the phone while Carlisle thought for a moment. "There's a woman named Gleason that is a deputy down there," he replied.

"She been there a while?" Max asked.

"Probably ten years," Carlisle answered.

"You got a number for her?"

"I don't, but she works evenings. You can probably call down there and get ahold of her if she's on duty," Carlisle responded. "Why?"

"We have a case that we're working on," Max explained. "We're trying to locate a woman named Angie Williamson, maybe Angie Grubber."

"You mean Snake Eyes Grubber's girlfriend?" Carlisle asked.

"Yep," Max continued. "She used to be Grubber's girlfriend, but when he died she was handed off, so to speak, to another biker that they call Billy the Kid. Snake Eyes's brother told us that Billy the Kid took her over to Oelwein. Then we don't know where she went. So we're looking for Billy the Kid to see if he can tell us where she might be."

"Billy the Kid?" Carlisle rolled the name around in his mind. "I think that he used to hang out down at Chris's in Cambridge sometimes. I kind of remember the name, but I don't really remember the guy. He must have stayed under the radar."

"Could have been a prospect, or whatever it is that they are before they get patched?" Max suggested.

"Could be," Carlisle replied.

"You don't know his real name, do you?" Max asked.

"I hardly ran into him at all," Carlisle answered. "But I mean, who forgets some biker named Billy the Kid? I'll ask around, though."

"That would be much appreciated," Max responded.

"No problem. So we're going to have a big wedding coming up here this summer." Carlisle said, changing the subject.

"Yes, we are," Max replied. "You going to come to it?"

"I'm going to be best man," Carlisle said.

"You are?" Max exclaimed.

"Yep," Carlisle said. "Milton asked me last month."

"I didn't know that," Max replied.

"Yep," Carlisle said, "I am."

Max said nothing.

"I'll check and see what I can find out about Billy the Kid, and get back to you," Carlisle said after a moment of silence.

"Thanks," said Max.

Carlisle ended the call. Max got on Gloria's computer, looked up the Fayette County Sheriff's Department and got a phone number. He punched it into his phone and pushed the call button. It rang once, then someone picked up.

"Fayette County Sheriff," the woman's voice answered.

"Hi," Max said. "My name is Max Mosbey. I'm a private detective in Ames and I would like to talk to Deputy Gleason if she's available."

"Deputy Gleason is in briefing right now," the woman informed him. "I can have her call you when she gets out."

Max gave the woman his phone number and ended the call. He sat back and started surfing the internet on Gloria's computer. Max had several interests, but the one that was most on his mind at the moment was playing his guitar. Max had taken up the instrument several years earlier, just before they had won the Powerball. He got on a site that sold them and started looking at the different sizes and shapes. His phone rang while he was checking out a $7000 Martin D28 acoustic.

Max picked up his phone. "Hello," he answered.

"Mr. Mosbey?" a woman's voice asked.

"Yes," Max replied.

"This is Deputy Gleason, I understand you wanted to talk to me?"

"Yes, I do," Max replied. "I'm a private detective for the G&B Detective Agency in Ames, and I got your name from Deputy Carlisle at the Story County Sheriff's Department. I'm looking for a woman named Angie Williamson or maybe Grubber. She might be in the company of a biker that they call Billy the Kid. I don't have a real name for him."

"William Bonney," Deputy Gleason responded immediately.

Max was taken aback. "Yeah, except I'm not looking for *that* Billy the Kid right now," Max replied with a chuckle, thinking that she was joking with him.

"No," Deputy Gleason said, recognizing Max's confusion over the phone. "The biker that you are looking for is named William Bonney, just like the Old West Billy the Kid. His parents' last name was Bonney and they named him William. He claims to be related to the original. I don't know if that's true, but his name really is William Bonney."

Max paused a moment to let it soak in. "That is pretty interesting. So I take it that you are familiar with Mr. Bonney?"

"He was quite the character for a while," Gleason answered. "He got caught up in a big meth ring bust, but I think he just got probation out of it. I haven't seen him for a while. He's still around, though, I think."

"I heard that you had a big meth problem around there," Max remarked.

"You probably read the book?" she replied.

"Yes, I did read it, a few years ago," he answered her.

"Don't believe everything you read," Gleason said. "It wasn't anything like the book says it was."

"That doesn't surprise me," Max laughed. "You don't sell books about the drug epidemic in Oelwein, Iowa, by saying it wasn't that big of a problem." Max waited a moment for a reaction, but didn't get one. "So if I come nosing around tomorrow, you think that I could find this William Bonney?"

"I don't know, but you might want to check with the probation offices over in West Union before you come over here. They might have an address on him."

Max heard Gloria come into the house. She called out to him, but he didn't answer.

"I'll do that," Max replied. "How about Angie Williamson? That's who I'm actually looking for. She was with him last we heard."

"I know who you're talking about," Gleason replied. "Blonde stripper, but I haven't seen her for a long time. The Oelwein police had a domestic assault case on Bonney for beating the hell out of her behind a bar one night. I don't think it went anywhere. She wouldn't testify. They filed charges, but I don't think that it ever actually went to trial."

Gloria came into her office to find Max sitting at her desk. She started to ask him what he was doing but saw that he was on the phone, so she busied herself putting away her stuff.

"To tell you the truth, both her and Bonney stayed in town and the Oelwein PD had most of the dealings with them. I just know what I picked up from them. Sorry, but that's about all I know about him."

"You don't happen to have a contact for me at the Oelwein PD, do you?" Max asked.

"Sergeant Fetters," Gleason offered. "He's a pretty good guy. I'm sure he will help you out with whatever you need."

"Thanks," Max started to end the call. "You've been a lot of help."

Before he could hang up, Deputy Gleason asked, "You aren't one of those Ames PD cops that won the Powerball a few years back, are you?"

"Yes, I am," Max replied. "We started a detective agency, and that's what we are doing now." Gleason didn't answer for a moment.

"You know an Officer Jackson?" she asked.

"Yes, I do," Max replied. "Milton. In fact, he's getting married to our receptionist this summer."

"Really?" Gleason exclaimed. "That's too bad."

"Why is that?" Max asked a little defensively.

Gleason laughed. "He's just a nice guy. It's always too bad when the guys like him get taken out of the available pool. I met him at a conference several years back. We've run into each other a few times, conferences, training, you know."

It was Max's turn to laugh. "I'll let him know that you were asking about him."

"Do that," Gleason replied and ended the call.

"What's up?" Gloria asked when Max put his phone down.

"We're working a case," Max replied.

"What?" Gloria exclaimed. "I thought that you guys learned your lesson with the last two."

"This one is for Monica. A gal that she used to dance with called her up out of the blue the other night and just said 'help me.' Then she hung up. So Monica put us on the scent. We're supposed to locate her and see what she needs help with."

Gloria snorted out a laugh. "You guys need to hire some real detectives to work for you. That way Monica could supervise them and you two could continue being worthless."

"That's harsh," Max said with a bit of mock hurt in his voice.

Gloria came up behind him and gave him a hug. "It's a harsh world out there, Max. Get out of my chair. I have some work to do."

Max got out of the chair and Gloria sat down in his place. Max left the room and went out to watch TV. He mixed himself a rum and Coke, then sat down on the couch. He turned on the TV and switched the channel to the local news, took his phone out of his pocket and started to search for the address of the Fayette County Probation Offices.

Monica stayed in the office after Max and Skip left. She continued searching the internet for any information that she could find that might help locate Angie, but she didn't even know what to look for. A patrol car pulled up in front of the G&B offices and parked next to her Nissan. She couldn't see who was driving because of the glare of the sun on the windshield. She assumed it was Milton coming back, and directed her attention to the computer screen again. She looked up when the door to the agency opened and a tall, slender officer with dark hair pulled back into a bun came through. Monica recognized her, but couldn't remember her name.

"Hey," the officer said when Monica looked up at her.

"Hey," Monica replied. "If you are looking for Max or Skip, they both left a little while ago."

"I didn't come in to talk to those two twats," she answered.

Monica had never heard Max and Skip referred to as "twats" before.

"I came in to ask you if anyone is throwing you a wedding shower," the woman said as she took a seat in one of the leather chairs across from Monica's desk. "Some of us at the PD were talking that maybe we should throw you a wedding shower, beings Milton works with us and all."

Monica had not thought about a wedding shower. She was sure that no one else she knew had, either. It was pretty much her mom and her daughter Essie, and Monica was sure that neither of them was planning a shower.

"That would be nice," Monica replied. "But you don't have to do it. I mean…" she trailed off.

"I know," the woman replied. "We want to do it. For Milton."

The remark had a bit of a sting to it. Monica wasn't sure how to take it. She came close to telling the woman that maybe they should throw a wedding shower for Milton then, but there was something intimidating about the woman that made Monica bite her tongue. Monica was not used to being intimidated. It was probably nothing, she thought, and let it go.

"A few of the women in records and dispatch thought that it would be nice," the woman continued. "A couple of female officers want to come, too."

"Well, thank you," Monica replied guardedly.

The woman waited a moment to see if Monica was going to continue. "We were wondering when might work for you and if you have anyone you want to invite. Milton said that your mother lives with you. Maybe she wants to come?"

Monica thought for a moment. She would probably invite Angie if Angie was around, but she couldn't think of anyone else. "I think that my mom would like that," she replied. "But she might have to take care of my daughter."

"Your daughter can come to the shower," the woman said. "Or if you don't want her to come, we'll do it when Milton's off and he can take care of her."

Monica hadn't thought about bringing Essie to a wedding shower. She hadn't thought about a wedding shower at all.

"Yes," Monica said. She dismissed her reservations. "I think it would be fun. I think that Essie would have fun, too."

"Okay," the officer said as she got to her feet. "Done deal. We'll get together and compare calendars. Find a time that works for everyone."

"I have a pretty flexible schedule," Monica piped up.

"I'm sure you do," the woman said. Monica thought that she heard that sting in her voice again.

"I just mean," Monica replied, "I know that you all have different shifts and days off. I'm just saying that I'm sure that I can make time for it whenever it works for you."

"That's nice of you," the woman said with the smile that Monica recognized as the one that people put on their faces when they want to be polite. "I'll get some dates and get back to you."

She turned and walked out the door. Monica watched her get into her patrol car and leave the parking lot.

Monica felt a bit uncomfortable. She had met the officer before, but she couldn't remember her name. The officer had been with Carlisle once when Monica and Milton had gone to a cop picnic. It was something they did nearly every week during the summer, just a picnic with cops, a few girlfriends and wives in the mix. Boyfriends, too, probably, although Monica didn't remember anyone being introduced to her that way. Nobody had said much to Monica, except Carlisle. She always felt a little uncomfortable at the picnics, like everyone was looking at her and wondering what the stripper was doing there. She wondered if the shower would be that way. But if the women from the PD wanted to throw her a shower for Milton, she wanted to enjoy it for Milton as well. She sat up straight and made up her mind: it would be fine. She would put her best foot forward and hope that things did not get awkward.

Chapter 5

Tuesday

Max pulled into the parking lot at Filo's just before eight, which was early for Max. He walked up to the counter and got into line behind two others waiting. Max stared out of the window toward the offices of G&B Detective Agency across the street. Skip's car was parked out front. Max suddenly found his thoughts interrupted.

"Max," the Barista called to him. Max turned to see him handing a cup of light roast over the display case to him.

"Thanks," said Max. "I'm taking it to go. I'll bring the cup back later."

The Barista nodded as he turned to help the people in line in front of Max. Max walked outside and got into his car. The cup that the Barista had given him was too big to fit in his cup holder, so Max drove with one hand, holding the hot cup of coffee in the other, trying not to spill it. He managed to make his way across the street and parked his Camaro next to Skip's Audi. He climbed out of the car with his cup of coffee and walked to the door. It was locked.

"Dang," Max said as he juggled his cup of coffee and slid the key into the lock. Max unlocked the door, put his keys in his pocket, then opened the door with his free hand.

"Dang," Max exclaimed again as the door bumped the cup in his hand and spilled hot coffee on his pant leg.

Max managed to get into the reception area without slopping any more coffee. He put his cup down on Monica's desk.

"Skip," he called out.

"What?" he heard Skip shout from his office down the hall.

"I'm here," Max called to him.

"I know," Skip shouted back. "I can hear you yelling at me."

Max took his cup and sat down in one of the chairs in the reception area to wait for Skip, watching the traffic go by on the street outside. Skip finally came up the hall with a leather jacket over his arm, a leather notebook in his hand and a Sig Sauer 40 cal pistol in a holster on his belt.

"Packing today?" Max observed. "Looks like you might be a little edgy these days after ol' Allan Proctor took a couple of shots at you, huh?" Max teased. Prior to the shootout with Proctor a few months earlier, Skip had seldom carried a gun. Max pulled up his own pant leg to reveal a .38 Special S&W revolver in an ankle holster. Skip looked down at the pistol. Max had been carrying that Smith and Wesson for as long as Skip had known him. Max looked up at him expectantly. Skip didn't say anything. Max let his pant leg drop and got up out of the chair.

"You driving?" Max asked.

"I think you should drive," Skip responded.

"Why?" Max asked as Skip was going out the door.

Just as Max was getting ready to follow, the phone on Monica's desk rang. Max looked at it and considered letting it go to voicemail for Monica to listen to when she got in, but he decided to answer it.

"G&B Detective Agency, we are not taking any cases currently," Max said into the phone.

"Who am I speaking with?" a voice on the other end of the phone asked.

"Detective Mosbey," Max responded. "To whom am I speaking?" he asked, emphasizing the "whom."

"Sheriff Kind, Boone County Sheriff's Office," the voice answered. "I hear you guys were up around Fraser and Ogden flashing your badges around like you were cops and asking a bunch of questions," Sheriff Kind said, dispensing with formalities and getting straight to his point.

Max didn't like the tone of his voice. "First of all, we don't have badges because we're not cops, so we don't need no stinking badges. Secondly, yes, we were up there yesterday, following up some leads on a case that we are working on."

"You guys ever think to check in with the real cops before you go running around investigating cases in our jurisdiction?" the sheriff asked with a sarcastic tone.

"You know anything about the whereabouts of an Angie Williamson who used to be Winston Grubber's girlfriend before he got busted and sent to prison?" Max asked pointedly.

"No," the sheriff answered, "I don't know any Angie Williamson."

"Well, that's why we didn't check in with you," Max shot back. "Because you don't know anything that might be helpful to our case. So we didn't want to waste your time or ours."

Max could tell over the phone that Kind was not used to being pushed back. He hesitated for a moment before he responded. "If you guys are going to go running around my county doing whatever it is you do, you need to be checking in with us here before you do it."

"Depending on what we find today, we might be back up there asking questions again tomorrow. Just checking in and letting you know," Max shot back.

"You've been advised," the sheriff replied.

"Noted," Max responded. "Anything else?"

"Not at the moment," said the sheriff, "but if you are snooping around up there and one of my deputies stops you, you might want to be a little more cooperative."

"I'll keep that in mind." Max hung up the phone.

Max locked the office door behind him. Skip was already sitting in Max's Camaro. Max opened the driver's door and slipped into the driver's seat. He pulled his phone out of his pocket and brought up the directions to the Fayette County Probation Offices, which he had entered into the GPS the night before.

"Where to first?" Skip asked.

"Fayette County Probation in West Union," Max replied. "Two and a half hours. You might want to take a nap."

"Where is Fayette County, even?" Skip asked.

"A ways north of Cedar Falls," Max replied.

"I'm going to take a nap," Skip replied.

Max pulled out of the parking lot and onto the street, heading toward US Highway 30.

"What took you so long?" Skip asked as he laid his head back on the headrest and closed his eyes.

"We got a call from the Boone County Sheriff on the way out the door." Max replied. "He was all pissy because we didn't let him know that we were nosing around his jurisdiction and asking questions."

"I suppose you smoothed it all over?" Skip asked.

"Not really," Max replied. "I kind of got into a pissing match with him. He accused us of flashing our badges around like we were real cops. I told him we didn't have badges. Things went downhill from there."

"Why am I not surprised?" Skip laughed. "He's got a point, though, Max," Skip went on. "We probably should have stopped in and given him a courtesy call before we went up there. I just didn't think of it. If we're going to actually do cases we might want to think about things like that. There is such a thing as protocol, you know."

"You're right," Max responded, a bit deflated, remembering how territorial they had been back when they were cops, and how they got upset when some other law enforcement agency came into Ames and conducted an investigation without telling them.

"I'll call him up later on, after he's calmed down a little, and apologize for you being such an asshole, and it will all be good." Skip said.

"That would be nice of you," Max replied. "And probably pretty easy for you, too, that me being an asshole part."

Skip just chuckled, his head still back on the headrest, his eyes closed. Max turned up the radio and drove on. He couldn't tell if Skip was sleeping, thinking, or if he had died.

Max pulled into West Union. The woman's voice on the GPS was giving him directions to the Fayette County Probation Offices. Max was carrying on a conversation with the voice on the phone. Skip had not opened his eyes but a few times to look around all the way. He and Max had talked a bit, but even though they were best of friends, after twenty plus years of riding around in the same car together, they didn't have a lot to say to each other.

"We're in West Union," Max told Skip.

Skip opened his eyes and looked around. "Looks a little dead around here," he observed.

Max pulled up in front of a building that looked like it might have been a store at one time. There was a sign over the door that said Fayette County Probation. Max checked the time on the car radio. It was eleven fifteen. The two got out of the car and walked into the building. The reception area was modern enough. A young woman looked up from her desk and greeted them as they came in. Three people sat in a waiting area to one side.

"Detectives Murray and Mosbey from the G&B Detective Agency," Skip said as he handed the receptionist their business card and gave her a moment to look at it. "We are looking for a William Bonney and an Angie Williamson. Deputy Gleason told us that they might be on probation with you here?"

The receptionist looked at the card again and turned it over. She smiled at the two detectives and was about to say something, but was interrupted by a phone call.

"Send Milly up," a voice said over her speaker phone. The receptionist looked at the three people sitting in chairs. A woman was already getting up and walking toward the offices down a hall to the right.

"I'm sorry about that," the receptionist said to Skip and Max. "We had William Bonney as a client here," she continued. "But he absconded about two months ago, and we don't have any knowledge of his whereabouts. If you would like, you can talk to his probation officer, but right now he has a client, so you will have to wait."

"We'll wait," Skip replied. Max was already taking a seat in the waiting area to the right. He picked up a *People* magazine and started paging through it. Skip sat down next to him.

"I used to get *Playboy* for the articles," Max said as Skip was sitting down.

"What does that have to do with anything?" Skip asked.

"I like looking through *People* for the pictures," Max laughed at his own joke.

"That's not even funny," Skip said.

Max looked over at the other two people sitting in the waiting area with them. "How's it going?" he asked. Neither responded to him.

Max and Skip did not have to wait long. A young man in work clothes came down the hall and stopped at the receptionist's desk.

"Need an appointment?" she asked him.

The man just nodded. The receptionist was tapping keys on her keyboard. How about the Tuesday the 14th next month?" she asked. "Same time?"

The man nodded again. The receptionist jotted something on a card and handed it to the young man. He looked around the waiting room as if he was looking for someone who wasn't there, then he walked out the door.

"There are two private detectives here to ask you some questions about William Bonney," the receptionist was saying into her phone as Max and Skip watched the young man leave.

"Down the hall, second door on the right," she said as she looked up at the two detectives.

Max and Skip stood and walked down the hall. The door to the office was open. Max peeked in and knocked on the door jam. "Howdy," he said.

A portly, balding, middle-aged man sat behind the desk jotting notes on a legal pad. He looked up and smiled. "Take a seat," he said. "Just give me a second here."

Max and Skip took a seat in the two chairs that occupied the cramped space between the desk and the door.

The man closed the folder, stood up and held out his hand. "Carl Robinson," he introduced himself.

"Skip Murray and Max Mosbey," Skip said and took Robinson's hand. Max handed him a business card as he shook Robinson's hand.

"Private detectives," Robinson reflected as he sat down and inspected the card. "What do you need from me?"

"We're looking for anything you have on William Bonney," Skip started. "Actually, we are trying to locate a woman who was with him, Angie Williamson. Her last known whereabouts was with Bonney, so that is why we are looking for him."

"Haven't seen either of them for two months," Robinson said. "I had him on a possession of controlled substance with intent to deliver, two years' probation, but he took off on me. I haven't seen the woman, either, since then. She used to come in with him."

"Any ideas at all where he might be?" Max asked.

"I only had him six or eight months," Robinson continued. "He wanted to go to Texas and finish his probation down there. He thought that I could just transfer him to some other probation office in Texas. When I told him it didn't work that way, he wanted to do his probation long distance over the phone. I told him that wasn't going to work, either. So then he just quit coming in. I went out looking for him after he didn't show up, but he had packed his bag and left. I figured that he up and went down to Texas like he was always talking about. But then a month or so ago I got a new client who said that he knew Bonney, and that he had gone to Boone County. So I put out the word to probation there, but I haven't heard anything on him. As it stands, there is a warrant out on him for probation violation and failure to appear. He missed a court date, too."

"Interesting," Skip remarked, "because we were over in Boone County yesterday asking about him and no one knew anything about him. They all said that he was up here."

Robinson shrugged his shoulders. "I got forty clients who have absconded on me and a hundred and eight who haven't yet. I have no idea where they all are. I don't have time to track them all down. I know that sounds bad, but there is only so much I can physically do."

"No," Skip replied, "were not questioning you, we know how it is. We used to be cops, we know what limited resources are."

"We aren't even that interested in Bonney," Max said. "We're looking for Angie. He's just a lead to her. You know anything about her, where she might be?"

"Not really," Robinson replied. "She was his 'woman,' if you know what I mean. He kept her close. He never showed up here without her. She always seemed a little afraid, and she was quiet, never talked to anyone in the office. But she was a stripper, and one of the conditions of probation was that Bonney couldn't drink or be on the premises of a bar or tavern, so that put her out of business. Because Bonney wasn't going to let her go strip without him around to keep an eye on her. I think that's the reason he wanted to go to Texas, or at least get away from here. Somewhere no one knew he was on probation."

"So, bottom line," Skip asked, "was he pimping her out?"

"I'm sure he was," Robinson replied.

"You think she was free to take off if she wanted?" Skip asked.

"Are you asking me if she was free to part ways with him and go on her own?" Robinson replied. "No, I don't think so. He had a hold on her, either physically or mentally, or maybe both, but it is one of those things. It wasn't something that I was dealing with. I was dealing with the conditions of his probation. I'm a probation officer, not a social worker." Robinson was getting defensive.

"But all the same," Skip continued, "wherever he went, she most likely went with him."

"I think that is a pretty good assumption."

"One other thing," Max said. "Bonney was in a motorcycle gang called the Hell Fighters. Was he associated with any motorcycle gang here?"

"He was," Robinson replied. "There's a Hell Fighters chapter here, and he was with them until he got busted. But a half dozen or more members were involved in the same bust. None of them are allowed to associate with each other or any other gang members, so the gang fell apart. There's still some ragtag remnants that didn't get picked up, but they are just a handful of wannabes who make it a point to stay away from the guys on probation, instead of the other way around. I doubt you could come up with one sporting his club colors right now."

"Interesting," Max said. "That's pretty close to the same story we heard in Boone County. They all got busted and the club broke up."

"Or that's what they say," Skip added. "I mean, maybe they are still active, just underground."

"Well, they all absconded from here," Robinson remarked. "Three went to prison, and we got three here on probation, and those three have all absconded to parts unknown."

"Could you give us names and whatever else you have on the other two?" Skip asked.

"Happy to," Robinson said. "I'll pull the files and copy them for you, if you want to go get a bite to eat and come back after lunch."

"That won't put you in a jam?" Max asked. "We don't want to compromise you."

"It isn't going to compromise me," Robinson snorted. "Just let me know if you run across any of them so that we can go pick them up. Hell, the county will give me an efficiency award or something for getting two private detectives to go out looking for these guys and not having to pay for it."

"We're on it," Max chuckled.

Max and Skip left the probation offices and got into Max's car. "Clients," Max shook his head. "They call them clients."

"I know, and they make appointments," Skip replied.

"We need to find somewhere to eat," Max said as he pulled out onto the street.

"I'll get the GPS on my phone to find us somewhere," Skip replied, swiping his finger up and down the screen of his phone.

Chapter 6

Tuesday

Skip talked Max into turning into a McDonalds after they left the probation office. Max would have preferred the greasy spoon café that his GPS had found, but Skip wasn't in the mood to sit and wait. So they stopped at the McDonalds and got something to eat. When Max was on the police department he would go through the drive-up regularly to grab a bite to eat on the go, but Gloria had nothing but disdain for fast food, so Max hadn't been to a McDonalds since they had won the Powerball and left the PD. He felt a little sick as they walked out to the parking lot. Skip seemed fine.

"Where to now?" Max asked, ignoring his queasy stomach.

"Let's check in with the Fayette County Sheriff's and let them know that we are in town doing an investigation."

Max gave Skip the eye.

"We don't need to alienate every law enforcement agency in the state," Skip suggested. "Let's just stop in and say hi. Maybe someone there can help us out."

Max got into the car and pulled out his phone to get directions to the sheriff's department. When he found it and pressed the screen, the same female voice that had directed them to the probation office started directing them to the sheriff's department. Max pulled out of the parking lot and drove, talking back to the voice as if it were a real person sitting in the cup holder between the front seats.

"Yes, ma'am," Max replied to the voice. "Did you say turn left at the next intersection? Yes, I'm going to turn left, I got my left turn signal on."

Skip ignored the conversation between Max and his phone.

Max pulled into the parking lot at the sheriff's department and parked. The two detectives walked into the building, into a small room with a plate glass window on the far wall. On the left wall was a line of 8x10 photos of the sheriff, the chief deputy, the dispatch supervisor and the chief jailor. Standard décor for the entrance to a county sheriff's offices. Behind the window sat a uniformed woman, who looked up as the two approached.

"Skip Murray and Max Mosbey," Skip introduced them through the metal grill in the middle of the window. Max could see that the glass was inch-thick standard bulletproof glass. Skip slid a business card under the window. "We're private detectives from Ames, and we are trying to locate a missing person. We just wanted to check in and let you know. We're going to go down to Oelwein and ask around, see if we can locate her there."

The uniformed woman was reading the card while Skip was talking.

"Everyone is at lunch right now," she said.

"Well, we don't need to talk to anyone, if you just let the sheriff know that we are on a case in this jurisdiction. We've already talked to Deputy Gleason about it over the phone. She is aware of what we are doing."

The uniformed woman looked at the card again, then tossed it in a basket with some mail.

"I'll let the sheriff know," she said.

"Thanks, appreciate that," Skip replied.

The woman sat looking at the two through the window.

"Thanks, again," Skip said.

He and Max went out through the door and into the parking lot.

"That was pretty exciting," Max observed.

"Covering our bases," Skip replied. "They can't say that we're digging around and flashing our badges without telling them."

"We don't have badges to flash," Max corrected him.

"I know," Skip replied back.

Max drove back to the probation office and parked. Skip jumped out, leaving Max in the car, and ran inside. A few minutes later he came out with a manila folder in his hand. Skip got in the car and shut the door.

"Got it." He opened the folder and started to examine the contents while Max drove out of the parking lot.

With the help of the woman's voice on his phone, Max made his way out of West Union and toward Oelwein. It was a twenty-five mile drive down Iowa Highway 150. He held the Camaro at just under ten over the speed limit. They pulled into Oelwein in less than half an hour. Though West Union was the county seat, Oelwein was the biggest town in Fayette County, with a population of a little over sixty-five hundred residents. Three times bigger than West Union. The whole county did not have much more than twenty thousand residents. It was a typical Iowa rural town, known mostly for their packing plant and their distinction as the meth capital of the world, a claim that was loudly denied by the residents there.

On the way down Skip had given the files for the three bikers a quick going over, but he could see that it was going to take more than a cursory scan to make any headway on them. Most of the notes were hand written, some of them along the borders of documents and court orders. Others were scribbled in incomplete sentences on legal size sheets of paper, and looked like Robinson had been trying to write while he interviewed the bikers at their monthly meetings. Skip gave up, closed the file folder and tossed it on the rear seat of the Camaro.

"This place is just weird," Max observed. "You ever spend any time here? It's like an *Outer Limits* episode. I mean, it's like everyone in town is an alien who took over someone's human body."

Skip looked down the street. It was one-thirty in the afternoon, and there was only one other car that they could see moving. "Pretty quiet," he replied.

"It's not quiet," Max observed. "It's silent."

Skip looked around and agreed, it was silent.

"You spend a lot of time in Oelwein?" Skip asked.

"Spent a night here a long time ago," Max said. "When we used to do that big bicycle ride across the state. We overnighted here. I got to tell you, it was spooky. I was actually glad to get out of here the next morning."

Skip looked around at the empty streets. It was midday, and nothing was moving. "Now you're starting to spook me," he said.

"You have reached your destination on the right," the voice on Max's phone informed them.

"Thank you very much for all your help," Max replied, pulling into one of the half-dozen empty parking spaces in front of the Oelwein Police Department. He picked up his phone and closed the GPS app.

"Why do you always talk to your GPS?" Skip asked.

"She has such a friendly and helpful voice," Max replied. "I'm just trying to be polite."

"So you're trying to be nice and polite to the voice on your phone, but you get in a pissing match with the Boone County Sheriff?"

"She is a nicer person," Max said defensively. "She doesn't start out accusing me of flashing my badge."

The two detectives got out of the car and went up to the door of the police department. It almost looked abandoned. Max was surprised when he pulled on the door handle and it opened. He walked in. Skip followed. A man in a uniform with sergeant's stripes on the sleeves sat at a desk behind a counter. He looked up as they came in.

"Would you happen to be Sergeant Fetters?" Max asked.

"Yes, I am," Fetters replied. "You the two detectives from Ames?"

"Yep," Max replied back.

Fetters stood up and reached across the counter to shake hands. "Deputy Gleason told me you guys might be showing up."

Skip shook Fetters's hand over the counter and gave him one of their business cards. Fetters turned and shook Max's hand.

"Skip Murray and Max Mosbey," Skip introduced them. "Desk duty?" he asked.

"Holding down the fort while the records clerk is at lunch. She hangs around during the noon hour because that's when a lot of people come in. I usually cover for her after the noon rush." Fetters laughed when he said "noon rush."

"Pretty quiet town," Max observed. "How many officers you have?"

"Six," Fetters answered, "plus four reserve officers." He paused. "Gleason told me that you guys are looking for Billy Bonney and his girlfriend?"

"We are," Skip replied.

"Can't help you much, there," Fetters said. "They just disappeared. They lived in a little rundown shack over on 6th Street, and one evening they loaded up and left. He was on probation for PCS with intent. Warrant came out on him, but he was long gone, that Williamson girl with him."

"No ideas?" Max asked.

"I heard from some of the mopes that they went back to Boone, but I don't know." Fetters replied.

"We were all over Boone County yesterday, and no one has seen him since he came here," Max replied.

"Well, I don't know if he went back to Boone or not," Fetters said. "That's just what we were told when we went looking for him. I mean, they would just as soon send me the wrong direction as the right direction. But I know that Fayette County contacted Boone County about the warrant, and as far as I know they didn't come up with him. Gleason would have known if they had."

"That doesn't surprise me," Max said. "They're not real cooperative around Boone County, either."

"They're fine," Skip interjected. "Max has been having a pissing match with the Boone County Sheriff," he explained. "How about Texas? His probation officer told us he talked about going to Texas."

Fetters shrugged his shoulders. "Who knows? He could have gone to Texas, or he could have been talking about it to throw Robinson off his trail. He could have gone to Minnesota or Nebraska. Those guys are real good at telling you one thing, then doing just the opposite. If he was talking about Texas, I would be more inclined to believe that he went back to Boone. But regardless, we don't know where he is."

"You know what he was driving when he bugged out?" Skip asked.

"Red 2006 Dodge Dakota," Fetters replied. "Had an old black nineties Harley with ape-hanger handlebars that didn't run half the time, too. I probably got the license number of both, if you want them."

"That would be great," Max replied. "So did you have much trouble with Bonney here in town?"

"Just a couple of domestic assaults. Nothing too serious. He would just get physical with Williamson sometimes. We would file on him, put him in jail, but the next day they would be back together again. Then we would arrest him for violating the no contact order, and on and on it went. Then she wouldn't cooperate or testify and the charges would get dropped and a month later we would be doing it all over again."

"Sounds familiar," Skip said, looking over at Max.

"The bikers read that meth book that guy wrote and decided to take over the meth business in Oelwein, and they got their asses busted for it. This is Oelwein. You don't sell meth in Oelwein and keep it a secret." Fetters shook his head. "Three of them went to prison, and three of them, including Bonney, got probation. But then they all three absconded. That's the last we had any contact with them."

"They all three abscond at the same time?" Skip asked.

"Pretty much," Fetters answered him.

"And you don't have anything on any of them?"

"Nope," Fetters said. "Nothing. I gotta tell you, we got a small department here and limited manpower. We don't spend a lot of time and money trying to find some bikers for the county who violated their probation and took off. As far as we are concerned, that's three shitheads that we don't have to screw around with anymore." He paused for a moment. "You know what I mean? I don't really care where they went, as long as they aren't here."

"We know where you're coming from," Max replied. "You do what you can with what you got."

"That's it," Fetters said. "You guys are welcome to snoop around if you want, but I don't think you are going to get anything more than we have. Honestly, I don't even know where to tell you to start."

Max and Skip could relate. "How about those plate numbers?" Skip asked. "That would help. Then we'll get out of your hair."

"No problem," Fetters replied. "I'll be right back."

Fetters went into a glass-sided office at the back of the room behind the counter. Max and Skip could see him rustling through papers on a desk. He jotted something on a piece of paper and came out with it in his hand. He passed it over the counter to Skip.

"Thanks," Skip said as he took the piece of paper. "If you do happen to hear anything, you got our number."

"Will do," Fetters said, reaching across the counter to shake hands again with the two detectives.

"Where did these guys hang out?" Skip asked as they turned to leave. "Is there a bar in town where they congregated?"

"Loopers, on the main drag just as you're going out of town to the south," Fetters replied. "Good luck getting anything out of anyone there, though. They aren't particularly forthcoming when it comes to answering questions about their clientele."

"Thanks for all the help, and stay safe," Max said as they walked out the door.

Max and Skip walked to the parking lot. Other than Max's Camaro it was still empty. They got into the car and Max hit the ignition.

"Where to now?" Max asked. "It's getting about time for Gleason to come on duty. We could go back up to West Union and talk to her."

"What's she going to add?" Skip replied. "She told you to talk to Fetters."

Max shrugged his shoulders. "How about stopping in at Loopers, just to check it out? We're here."

"Nothing to lose," Skip remarked. "I could probably use a beer."

Max headed the Camaro south. Just as they came to the city limits, Max spotted the bar on the left side of the street. It was a Butler building that looked like it had been a convenience store at one time. The overhead awning that once sheltered the gas pumps was still there. The pumps were gone. The lot held two cars and two pickup trucks that looked like farm trucks. The building was nothing fancy. The front was lined with windows. Without the temporary marquee mounted on wheels out front and the neon beer signs in the windows, one wouldn't know that there was a bar inside. There were no markings to indicate parking spaces. Max parked under the awning, away from the other vehicles where he might get a door ding in his new car.

"I think there's a place over there that's a little farther away," Skip said.

"A little exercise might be good for you," Max responded.

The two detectives got out of the car and made their way toward the door of the bar. Max went in first and looked around. The interior looked unmistakably like the interior of a convenience store that had been transformed into a bar. Six booths lined up along the windows on the left, with a kitchen on the end, at the back of the building. On the right, a scarred wooden bar took the place of the checkout counter.

Four men dressed like farmers occupied one of the booths. A man and a woman who did not look like farmers sat on stools at the bar. A big man with a mullet was bartending. Max nudged Skip and tilted his head toward the bar. Skip was trying to decide if Max was pointing out the bartender's choice of hairstyle or if he just wanted to suggest that they belly up to the bar. Skip decided it was the hair.

The two sat down at the bar. The man and woman looked their way. Skip nodded to them. "Looks like the happening place in town."

"What'll you have?" the bartender asked. The two customers turned their attention away from Max and Skip and toward each other.

"Miller Lite," Skip replied.

"Same," Max said.

The bartender went to the cooler on the wall behind the bar and took two bottles of Miller Lite out with one hand, and with the other he pulled a bottle opener out of his pocket and deftly popped the caps off the bottles. He put them on the bar in front of Skip and Max.

"Anything else?"

"Nice little place you got here," Skip remarked. "I'll bet it's hopping on the weekends."

"Live music on Saturday nights," the bartender replied.

"Get a lot of motorcycles in here when it gets a little warm?" Skip chatted up the bartender. "We heard that there is a motorcycle club here in town.

"We get a few," the bartender responded. "Not as many as we used to, though. The Hell Fighters used to come around, but they pretty much scattered. A bunch of them went to jail on some drug charges."

"No kiddin'?" said Max. "Hell Fighters? I used to actually know some Hell Fighters that lived in Boone. A guy named Billy Bonney." Max paused for a moment. The bartender said nothing. "Yeah, that was his real name, same as the Old West outlaw. Billy the Kid. I think he even went by that."

The bartender didn't respond. "What's the name of that other guy that used to hang out with Billy?" Max asked Skip.

"Grubber," Skip replied to Max. "I can't remember his first name. I think they called him Snake Eyes. He wasn't a bad guy. I mean, you didn't want to get on his bad side. But I used to see him around."

"Didn't he have a girlfriend who was a dancer in one of the bars?" Max picked up the conversation. "I can't remember her name. Cute little gal, though."

"Yeah, that's him," Skip answered Max.

The two turned back to the bartender, who was listening.

"You ever have dancers in here?" Max asked.

"We used to," the bartender replied. "Not much of a draw, though. Live music brings them in. Around here you don't bring your wife or girlfriend to a strip bar, but live music is different. It has a wider appeal," the bartender deadpanned.

"I can see that," Skip agreed. "I wonder what happened to Bonney?" Skip turned back to Max. "He just sort of disappeared."

"No idea," Max shook his head.

The two looked up at the bartender.

"Never heard of him, if that's what you're fishing for," the bartender said.

"Not fishing for anything," Max said. "Just talking."

"Right," the bartender responded as he turned and walked down the bar to where the couple was sitting. He leaned over the bar and talked to them in a low voice. The man glanced over at the two detectives, then took his eyes away from them when he saw them looking over at him.

Max took a big swig from his bottle, looked at Skip and motioned toward a pool table that stood opposite the booths where the farmers were gossiping. Skip got up and walked over to the table with him. Max dug in his pockets and came up with two quarters. He held them out toward Skip. Skip put his hand in his pocket and came out with a handful of change. Max took two more quarters from Skip's hand and plugged them into the pool table. Balls fell into the tray below. Skip found a straight cue from the rack while Max was racking the balls. When he was finished, Skip broke them.

Max had taken a cue at random from the rack and was chalking it up.

"I think he figured us out," Max said, referring to the bartender.

"He's been around the block," Skip replied.

Max had taken a shot. "I got stripes."

Skip leaned on the table.

"I'm still shooting," Max told him.

"Of course you are," Skip stepped back as Max put a ball in the corner pocket.

Max chalked the cue as he went around the table and set up for his next shot. Skip stood drinking his beer while Max put another ball in the side pocket.

"Finish her up," Skip said. "Let's head home."

Max took another shot. The eight ball went in the same pocket as the ball before it. "You win," Max said. He turned and put his cue in the rack. Skip replaced his cue as well when Max stepped away, and followed him out the door. They left the two half-empty bottles of beer sitting on a shelf on the wall beside the pool table.

Chapter 7

Tuesday

Max pulled his car up in front of Skip's Audi and put it in park. As they had turned onto the street that ran in front of the G&B Detective Agency, both men had looked for Monica's car parked in her reserved space, but it was not to be seen.

"Going in?" Max asked as Skip was opening the door of the Camaro to get out.

"What time is it?" Skip asked.

"Time for a rum and Coke," Max replied.

"Why not?" Skip answered, closing the car door again. Max pulled into the parking space next to Monica's reserved space and parked. The two got out of the car and walked to the door of the agency. Skip had his keys in his hand and opened the door. He didn't bother to lock it behind him. Max made a beeline for the break room and the bar that occupied much of one wall. He took two glasses from a shelf and placed them on the bar.

"Lime?" Max called out to Skip.

"Sure," Skip called back from his office.

Max heard the front door open.

"Hello," he heard a voice call from the reception area just inside the door.

"Back here," Max shouted. Skip came out of his office and walked past the bar toward the front.

"They sent me over to get coffee cups," a college-aged woman said when Skip came into the reception area.

"Girl is here from Filo's looking for coffee cups," Skip shouted back to Max.

Max came out of the break room with a cardboard box that held a half dozen coffee mugs.

"Didn't get a chance to wash them," he said as he handed the box to her. "Sorry."

The girl took them.

"You new?" Max asked.

"Yes, I just started last week," she replied.

"Yeah," Max said, "I am always going to bring them back, but for some reason I never do."

"It's alright," she replied as she turned and went out the door with the box of cups in her hand.

"Do you think I should have given her a tip for coming over and getting those?" Max asked Skip as they watched her cross the street.

Skip just shrugged his shoulders and took a seat in one of the easy chairs that sat opposite Monica's desk. Max went back to the bar and returned a few minutes later with their drinks in his hand.

"What now?" he asked Skip.

"I don't know," Skip replied. "I think that we have to go back over to Boone County and do some more investigating. Everything we have right now makes a circle that sends us right back to where we started. Someone over there has to know something. I think that we need to widen our net."

"I think that, right now, that is the only direction we have to go on," Max agreed. "At least our sources in Fayette County seem reliable enough. I think maybe yesterday we got the runaround."

Skip got up and went to Monica's desk. He picked up her office phone and dialed a number.

"Who are you calling?" Max asked.

Skip held up his hand, palm toward Max.

"Yes, this is Skip Murray, and I'm wondering if Sheriff Kind is still in?"

Max gave Skip a bit of a glare. Skip held his hand up again.

"Sheriff Kind," Skip said into the phone. "Skip Murray here, G&B Detective Agency. I heard that you and my partner had a talk today that didn't go well. I just want to start by apologizing for him. He sometimes opens his mouth before he engages his brain."

Max stood up and walked toward the desk. Skip held up his hand a third time.

"Yes, well, we really didn't plan on getting that involved over there in our investigation yesterday. We just sort of fell into a rabbit hole. In hindsight, I wish that we had thought to touch base with you before we let it go that far. But again, I apologize."

Max paced the floor. Skip looked up and mouthed the words, "sit down." Instead, Max walked down the hall toward his office. He could still hear Skip talking on the phone.

"Yes sir, well, we are trying to locate an Angie Williamson who hasn't been seen by her friends and family for a while. One of them hired us to locate her. That's pretty much all there is to it. We're not looking to cause any problems for anyone. We just want to find her and make sure she is alright."

Max went to the bar and started mixing another rum and Coke.

"Yes, sir," Skip said. "We just went up to Fraser to look for her because that is the last place that her friends knew of her whereabouts. But then we ended up in Odgen talking to her old boyfriend's brother to see if he knew where she might be. Anyway, we were in West Union and

Oelwein today, following up the leads that we got yesterday, and they are all pointing back to Boone County. We were thinking that tomorrow we might come back over and do some more investigating. See if we can find something a little more substantial about where she might be, so we're not out there stumbling around."

Max came out with his drink and sat down in one of the chairs opposite Monica's desk.

"Yes, sir," Skip continued. "No doubt. We don't want anyone thinking that we are affiliated in any way with any law enforcement agency. We make sure that is clear, that we are private detectives. We made sure everyone we talked to yesterday knew that."

Skip paused for a moment.

"Thank you, sir, I appreciate it. And sorry again about this morning."

Skip hung up the phone. "What a condescending asshole," he declared.

"What did I tell you?" Max exclaimed.

"Yeah, well, we have to work in his jurisdiction, not the other way around," Skip replied. "Like it or not, we have to get along with him if we are going to go over there and try to do anything."

"No, we don't," Max said.

"Yes, we do," Skip replied.

Max was going to argue again, but Skip was dialing the phone. He put it on speaker as it rang.

"Monica," Skip replied to Max's questioning look.

"Hello," Monica's voice came on the phone. "You guys come up with anything today?"

"Not much," Skip replied. "Made a full circle. Everything pointed right back to Boone County." Skip paused for a moment. "You come up with anything in your research?"

"A bit," Monica said. "I found an obituary that listed Angie as a daughter. There was also a surviving husband, a surviving son, Ronald, and a surviving sister. I came up with the husband's phone number, and I talked to him for a while. He didn't have much good to say about Angie. He was a second or third husband, and he married her mother after Angie had moved out. He said that he only talked to Angie a couple of times, and that she and her mother didn't see each other, he didn't know why. She didn't come to her mother's funeral, but she sent flowers, and that was five years ago. So that would be before I even knew her, and she never mentioned her mother to me. He also said that Ronald, the surviving son, is Angie's older brother, but he hasn't seen nor heard from him since his mom died. So basically, he wasn't any help at all."

"Did you find anything on Ronald?" Max shouted at the phone.

"Just some guy in South Africa, a musician." Monica answered. "I'm pretty sure it isn't the same guy. I'll look more, though. There are lots of Ronald Williamsons, but the guy in South Africa comes up most of the time. When you run the name, I mean."

"Do you know that the Ronald we are looking for is a Williamson?" Skip asked. "Could be from a different sperm donor."

Monica didn't say anything for a moment. "Was that supposed to be humorous?" she asked. "Because it isn't. People can't control where they come from."

"I'm just saying," Skip answered in defense of himself. "Did you ask the stepdad?"

"No," Monica replied. "I'll call him back and make sure."

The two detectives listened to see if Monica had anything to add. "Okay," Skip finally said, "That's something. Keep looking for anything else that you can find. We're going back up to Fraser tomorrow and start all over again."

"I was thinking," Monica responded. "Why don't I do some leg work, too? Maybe I can hit some of the strip clubs down toward Des Moines. Pose as a dancer looking for work, throw Angie's name around. See if anyone says that they know her."

Max and Skip thought about it a moment. "I don't know about that," Max said. "How do you think that your intended would feel about that?"

"I'll talk to him," Monica said. "It's just undercover work. How did it set with Gloria back when you two were doing prostitution stings on the PD? That probably wasn't a consideration then. What's the difference?"

"Two things," Max countered. "One, we were already married, and two, it was my job."

"Well, this is my job," Monica replied.

"Your job is taking care of Essie, going to college, getting married to Milton and answering the phone to tell people that we aren't taking any cases. In that order. You're a busy girl." Max said.

"And Angie was my friend," Monica replied. "I think that I am a big part of this investigation, and I don't want to sit on the sidelines for this one. Milton will understand."

"What about school?" Skip asked.

"I'm on spring break."

"How about studies?" Max tried. "Don't you have a paper to write or a project to do over spring break?"

"Why don't you let me worry about that?" Monica said with a bit of anger in her voice.

The three were quiet for a moment. Max was looking at Skip, waiting for some support. Skip did not say anything.

"What do you think?" Monica broke the silence.

"I think that you should at least talk it over with Milton before you go off posing as a stripper," Skip replied. "After all, you've been trying to put that part of your life behind you. Do you really want to go do that?"

"I'm going to see him tonight," Monica sighed.

"Monica," Skip said in serious tone. "Another thing: going undercover is risky. You don't just go out and pretend you are someone or something and start asking questions. You need a plan, you need backup. Don't go out on your own. It isn't smart."

"I won't," Monica assured him.

"Talk to you first thing in the morning. We'll all meet up here." Skip ended the call.

"I don't think that is such a good idea," Max said to Skip as he hung up the phone.

"I don't, either," Skip replied. "But you can't tell her what she can do and can't do. This whole case is about her. We can't cut her out of it. Maybe Milton can talk her out of this undercover idea of hers, but I doubt it."

"You're right," Max sighed. "I just don't like it. She's too close to this—too emotionally involved."

"Well, we haven't made much headway up 'til now," Skip shrugged his shoulders.

The two sat looking out the window at cars driving by on the street, sipping their drinks, both lost in their own thoughts. Max was checking the vehicles parked across the street in front of Filo's. He caught sight of Gloria's little red sportscar driving through the parking lot from the direction of the fitness center in the building next to the coffee shop. She must have been at a class, Max thought.

"Probably a yoga class," Max said aloud.

"Probably," Skip replied. "Okay, tomorrow we meet up here with Monica. We'll take Monica with us. That will help her feel like she is doing something. Go back up to Fraser, talk to the guy up there again, then to Ogden, then let's go into Boone and just start hitting bars. See what we can find out. I think there's one right north of the tracks that I used to see a lot of Harleys parked out in front of, the few times I was over there. Anyway, we just keep asking questions. If we don't come up with anything, we go south. We start hitting the strip clubs south of Ankeny and north of Des Moines. There's three or four of them that I remember. We'll let Monica do her thing. We'll watch her back."

"She doesn't get out of our sight," Max said.

"That's right, she doesn't get out of our sight," Skip agreed. "That's going to be the conditions."

Angie sat on her bed, looking out the window at the woods below. The house where she was staying was nice. It was huge, by any standards. She heard men's voices outside the door, but she couldn't make out what they were saying. She was tempted to open it a bit and peek out. They were probably playing poker. They usually started early and played through the night. When they took breaks, some of the players would come up and visit her. She would give them whatever they wanted, and when they left, satisfied, she would clean herself up, sit on the bed and wait.

They always told her to stay there and to keep the door closed unless they called for her. She knew what awaited her if she got caught trying to pull something, and she was always afraid. She looked across the room and into the bathroom. It wasn't so bad, she told herself. It was a nice room, with a king sized bed, its own bathroom and a nice view of the forest that lay behind the house. Sometimes she opened the window at night and she could hear the river flowing beyond the house. What else should she want? She was lucky. It could be a lot worse. It could be a whole lot worse. It had been a lot worse when she and Billy were living in a trailer in Oelwein. There was nothing wrong with this, she convinced herself.

Angie went to the door and pressed her ear against it, trying to hear what was going on downstairs. She couldn't tell. She went back and sat on the bed. She wished that she had a TV. She looked out the window and thought about how much she had loved Winston. But Winston was gone now. He died in prison, leaving her in Billy's care. She hadn't loved Billy, but he treated her okay. A few times he got high or drunk and slapped her around for reasons that he imagined, and the neighbors would call the cops. The cops just made things worse. But most of the time he took pretty good care of her. Angie didn't expect more. She was second fiddle, and she knew it. She couldn't complain.

Then one day Billy had come into their trailer with another man, just as he often did. Angie had gone back to the bedroom to wait. She was surprised when Billy came back to her room and sat beside her. He told her that he liked her a lot, but that he was leaving town and she wasn't coming along. Then he had sat beside her for a long time, holding her hand. When he got up and left the room, the man that had come to the trailer with Billy came into the room. He and Angie had sex on the bed. When they were done, the man stood up and told her to pack whatever she wanted to take with her. She did as she was told. When she came out of the room, the man was waiting and Billy was gone.

Outside the trailer was parked a black Ford Escalade with tinted windows. The man opened the back and put her suitcase inside. Then he opened the passenger door and held it for Angie. It was the nicest vehicle she had ever ridden in. The man told her his name was James. He said that Billy had owed him a lot of money, and that now he was going to take care of Angie. That she would be with him instead of Billy. Angie had wanted to ask him how long, and if she would ever see Billy again, but she didn't. She didn't know James well enough to risk it. So she had sat in silence, watching the road in front of them as they drove.

Angie didn't know how long they were on the road, maybe a couple of hours, but they hadn't stopped. They drove into the night. Finally, they took a paved lane off of a blacktop road that had looked a little familiar to her, and came to a large house overlooking a river. It was beautiful, actually. She had gotten out with James, and he had called her to the back of the Escalade. He unloaded her suitcase on the ground and left it for her. She followed him into the house and looked around. It was open, and she could see that the back of the house, overlooking the river, was all glass. She couldn't see much in the dark, but she was sure that the view would be gorgeous during the day. James told her to follow him. He took her up a flight of stairs to a bedroom. It was huge compared to the bedroom in the trailer back in Oelwein. He told her to unpack, make herself at home, and not to come out of the room unless he told her to. She had done as she was instructed.

Angie had waited for James, but he didn't come back that night. She had fallen asleep. James woke her in the morning with a cup of coffee, two scrambled eggs, three pieces of bacon and toast. He set it on the dresser and left. When she finished eating, Angie had gathered up the plates and the coffee cup and left the room with them. She was looking for the kitchen when James found her. He asked her what she was doing, and she told him that she was taking the dishes to the kitchen. James took them from her and told her to go back to her room and not to come out again. She spent the rest of that day there.

That evening a woman had entered her room without knocking. The woman hung some dresses in the closet and put some other clothes in the dresser. When she was done she stood in the doorway, arms crossed. She explained to Angie that her job was going to be to make the customers happy, in whatever way she could. That sometimes she would be invited into the salon with the customers, but otherwise she was to stay in her room and wait. She asked Angie if she had any questions. Angie knew exactly what the woman was talking about. The woman left, and Angie waited as she was told. Three men visited her that night. The woman came in after the third left and told Angie that she wouldn't have any more visitors that night. She told Angie to go to sleep. Angie asked the woman her name. The woman turned and left, shutting the door behind her. Angie had taken a long shower and gone to sleep.

In the morning, another woman, who told Angie that her name was Jean, brought her breakfast. A few hours later, Jean brought her a ham and cheese sandwich, a salad and some chips for lunch. That evening she had pork chops, a baked potato and French cut string beans. Angie had not had three good meals like that in one day for as long as she could remember. Angie did not leave her room the whole day. The third day, when Jean brought her supper, she told Angie to expect some visitors. Angie went through the wardrobe that the woman had brought the first day and picked out a cute outfit. She got dressed and waited.

Her life had continued that way for a long time, now. Angie didn't know how long. The days ran together after a while. Angie didn't get out of her room much. On the evenings that there were customers, which was more often than not, Jean brought Angie something to eat, then came back for the plates an hour or so later. They fed her well enough, although not a lot. Angie knew that she was not putting on any weight, even though she spent almost all of her time in the bedroom.

Sometimes Angie got to be a hostess, which meant she was allowed to leave the room. Besides Jean and the first woman, whose name Angie still did not know, there were two other women in the house, but they did not talk much. The woman that Angie did not know her name made sure of that. Whenever the three were in the salon, they were watched closely. Once in a while they would go to the kitchen and eat together, or on rare occasions, when there were no customers, they would be allowed to watch TV in the room where the poker tables were set up. Jean would chatter away with them, bring them tea or water, but if they tried to hold a conversation with each other it was always cut short by the woman with no name. They were never allowed together without her being present. But every day Angie would hear Jean down the hall talking to the other women in the same manner as she visited with Angie. It seemed that Jean was the only one allowed to chat, but she never said anything, really. And no one said much to Jean. Just meaningless chatter.

Although she tried desperately to push the thought out of her mind, Angie realized that she was a prisoner in the house. She began to worry about when she was going to leave, and she was aware of the possibility that she wasn't going to. At least not alive.

Chapter 8

Tuesday

Monica was sitting on a park bench at the edge of the neighborhood playground, watching Essie play on the equipment. Next to her sat Milton. He was a big man, but not big in the sense that he was overweight—just the opposite, Milton was physically in the prime of his life. Monica wanted a marriage that lasted forever. She didn't want to end up like so many people she knew, never having a relationship that stood the test of time. So she thought about it a lot, and often wondered what it would be like to grow old with each other. What would life be like when Milton got a paunch, and when she put on some weight and got a wide bottom like her mom? She tried to picture them as parents, and even grandparents. It made her comfortable to think about it in those terms. But it also scared her to think that her dream might be just that: a dream.

"Well, what exactly do you want to do?" Milton was asking. "Are you actually thinking of dancing again? Because if that's the case, I'll tell you right now that I'm not good with that. In fact, I can't even talk about that."

"No, Milton," Monica replied, "I'm not talking about dancing, I'm talking about posing as a dancer who's looking for a job. Asking some questions, getting some information that the clubs probably wouldn't give the guys. Nothing more. Just going in and posing as a dancer looking for work."

Monica could tell that she was not selling it to Milton. "Listen, Max used to do prostitution stings, right?"

"Yes," Milton answered, a little reluctantly, knowing where she was going with it.

"Did Max do the dirty with the prostitutes?"

"No," Milton said with the same tone.

"So that is what I want to do: just work with the guys undercover to get some information. Because no one is going to talk to them, but I think I can get them to talk to me."

Milton didn't reply.

"I just want to help, to play an active role in this case. My life is different now, and I'm a different person than I was when I was dancing. I know that I'm getting married in a few months to a police officer and I'm so proud of him that I tell everyone that I'm marrying him. But—"

"Here comes the 'but,'" Milton interrupted.

"But Angie is in some kind of trouble. I'm the person she called for help. I work for a detective agency that is investigating it, and I want to have a role in this. You understand that, don't you?"

"Yes," Milton replied. "I do understand it. I understand it well. But I still am not happy about you even pretending to go back to that life. Understanding your reasons doesn't make it go down better."

Monica could see that Milton was forming something up in his head, and she waited.

"So here's the deal," Milton continued. "I know that the chances of Max and Skip getting anyone to give up any information worth shit to this investigation is not good. As soon as they start asking questions, people smell cop." He raised his eyebrows and she nodded. "But the thing is, you're a girl. You're an attractive—no, you're a very hot-looking girl. So you can pretend you are a dancer, or you can *actually be* a detective, just like Max and Skip, working on a case. And guys are still going to spill their guts to you. So why don't you just be who you are, instead of pretending to be who you were? I'm happier with you being who you are now."

Monica thought about it. Milton was making sense. "Do you think that the guys will let me do that?"

"Yes, I think they will, if you explain to them how important it is to you," Milton replied.

Monica thought about it a little more. The lights came on around the playground and along the sidewalk that wound its way through the townhomes. It was still spring and it still got dark early. It was getting cold.

"Fair enough," Monica said, nodding. "Fair enough. I'll be a detective."

"I think that you will make a good detective," Milton responded with a smile.

Monica called to Essie as they stood up and turned toward home. Milton hadn't told her what to do and expected her to obey; he had disagreed with her idea and respectfully presented a better one. This relationship was worlds away from the one she had observed between Angie and Winston. She felt like she and Milton were becoming one, cementing the partnership.

Essie wanted to ride on Milton's shoulders. He picked her up like she was a feather pillow and threw her behind his head, her little legs over his shoulders, her hands clasped together around his forehead, laughing in her excitement. Milton held both her ankles, keeping her in place. Monica reached up and put her arm through his as they walked toward her townhouse. Monica had never felt so close to Milton.

"What would I do without you?" she asked him.

"Well, I hope you never have to find out," Milton said lightheartedly.

"I want some ice cream," Essie called out from her perch on Milton's shoulders.

"Should we go get Grandma and take her along?" Milton asked.

"Only if she can behave herself and not talk too much," Essie said in a serious voice.

"I wish that you wouldn't teach her that kind of stuff," Monica said. "You know she says that stuff to Mom."

Milton laughed.

"Do you think that you could at least try?" Monica asked him. "Why do you have to stir the pot?"

"I'm not stirring the pot," Milton replied. "It's all in fun. We're just having fun."

"Well, it isn't fun for Mom, so quit it," Monica rebuked. "And you've been on thin ice with her since day one. You aren't helping yourself any, Buster."

"Well, she's not been real subtle about letting everyone know it, either." Milton defended himself.

"So you be the big boy about it, then," Monica said. "She was here long before you were."

"Essie, Grandma can come along even if she doesn't behave herself and talks too much," Milton told the little girl. "We both love Grandma, don't we?

"Yes," said Essie.

"See?" Milton said to Monica.

"You're on thin ice," Monica replied. "Remember that."

"Why is daddy Milt always in trouble?" Milton asked Essie.

The three walked along the lighted path toward home.

"You know that officer, I think that her name is Sarah?" Monica asked. "She was with Carlisle once at a cop picnic."

"What about her?" Milton asked casually.

"She stopped by the office today, and she wants to have a wedding shower for me. Said that she and some of the other women at the station want to have one," Monica explained.

"Well, that's nice of them," Milton said.

"Did they talk to you about it?" Monica asked.

"She mentioned something about it," Milton replied. "First I've heard that she talked to you about it."

"Why didn't you tell me?" Monica asked. "I'm kind of excited about it. It makes me feel good that they want to do that for me."

"Not my thing," Milton replied. "It's their thing."

"Well, I wish that you had told me. She caught me by surprise and it felt kind of strange," Monica remarked. "I wasn't prepared for it." Monica reflected for a moment. "She and I don't know each other all that well. Maybe that's all there is to it."

Milton did not reply. They were walking up to the patio in the back of Monica's townhouse. They could see Shawna sitting on the couch in the living room watching TV.

"Let's get Granny and go for ice cream," Milton said, lifting Essie over his head and putting her on the ground.

The man had come to visit her after dark. He was in his fifties, Angie guessed. He was sweaty and he smelled a little. After he had sex with her, he asked her if he could take a quick shower. He must have been able to smell himself, she thought. She told him that he could do whatever he wanted. While he was showering, Angie looked over at his clothes sitting on the chair and saw the imprint of a cell phone in his pants pocket. After a moment of indecision, she fished it out of the pocket and dialed a number from memory that she hadn't dialed for years. She waited while it rang and a familiar voice answered.

"Monica, help me," she had said into the phone. "This is Angie. Can you guys help me?"

The voice on the phone had started to speak, but Angie had heard the man get out of the shower, so she ended the call. She worried that Monica might try to call back, and panicked. Angie hurriedly turned the phone off and replaced it in the pocket where she had found it. The man came out of the bathroom with a towel around his waist. "Were you talking to me?" he asked.

"No," Angie had replied. "I was just singing a little song."

The man had looked at his clothing laying on the chair. He checked the pockets, making sure his phone was still there. He got out his billfold and looked in it, counting his money and his credit cards. He gave Angie an accusatory look. Angie sat still, her face as blank as she could make it. He took his clothes into the bathroom and came out five minutes later, dressed. He put a twenty-dollar bill on the dresser.

"A tip," he had said. "Thanks for the shower," he added. "It woke me up a little. I lost some tonight that I need to catch up on."

Angie had smiled at him. After he had left, Angie took the bill and put it inside a pair of grey socks in the top drawer of her dresser, then she had sat on her bed and waited for the next customer.

That had been three days ago. Angie thought about Monica. She thought about how Monica had found a way out of the stripper life. She remembered that day when she and Billy had stopped in Ames on their way to visit friends in Pilot Mound, and she had run into Monica in the grocery store. Monica had looked so great. She was happy and full of life. She was back in college. That was all Monica used to talk about, going back to college. And she had a steady job at a detective agency. Angie couldn't believe it. Monica was telling her about the two cops who had started a detective agency and had hired her to work for them, when Billy came around the corner from one of the aisles and saw her. Angie had told Monica that she had to go. She wished that they could have talked longer, maybe even sat down in the food court in the corner of the store with a cup of coffee to catch up, but Billy would have pitched a fit. Angie said her goodbyes quickly and caught up with Billy in the checkout line.

"Who was that?" Billy had asked when they left the store. Angie had told him that she and Monica had danced together. Billy had laughed. "I'll bet she got all the tips," he had said. "She's a friggin' knockout." He had laughed again. Angie had felt the sting, but she didn't say anything. She knew that nothing but grief would come from it if she did. So she let it slide. Besides, he was right. Angie had made most of her tips in the parking lot. She didn't have any competition there.

The door to Angie's room opened. She looked up, expecting to see a customer, but instead it was James. She didn't like the look on his face.

"Angie," James said to her. "The other day, did you try to call someone from one of the customers' phones?"

Angie didn't reply. She smiled at James, but she was not smiling because she was happy. It was a nervous smile. She was afraid.

James came toward her and she turned her head, expecting him to hit her.

"I'm not going to hurt you, Angie," James said in an even voice. "That's not how I take care of things. I don't hit people." James sat down on the bed next to Angie. She was shaking.

"Angie, you got it pretty good here, don't you?" He waited for an answer. "Don't you?" he repeated when he didn't get a response.

"Yes," Angie replied.

"You got this nice room, you got clean sheets, you got your own bathroom, you got nice clothes, don't you?"

"Yes," Angie whispered, looking at the floor.

"You get fed well, don't you?"

"Yes," Angie whispered again.

"Angie," James said in a slow, even voice, "you try to pull some shit again, any shit, and I'm going to pack you up in a box, and I'm going send you down to some shitheads in Mexico who will let you live in a barn while they make movies of you so they can post them on the internet for perverts to watch. Do you want to live like that?"

"No," Angie whispered. She was shaking, holding back tears.

"Who were you calling?" James demanded.

"Just a friend," Angie replied. "I just wanted to talk to my friend, that's all."

"Listen here, Angie," James continued. "I don't want you calling your friends or anyone else, do you understand me? I'm your only friend. Angie, you have value to me right now. You help me keep my customers happy, and when they're happy because of you, they aren't quite so unhappy about losing money at the tables to me. And your job is to continue making them happy.

Whatever they want to do, you do it." James stopped talking for a moment to let Angie think about what he was saying. "But if you don't do your job, I can't do my job, and then you aren't of any use to me, Angie. When you aren't of any use to me, I'll ship you down to Mexico so fast it will make you dizzy."

Angie was sobbing.

"Are we understanding each other?"

"Yes," Angie sniffed.

James sat for a moment beside her. "Clean yourself up," he told her. Angie got up and went into the bathroom. James left and shut the door behind him.

Angie got dressed and sat on her bed waiting. She was feeling a little sick. She thought about Monica again, and wondered if Monica was going to try to help her. Angie hoped that she wouldn't. She started to get scared. What would happen to her if Monica tried to help? What would happen if those detective friends started nosing around and James found out? Angie wished that she had never tried to call. She wished that she had just one more chance to call Monica and tell her not to help, not to look for her, just to forget that she had ever called in the first place. If Angie just made one more call, she would never call again. But Angie knew that she wasn't going to get that chance, and even if she did, she wouldn't try again. There was no way out. Her fate was sealed. Angie told herself that she existed for one thing. For Monica it was school, her daughter, her boyfriend, her job; that was Monica's life, not hers. Angie existed to make the customers happy. That was all there was. She smiled. She was good at making the customers happy. That was one thing she had going for her. She had to quit thinking about Monica and start thinking about herself.

Two men came into Angie's room, closing the door behind them. Angie looked up from the bed at the two of them and smiled.

Chapter 9

Wednesday

Monica pulled into her reserved parking space in front of the G&B Detective Agency and killed the engine of her car. Skip's Audi was parked on the other side of the parking lot under a tree, where he usually parked. It wasn't often that Skip didn't beat everyone to the office. Monica usually arrived around eight o'clock. Her schedule said nine, but it wasn't actually a schedule, it was more of a suggestion. Monica set her own hours, normally around her classes at the university and her duties as Essie's mom, but Monica was ever mindful that she was employed as the office manager at G&B Detective Agency, and that she had duties. She appreciated the job that Max and Skip had given her when they won the Powerball and started their detective agency, and she appreciated even more the support the two gave her with her classes and with Essie.

Monica often thought back to that night when Max had offered her the job. She had been dancing at the local strip club, trying to make enough money to go back to school, but barely earning enough to make ends meet. Then Max came strolling in, sat down during her break and shot her a deal. A good wage, good childcare for Essie at the daycare down the street and what Max had called "a full ride scholarship" to the university to continue her studies. It was as if she had won the lottery, too.

As far as Max and Skip were concerned, her job was to answer the phone messages left at the agency and tell people that they were not taking any cases. The guys didn't want to work, they just wanted a detective agency. But people called daily for more reasons than to hire a private investigator. People would call wanting to talk to Max or Skip about some deal. Scammers, panhandlers, people who were taking a long shot with some outlandish scheme or product that they were sure would make them rich and the two millionaires even richer. It became Monica's job to screen them. If she thought that the guys might be interested, she put them in contact. If she didn't, which was most of the time, she told them thanks, but no thanks. Slowly, over the first year, Monica became an important part of Max and Skip's lives, and to some extent their wives' lives as well. She handled almost everything that they didn't want to handle for themselves. And she was loyal to them to a fault. They were as much a part of her life as she was of theirs. To her, that relationship was important, so she came in before class every day, just to make sure that there wasn't anything important that needed attending to before the guys eventually wandered in.

Monica walked into the offices, and the first thing she saw was Max's bicycle leaning against her desk. She wheeled it down the hall to the back. Max was not in his office, probably at Filo's coffee shop across the street. Skip was in his office, doing whatever work he did there. She wasn't quite sure what he had to do, but Skip liked doing his office work and that was enough for her. It wasn't her job to get an accounting from Skip.

"What's up?" she asked as she rolled the bicycle down the hall past Skip's open door.

"Max says he'll put that in the back when he is done having coffee at Filo's," Skip replied.

"I'm sure he was going to do that as soon as he comes back, whenever that might be," Monica remarked a bit sarcastically. "I talked to Milton last night about our proposition," she changed the subject.

"And?" Skip replied.

"And he isn't particularly supportive of me going undercover as a stripper looking for work," she said.

Skip didn't look surprised. "So you're good with not doing that?"

"Yep," Monica replied. "I am, because Milton thinks that I don't need to go undercover. He thinks that I would make a good detective. He thinks that you two need me on the case with you in that capacity. So that's what I'm going to do."

Skip looked at her askance. "I see. How exactly is this going to work?"

"I have the rest of the week off from school, so I'll just go with you guys and start investigating with you. Pretty simple plan." Monica replied. "And it just makes sense."

"What about Essie?" Skip asked. "You have some studying to do over break, don't you? A paper to write? When are you going to do that?"

"When are you two going to spend a little time with your wives?" Monica countered. "Spending time with your wives is important, too. I'll have time to study, and I'll have time for Essie. This isn't a permanent thing. It is a case we are working on right now. When we get it solved, we can all go back to what we were doing before."

Skip didn't answer.

"I'll make sure that we have a balance," Monica said. "I just need to be a part of this case. Milton thinks that I'm more valuable as an investigator."

"I'm sure he does," Skip remarked.

"Do you think he is wrong?" Monica asked.

Skip thought for a moment. Monica waited.

"I think Milton is right," Skip finally acquiesced. "The undercover thing wasn't feeling right, anyway. I don't want to say it, but it does make sense for you to get directly involved in this one."

Monica leaned the bicycle on the wall, walked into Skip's office and gave him a hug as he sat in his chair at the desk. Skip scrunched into his chair and tried to avoid her. Skip wasn't a hugger.

"You could get yourself in trouble, hugging a fellow in the workplace like that," Skip said as she stood up.

Monica laughed as she went out into the hall and wheeled Max's bicycle to the back room. She leaned it against the slide that occupied one end of the big room, along with the other playground equipment Essie used when Monica brought her into the office.

As she came back past Skip's office, he looked up.

"Don't worry, I won't hold you up or get in the way," Monica said. "Think about who all might be more likely to talk to me than to you guys." She paused. "What do you think?"

"You're right, you're right. I think that everyone would rather talk to you," Skip sighed.

Monica smiled and made her way back to her desk. She picked up the phone and dialed Max's cell number. Skip continued to check the overnight markets on his financial feed.

"*Que pasa*?" Max answered his phone.

"Are you coming over here so that we can get to work?" Monica asked.

"What work?" Max asked.

"Our case," Monica told him. "We're waiting for you."

Max was already up and heading to the door. "I'm on my way," he replied, ending the call.

Monica sat down at her desk and began searching the internet for anything that she could think of that might be of value to the case, but she was aware that she was just shotgunning it. She just needed to feel like she was doing something.

"Hey, did you see where my bicycle went?" Max asked as he came through the door.

"I put it in the back," Monica replied.

"I was going to do that," Max said a bit indignantly.

"I told her that," Skip said, coming up the hallway. "But she did it, anyway."

"Why does she do that?" Max asked. "We're not babies."

"I'm sitting right here," Monica said to Max.

"Yeah, well, guess what?" Skip said. "Monica is on the case now."

"She's not going undercover," Max replied.

"She's not. She's going along to help interview." Skip answered.

"She's going to be a detective?" Max asked.

"That's what she wants to do," Skip answered.

"So what do you think?" Max asked.

"You know," Skip replied, "at first I was thinking that it wasn't such a good idea. But then I remembered that she is streetwise. Possibly more streetwise than either of us, because she's seen it all from the other side. And she is smart. She's smarter than a whip. She reads people like a book."

"She's sounding pretty cliché," Max said a bit sarcastically.

"I'm serious," Skip said. "I think that she can be an asset. She's worked two cases for us from the back side, and she has good intuition. Plus, think about how well she handles all the cons who try to separate us from our money. Like I said, at first I was a little closed to it, but the more I think about it, the more I think we could use her."

Max shrugged his shoulders. "I guess that I don't have a problem with it. But I don't want her all tangled up in this and falling behind in school."

"I don't think anybody wants that," Skip replied. "She wants to do it, though, and I say give her a chance. If it doesn't work out, it doesn't work out. She's smart enough to realize if it doesn't."

"Hey, you two," Monica interrupted. "I'm still sitting right here while you talk about me."

Max looked over at her and shrugged his shoulders. "What's the plan, then?" he asked.

Skip stood silently for a moment.

"Here's a thought," Max continued when Skip didn't answer him. "There's a couple of Boone-ites working over at ISU Police. They've been there for years. I know them from the early days when I was on nights. I'll bet that they're still there. I mean, those ISU guys never retire. And I'll bet that they work days. Let's go find them and see if they know anything. They've lived in Boone all their lives."

Skip sat up. "I know who you're talking about. Jones is one of them."

"Gary Jones and Bill Langston," Max said.

Skip was already dialing his phone.

"You know the ISU Police number off the top of your head?" Max said with a little surprise in his voice.

"It's in my speed dial," Skip replied. "I used to call them up all the time about cases."

"Hello," Skip said into his phone. "Hey, this is Skip Murray. I used to be on Ames PD. I retired."

Skip paused for a moment. "I think that you can help me. I'm trying to find Jones or Langston. Either one of them working today?"

There was another pause as Skip listened into his phone.

"Any way that I can twenty-five them somewhere over here on the west side?"

Skip listened again. "She's checking on his twenty," Skip said to Max in a hushed tone. "I can hear him on the radio. Sounds like he can meet us at the old dairy farm."

"Which one?" Max asked.

"Thanks," Skip said into the phone. "Tell him five minutes."

Skip ended the call. "Langston," he replied. "Let's go, you're driving."

"I rode my bike," Max informed him.

"I'll drive," Skip said, standing up and reaching for his jacket.

Max followed him out the door, Monica right behind him, locking the door to the agency as she went out. Skip was already in the Audi. Max jogged across the parking lot and got in the passenger side. Monica got in the back. Skip pulled out of the parking lot and turned east onto Mortenson Road. He waited for the light to turn green at Dakota, then continued toward the old ISU dairy farm, just a mile or so down the street. Back in their earlier years on the police department, the dairy farm had been a common meeting place for officers on patrol. It was not unusual to see two patrol cars pulled up beside each other, the officers having a confab, the code for which was ten-twenty-five, or twenty-five for short. Be it for exchanging information or just for someone to visit with out of boredom, it was common for an officer to hear their call number over the radio and the voice at the other end ask them their twenty, where they were, and then ask if they wanted to twenty-five. On the west side of town it was either the dairy farm or the parking lot behind the Methodist church on Hayward.

When Skip got close to the old dairy farm parking lot he could see an ISU Police patrol car sitting there parked, facing the street. Skip pulled into the lot and brought his car up next to the ISU officer's car, driver's door to driver's door, expertly missing the rearview mirror with his own by no more than an inch.

"What's up?" Langston asked in a friendly manner when Skip lowered his window. Langston looked across the car to see Max sitting in the passenger seat and a young black woman in the back seat leaning forward between the two ex-cops and giving him a serious look.

"Not much," Skip said. "What's up with you?"

"Same old thing," he answered. "Heard you guys opened up a detective agency."

"Yes, we did."

"Why?" Langston asked.

"Well, it seemed like a good idea at the time," Skip chuckled.

Max laughed, too. "But we're starting to rethink it," he called from the passenger seat across the car.

"Who you got there in the back seat?" Langston asked.

"Our associate, Monica," Max replied. "Monica, Langston; Langston, Monica."

Langston nodded toward Monica and smiled.

"What do you need?" Langston asked. "I'm thinking that this isn't a social visit."

"We want to get a little background from you on a case we're working." Skip replied. "You're still living in Boone, aren't you?"

"I am now," Langston replied. "I used to have a nice little acreage just outside the edge of town, but now the edge of town is west of me a ways. Now I live in town."

"That sucks," Max said sympathetically.

"Not really," Langston replied. "I had ten acres, sold off five to a developer, told my ex-wife to find somewhere else to keep her stupid horses, and now I'm debt free and I still got enough land that I don't have a next-door neighbor. It all worked out."

"Glad to hear that," Skip said. Max and Monica were nodding their heads in agreement. "Here's the deal," Skip continued. "We got a missing person case that we're working on. A gal that used to be a stripper called our associate here asking for help, and then hung up. Angie Williamson is her name. She was living up in Fraser with some Hell Fighters. But then the guy she was living with got sent up in that stolen car ring that they busted a few years back, and she got connected up with another shithead called Billy the Kid. No shit, they call him Billy the Kid. That's the story that we got on Monday. So then this Billy the Kid and Williamson went to Oelwein. But when we went over there looking for her yesterday, everyone we talked to said that they both came back to Boone." Skip paused for a moment. "So that's it. We are right back where we started. We went in a circle. If it was your case, where would you look, being from there?"

"Who did you talk to in Fraser?" Langston asked.

"We talked to a deputy named Duffy in Fraser. He didn't seem to know much. Then we talked to a bartender at a bar in Pilot Mound. He was less than helpful, but we ran into an ex-biker there named Byron Grubber. We had to go down to Ogden to talk to him, because he didn't want to be seen talking to us in Pilot Mound."

Langston snorted. "Duffy is just a good ol' boy. Nice enough guy, but he rides both sides of that fence. He's the kind of guy who will tell you something about someone, then go back and tell them you were asking. And Grubber is an idiot."

"Okay," Skip replied. "So who do we talk to?"

"Boone County is a hard nut to crack. The railroad has been its lifeline since the town was founded, still is. Boone is big city for a lot of those hicks up there in the north part of the county, so they come to town to get a little taste of it. There's a few bars just north of the tracks where they like to go. The regulars there don't have as close ties to the bikers as they do in Fraser and Pilot Mound. You're more likely to find someone there who wants to impress you with something they heard or something they know."

"The bartender in Pilot Mound was pretty friendly," Max called across the car. "You ever get up that way? You happen to know him?"

"No," Langston laughed. "Maybe he is worth talking to again, if you got something going with him. I just don't see a bartender in Pilot Mound giving you much, though. I would hazard to say that he's feeding it to you. Sending you off on a goose chase."

"Well, we went in a circle yesterday," Skip admitted.

"I'd start with those bars north of the tracks," Langston suggested.

"Do you know anything?" Skip asked. "I mean, you've lived there all your life."

Langston reflected. "Most of those guys you are talking about, I know who they are. But honestly, I'm not one to rub shoulders with those guys. I live a pretty quiet life and mind my own business over there. I don't go up to Fraser or Pilot Mound, and I don't frequent the bars. I'm not into motorcycles, bikers and stuff like that. If I do get out of Boone, I come over here to Ames. If I could help you, I would sure do it, but I don't have anything."

Skip leaned back and looked over at Max. "You got anything to add?" he asked.

Max shook his head.

"Monica?" Skip asked.

Monica shook her head no.

"Do you know where our offices are?" Skip asked.

"Across from the coffee shop west of here," Langston answered.

"Stop by if you get a chance. We can always put on a pot of coffee," Skip said. "We like visitors."

"I'll do that," Langston replied. "I'm really sorry that I can't give you more. I just don't hang around with anyone associated with that crowd."

"No problem," Skip replied. "I wouldn't expect you to be hanging out with those guys. We'll check those bars north of the tracks."

Langston put his patrol car in gear to pull away.

"What do you think of Kind over there?" Skip called out before Langston pulled forward.

"I like him," Langston replied. "He's hard core, but you can get that way sometimes. Boone County isn't an easy place to be sheriff."

Langston pulled away.

"Nice guy," Max muttered.

Chapter 10

Wednesday

Skip drove out of the dairy farm parking lot behind Langston and turned west.

"What now?" Max asked.

"It's early," Skip said. "Probably none of those bars he was talking about are open yet. Go back to the office?"

"Might be like the Tip Top," Max suggested. "Maybe they cater to the night shift crowd when they get off work. There's nothing at the office."

"That's a good point," Skip replied. "Might as well go over and check it out. We gotta start somewhere. What do you think?" Skip called back to Monica.

"I'm just learning the ropes right now," she answered.

Skip turned onto Dakota and drove on to Highway 30 toward Boone.

"So," Max leaned his head back and turned toward Monica in the back seat. "I heard that Carlisle is going to be Milton's best man?"

"Yep," Monica replied.

"I thought maybe Milton would want me to be his best man."

"Well, he asked Carlisle." Monica said.

"Maybe I could be the maid of honor?" Max suggested. "I've heard that they do that these days."

"Mom's going to be my maid of honor," Monica replied.

"You've been doing some planning, then?" Max asked. "Well, Skip and I thought that we would just pick up the bill for your wedding and all, and this is the first we've heard anything about all of this."

"Leave me out of this," Skip interjected.

"We don't want you to pick up the bill," Monica said. "We're going to do it ourselves. Nice little intimate ceremony at Ada Hayden Lake. Milton has a cop friend who is an ordained minister, and he is going to do the officiating."

"So are we invited?" Max asked.

"Of course you're invited!"

"What cop?" Skip asked. "Not that Bible thumper that talks in tongues!"

"I don't know," Monica replied. "Milton is lining that up. I'm sure it's going to be fine. You guys are being obnoxious."

"I'm not being obnoxious," Skip interjected.

"So Shawna is the maid of honor," Max reflected.

"Actually, she is doing some of the planning. It's a good opportunity for her and Milton to get to know each other. I think it will be good for both of them. Besides, they are already getting along better."

"Do we have any official duties in this wedding?" Max asked.

"You're going to come to my wedding, bring your lovely wives, behave yourselves and support Milton and me," Monica replied. "Maybe give us a nice wedding gift," she added.

"Got honeymoon plans?" Max asked. "Maybe we can give you a nice honeymoon for a wedding present."

"We're going to Lake Tanneycomo in Missouri, and Milton is going to teach me how to fly fish for trout."

"Since when are you interested in fishing?" Max laughed.

"Since I met Milton," Monica replied. "He likes fishing. He hasn't done it for a long time, though. It's something I think we can both enjoy. It's something we can do with Essie. I think it sounds like a good thing for us to do."

Max shrugged his shoulders. "What's Shawna going to do when you get married?" he asked.

"She's moving in with us," Monica replied. "We're going to sell my townhouse and we're going to buy a house with a yard. Ideally a house big enough for Mom to have her own space."

"Milton is good with this?" Skip asked.

"Built-in babysitter," Monica replied. "Besides, I don't want Mom living on her own. She needs some structure."

Monica paused for a moment. "You know, neither one of them wants to admit it, but I think Mom and Milton are starting to like each other. They still snipe at each other some, but she and Essie have taken to siding with him all the time when we are all four together. It's like me against the other three."

"You met Milton's parents?" Max asked.

"No," answered Monica, "have you ever met them?"

"No," Max replied. "He's never even talked about them, that I remember. I think they are super religious."

"Milton says that he doesn't think they will come to the wedding," Monica replied. "His sister and her husband live in Oklahoma, and they're coming. They're actually coming a week early, just to help out. Milton is really excited about that. But he doesn't talk much about his parents. I don't think that they get along, or something."

"How about the reception. Do you have any plans for the reception?" Max asked.

"We haven't gotten that far, yet," Monica answered.

"How about Skip and I throw a reception for you?" Max asked.

Monica thought for a moment. "I'll discuss it with Milton," she replied. "We want to keep it low key. I'm afraid you guys might go overboard."

"We won't go overboard," Skip said.

"I'll talk to Milton about it." Monica repeated. "I know that you guys are itching to do something."

Skip was driving up Story Street in Boone, toward the bars. They passed the stores on either side of the street that made up the "historic" downtown business district. They crossed the railroad tracks at the north end of the downtown businesses and spotted a bar on the left. There were a half-dozen cars parked in the lot to the side of the building. Skip pulled into the lot and parked on the opposite side from the old pickup trucks and the beat-up clunkers that were parked closer to the entrance.

"Good call," Max said to Skip.

The three got out of the car and walked to the entrance. Max was right, the bar was hopping for that time of the morning. There was a lot of industry in Boone, not to mention the Union Pacific Railroad had a yard there. It was a blue collar town, and the bar was filled with blue collar night shifters having a drink or two after work.

"What do ya need?" the bartender asked as the three took up stools at the bar right next to the taps.

"Three Miller Lite draws," Max said, a little louder than necessary.

The bartender turned three beer glasses up and placed them on the bar next to the tap. He took one of the empty glasses and started to fill it.

"We're private investigators, working for the law firm of Hupster and Abercrombie," Max informed the bartender. "You probably heard of them. They have commercials on TV all the time. We're looking for some people who might have gotten screwed over by the UP. Hupster and Abercrombie is representing them in a class action suit over it. Looking for a guy named William Bonney. He's from around these parts. Sounds like he might be in for a big settlement, if we can find him. You don't know him, do you?"

Monica gave Skip a curious look. "What's he doing?" she whispered.

"Let him go," Skip whispered back. "Just play along."

"So who are you shitting?" the bartender asked Max. "William Bonney? You mean like Billy the Kid?"

"Yep," said Max as the bartender filled another glass. "Just like William Bonney, Billy the Kid. This guy we are looking for is actually named William Bonney. I get this every time I ask about him. I don't know, maybe his parents thought it was clever, but we aren't concerned with how he ended up with that name, we are looking for the William Bonney who supposedly worked for the UP five years ago, and who might be looking at a pretty good cash settlement."

The bartender put the beers in front of the three. He smiled at Monica as he put a coaster under hers and gave her a napkin. Skip was wondering if he was going to give her a stir stick and a glass of ice water just for a reason to keep smiling at her a while longer.

The bartender looked down the bar at the four other patrons sitting on the stools at the bar.

"Anyone know William Bonney?" he asked.

"Used to be a biker up in Fraser called Billy the Kid," a woman two stools down answered. "I haven't seen him around here for a long time. Might be the same guy. I don't know that he ever worked for the railroad, though."

"What's this suit about?" the man next to the woman asked.

"Don't know anything more than it's about benefits they were supposed to get that they didn't. Something about them being treated like part time or temporary employees when they were qualified for full time benefits. Hupster and Abercrombie didn't hire us to deal with that, though. They hired us to find people who might be a part of the suit, and right now we are trying to find William Bonney. So that's about all we know. We got some paperwork to give him, but it is all sealed up in envelopes. We just gotta give him the envelope."

"I might know this guy," the man announced. "There a reward or anything for finding him?"

"Nope, don't think so," Max replied. "It's a class action suit, it isn't a criminal investigation. If we don't find him, we don't find him. He gets left out."

"Well, good luck on that," the man replied. "Because there's an arrest warrant out for him and he ain't making himself available to private detectives, or anyone else that he don't know."

"Well, maybe if you know this guy, you can tell him that we are looking for him and let him decide if he wants to talk to us." Max answered as he passed a business card down the bar.

The guy took the card and looked at it.

"If I see him, I'll let him know," he said.

All of a sudden Monica spoke up. "We have information that he is living with a woman named Angie Williamson. Maybe if we find her, we can find him. If anyone has any information about her, it might help."

"She's a stripper," the man replied.

Monica didn't answer.

"You're a stripper, too," he added.

Monica was taken aback a bit. "I'm not a stripper, I'm a private detective."

"You look like a stripper that used to dance in a club over in Ames," the man challenged her. "I used to go over there all the time. You're her."

"I'm not a stripper," Monica replied.

"Hey," Max butted in. "We're not looking for strippers, we're looking for William Bonney. That's all. If you know him, we would appreciate it if you would give him our card so that he can call us. We don't care about any warrants. We just want to give him an envelope."

Skip was getting up off his stool and had Monica's arm, urging her to do the same. Max downed the rest of his Miller Lite in one gulp and got up as well.

"Okay, good to meet you all," Max said to the remaining people at the bar. He followed Skip and Monica out the door into the parking lot. Skip had his arm around Monica's shoulder and was talking to her. He gave her a squeeze. Max trotted up beside them and saw tears rolling down Monica's cheeks.

"Hey, what's the matter?" he asked.

"Monica is just a little upset," Skip said. "It'll pass."

They got to Skip's car and he held the passenger side door open so that Monica could get in the front seat. Max climbed in the back.

"This about that guy calling you a stripper?" Max asked. "Because he's just a jack off. Just let it go."

"What am I going to do if Milton and I are sitting in some restaurant or bar and a guy like that shows up and starts in?" Monica sniffed.

Max handed her a tissue that he found in a box on the back seat.

"Milton can punch him out," Max replied.

"I don't want Milton to punch people out," Monica answered. "I don't want Milton to have any reason to punch people out because of me."

"Milton's a big boy," Skip said as he put on his seat belt. "You don't need to worry about Milton."

"What's he going to think if something like that happens?" Monica sniffed again and Max handed up another tissue.

"Milton's going to think that you're the prettiest girl he ever met and that he's so lucky to have you that he can hardly stand it," Skip answered her.

Monica wiped her nose and looked out the window as Skip pulled out of the parking lot.

"What's next?" she asked.

"Let's see if we can find another bar. Sounds like Billy the Kid is around here somewhere, if that fellow back at the bar is going to deliver him a message."

"In the meantime," Max added. "We should probably keep in mind that Monica is right: we aren't looking for Billy the Kid, we're looking for Angie."

Skip drove along the street that ran parallel to the railroad tracks until he found himself in a residential area with the tracks on one side of the street and homes on the other side. Skip turned around and headed back toward the main drag. When they got to Story Street, Skip stopped at the stop sign and looked up the street.

"You know this town at all?" Skip turned toward Max in the back seat.

"Kind of," Max said.

"Well, I don't see any more bars around here. You know of any other dives in town that might be open at this time of the morning?"

"You ever been to the county courthouse?" Max asked Skip.

"Not that I remember," Skip answered. "There a bar in the courthouse?"

"No, but there's a bar over by the courthouse. Go back south on the main drag," Max replied.

Skip did as Max instructed him. When they got to the intersection with Story Street, he proceeded south over the railroad tracks and through the business district from the opposite direction.

"Wanna stop in at the Boone PD and tell them what we are up to?" Max asked. "I suppose we should introduce ourselves. No use ruffling more feathers."

"Good idea," Skip answered. "You know where it is?"

"Just passed it," Max replied.

"Where?" Skip asked.

"On the right," Max answered. "Go around the block."

Skip turned right and drove around the block. He found a place to park on Sixth Street.

"We all go in, or what?" Skip asked.

"Why don't you just go in," Max replied. "I'm kind of stuck back here. Maybe you can go in there and use some of your bullshit diplomacy, like you did with Sheriff Kind."

Skip didn't answer. He turned off the ignition and left his two associates sitting in the car. He walked around the corner to the front of the police station and went through the door. Inside was a counter, and behind it a woman sitting at a desk staring at her computer screen. She looked up as Skip approached.

"May I help you?" she asked.

Skip placed his business card on the counter and slid it across to the woman.

"Skip Murray, G&B Detective Agency. My associates and I are in town on a missing person investigation and I just wanted to stop in and let you know we are here."

The woman stood up and came to the counter.

"Who are you looking for?" she asked. "We haven't had any missing person report."

"Probably not," Skip replied. "This is a friend who is reporting it. It doesn't meet the requirements for an official missing person's report, but our client is simply concerned about her friend and asked us to look into it."

The woman frowned. "So what are you looking for from us?" she asked.

"Nothing, really," Skip replied. "Just letting you know that we are in town."

The woman was reading Skip's card.

"Does this person you are looking for have a name?" she asked without looking up from the card.

"Angie Williamson," Skip replied.

The woman turned her eyes toward Skip.

"I know her," she remarked. "I mean, I don't know her personally, but I know who she is. Used to run around with a pretty rough crowd. Mostly bikers."

"That would be her," Skip replied. "Have you seen her lately?"

The woman shrugged her shoulders. "I can't recall seeing her lately." She paused, thinking. "I haven't seen her, but..."

The woman had sat down at her computer and was typing on the keyboard. Skip waited quietly while she searched.

"I think one of our officers did a warrant check on her probably two weeks ago during a traffic stop," the woman said absently as she continued to read the computer screen.

"Was she driving?" Skip asked.

"Passenger, I think," the woman replied.

"Got a name on the driver?" Skip asked.

The woman continued typing. "I can't seem to find it in the computer," she replied.

"Got a license number?" he pressed. "Or a description of the vehicle?"

"Black late model Escalade, if I remember right," she said. "Stopped for tinted windows and got a warning. That's probably the best that I can do for you right now." She looked up from her computer and shrugged her shoulders. "I'm just remembering something I read two weeks ago on the log. It was a routine traffic stop. I recognized the name."

"Is there anyone I can talk to who might be able to give me a little more?" Skip asked.

"Sorry, no one at the moment," she apologized.

"Can you tell me if she was okay?" Skip asked.

"I don't remember it saying that she wasn't okay," the woman replied. "I can't find it right now; I'll have to go back and check with dispatch to see if they know where it is."

Skip stood a moment. "Thanks for looking," he told the woman. "I appreciate it. Could you put the word out to your officers that we are looking for this Angie? If there is any info that they can give us, they can call me at that number."

The woman had laid the business card on the counter. Skip picked up a pen and wrote his cell number on the back.

"That's my cell number. They can call me there anytime."

The woman pondered the number for a moment. "I'll pass this on to the officers and see if anyone can remember the stop."

"That's all I can ask," Skip replied.

Skip left the PD, walked around the corner and got into his car.

"What took so long?" Max asked.

"An officer called Williamson in for a warrant search during a traffic stop two weeks ago. The lady in there thinks that it was a black Escalade with tinted windows," Skip replied.

"What does it mean that they did a warrant search on her?" Monica asked.

Skip had pulled up to the intersection at Story Street and was waiting for traffic.

"South?" he asked.

"South down to Mamie Eisenhower, then right," Max instructed. "Just that," he continued, speaking to Monica. "The officer is out there driving around, sees a vehicle that catches his attention, pulls it over for whatever minor infraction that he can spot that gives him cause to make a traffic stop. Then he looks around, IDs everyone inside, does a warrant search through NCIC on everyone, maybe asks to search the vehicle, maybe not. If there isn't anything there, he gives them a warning and sends them on their way. Then he looks for another random car to pull over." he explained. "It's called fishing."

"Interesting," Monica replied. "That's sneaky. So what did they say about Angie? Was she okay?" she asked Skip.

"Evidently," Skip replied. "I mean, the officer cut them loose. If there was anything hinky going on he would have followed up on it. That's why he's doing it."

"Anything else?" Max asked.

"The lady there either couldn't or wouldn't give me anything else. She couldn't seem to find anything in her computer about the stop, but she said that she's going to pass it on to the shifts and the officer who did the stop can call us," Skip answered. "Maybe."

"We'll see if that happens," Max remarked.

"Well," Skip replied. "It's the closest we've gotten to her so far."

Chapter 11

Wednesday

Milton stopped by the detective agency as usual for his morning break. He parked beside Monica's car and walked to the door. It looked dark inside. He tried the door, but it was locked. He cupped his hands over his eyes and peered through the window, but he couldn't see any signs of movement inside. He paused for a moment, then went back to his patrol car, opened the door and before he got in, he looked across the street at Filo's. He got back into his car, drove across the street and parked by the door.

"Ames one-twenty-five, out at Filo's for break. I'll stay on portable," Milton called into the microphone.

"Ten-four, one-twenty-five, zero-nine-fifty-six," came the response.

Milton got out of the car and walked into Filo's. There was a college-age couple sitting at a corner table absorbed in their studies. Milton walked up to the counter and rang a bell that sat there. The barista came out from the back.

"Hey," he addressed Milton as he came up to the counter. "How are you today, Officer Jackson?"

"Fine," Milton replied, looking through the window and across the street at the agency. "Pretty quiet over there this morning," he observed.

"Haven't seen anyone over there," the barista answered.

"Medium light brew to go," Milton said.

The barista pulled a white paper cup from the stack on the counter and started to fill it from the air pot behind him. Milton continued to stare out the window at the agency. The barista placed his cup of coffee on the counter and got his attention. Milton paid for the drink.

"Well, have a good one," he said to the barista, who was staring out at the agency as well.

Milton chuckled. "Why the hell are we standing here looking over there?" he asked the barista.

"I don't know," he laughed. "Max comes over here and does it almost every morning. I guess it's contagious."

Milton shook his head and walked out of the coffee shop to his patrol car. He placed the cup of coffee on the roof of the car and unlocked the door. He climbed inside and got himself situated as comfortably as he could in his seat with all his gear around his waist and his bulletproof vest binding him, fastened his seatbelt and picked up the mic.

"Ames one-twenty-five, ten-eight," he said absently into the mic.

"One-twenty-five, ten-four, ten-eight, ten-zero-four," came the response from dispatch.

Milton turned to look through the cage and under the shotgun that was mounted behind his head as he backed out of the parking place. As he did so, he heard something roll across his windshield. He hit the brake and turned his attention toward the front just in time to see his cup of coffee slide off the hood and onto the ground.

"Fuck," he shouted.

He turned on his windshield wipers to clear the coffee that had spilled all over the windshield as the cup had tumbled over it.

"Damn it," he said out loud.

Milton looked back again for traffic, and then backed out of the parking space and drove out onto the street. He looked over at the empty offices across the street as he went by. As he pulled up to the stoplight, his phone rang and he fished it out of the pocket of his vest. A quick glance at the screen showed him that Monica's mother, Shawna, was calling.

"Hello," Milton answered.

"Milton," Shawna responded. "What about flowers and a cake?"

"What about them?" Milton replied.

"Well, where do we get them, and who pays for them, the bride or the groom?" Shawna inquired.

"I would guess that we could get them both at HyVee," Milton suggested.

Shawna didn't say anything. Milton could tell that she was thinking about it.

"Maybe the cake coming from HyVee would be okay, but do you think that Monica would want flowers from a grocery store?"

It was Milton's turn to think about it.

"Probably not," he replied. "Probably not. Maybe we need to look around for a real florist to do the flowers. What are you thinking for that?"

"I don't know," Shawna answered. "First thing, she needs a bouquet. A corsage for the bridesmaids and a corsage for me. A boutonniere for you and one for your best man, whatever his name is. And the groomsmen."

"Carlisle," Milton responded.

"Yeah, one for Carlisle," she added. "Are you writing all this down?"

"No," Milton replied. "I'm driving a patrol car."

"Okay," said Shawna. "I'll make a list. So you don't think that your parents will come to your wedding? I mean, that's what Monica said."

"I really don't think so," Milton replied. "They didn't come to my sister's."

"Monica says they don't like it that you are marrying a black woman," Shawna stated with a bit of contempt in her voice.

"You know, Shawna?" Milton said. "I don't know what they think, because I haven't talked to them about it. And I really don't care what they think. That's their problem. They have to live with themselves."

"Are you embarrassed to tell them that you're marrying Monica?" Shawna challenged.

Milton paused for a moment.

"Why are you thinking, Milton?" Shawna asked.

"No, I am not embarrassed of Monica," Milton finally spoke. "I'm embarrassed of my parents. I'm embarrassed of my parents because they are not capable of understanding what a wonderful, warm, loving, caring person Monica is. I'm embarrassed for them that she is so much better than they are."

It was Shawna's turn to take a moment to reflect before she answered.

"Good answer, Milton. You get a gold star for that one. You get a few more and I might actually think that you are worthy of my daughter."

"Cake," Milton changed the subject back. "Maybe we should look around for a baker to do the cake. I think a HyVee cake is fine, but it isn't about me, it's about Monica. I want her to feel good about our wedding. I'll ask around and see what other people do. There's a couple of cops on night shift that got married last year and the year before, I'll ask them what they did."

"Back to flowers?" Shawna asked.

"Bouquet for the bride, and then let's just start a list of who gets what as they come up. Monica, you, me, Carlisle, bridesmaids, groomsmen, my sister, let's go from there."

"Who's paying for what?" Shawna asked.

"I'm paying for it all," Milton answered. "Look, we already decided that we are going to pool resources when we get married. So I'll pay for it all and in the end it all evens out."

"Yeah, well, I told her that she needs to keep some of her resources in reserve, just in case she has buyer's remorse later on," Shawna replied. "I've been there."

"I know what you told her," Milton sighed. "But we're not going to have buyer's remorse. We are going to put our finances together. And we're not you."

"That was a mean thing to say," Shawna replied.

"Well, you started it," Milton said, becoming a bit exasperated with the direction that the conversation was going.

"I guess I did," Shawna said. "Okay, I'll start making a flower list, you work on where to get the cake."

"Okay," Milton replied. "That it?"

"For now," Shawna answered. The phone went dead.

At least she admitted that she started it this time, Milton thought as he stuck his phone back into the pocket of his vest. That's progress.

Milton realized that he had been making a big circle around the west side of town and was driving back toward the agency from the north. When he got to the intersection, he turned left onto the street that went past the agency. It was still dark. Monica's car was still parked out front, just as it had been ten minutes ago. As he drove by, he thought that he couldn't just circle around all day until Monica came back. He knew that she was out with Skip and Max. Milton realized that he was a little jealous that she was out there doing an investigation with them while he was driving around in circles waiting to hear what they found out.

Milton continued through the intersection at Dakota, determined not to change directions until he got to the other side of the city limits. Milton drove on, past the ISU dairy farm, past the stadium, and made his way toward the truck stop. He looked at the dash clock. It was close to Carlisle's break time. He continued on his path.

Milton spotted Carlisle's patrol car in the corner of the parking lot, partially tucked behind an idling semi. There was room for Milton to pull up, driver's side window to driver's side window, where they could chat.

"Hey," Carlisle said as Milton rolled down his window. "What's up in the big city?"

"Nothin'," Milton replied. "You been up to anything?"

"Not really," Carlisle responded. "Was down in Slater earlier today and some weird guy at the Casey's store was telling me about this big house back in the woods up north of Boone on the Des Moines River, where supposedly they have themselves a regular high stakes poker thing. He says that high rollers from all over the place go up there at night and they have five or six tables going, craps and roulette too. According to this guy, a lot of money changes hands. Said that they also do some sports betting, said that you can bet on about anything."

"That's interesting," Milton replied. "Say anything about drugs or hookers? Those three go together most of the time."

"Didn't think to ask," Carlisle answered. "He didn't really know much about it, other than it was up north of

Boone. I got the impression that he hadn't actually been there. He was just telling me what he had heard."

"Interesting," Milton replied again. "Little out of my jurisdiction, though."

"Mine, too," remarked Carlisle. "But I'm going to twenty-five a Boone County deputy here in a while and let him know what this guy told me. I'll see what he says. Maybe they already know about it."

Carlisle took a bite out of his burger and washed it down with Coke.

"I'm just waiting for him to get back over this way," Carlisle continued. "He's over on the other side of the county right now."

"Monica is over in Boone County today with Max and Skip, looking for a missing gal that she used to know," Milton remarked dejectedly.

"Stripper?" Carlisle asked, wishing that he hadn't as soon as he said it.

Milton frowned. "Yeah," he answered.

"Why's Monica with them?" Carlisle asked.

"She's bound and determined that she's going to help look for her, so the guys loaded her up and took her along," Milton answered. "I mean, those guys are like her big brothers. If she wants to tag along, they don't care."

"How's school going?" Carlisle asked.

"Spring break," Milton answered.

"Well, what else is there for her to do on spring break?" Carlisle continued. "I suppose it's better than leaving ol' Milton to work while she goes down to Panama City and parties with the rest of the college kids."

"Funny," Milton replied.

"Just saying," Carlisle came back. "You got a good deal with her, I wouldn't get too pissy about her doing a ride-a-long with Max and Skip while she's on spring break."

"You're right," Milton said with resignation. "Maybe I'm just feeling left out."

"Probably," Carlisle replied. "Hey, I heard that you talked Sarah into throwing a wedding shower for Monica," he changed the subject.

"I mentioned it to her," Milton replied. "I thought that it might be nice, let them get to know her. She's going to be around quite a bit more after the wedding. She's going to be one of the cop wives, you know. It would be nice for her to feel like she's included."

Carlisle didn't say anything.

"Why?" Milton said after a moment of silence. "She say something to you about it?"

"Just that you suggested that she throw a wedding shower for Monica," Carlisle said.

"Is that all she said?" Milton asked. "Was she pissing about it to you or something? Because you're being a little closed-lipped about it."

"I'm not being anything about it," Carlisle said defensively. "You're the one pissing about it right now."

Milton didn't respond. Carlisle was right. But when Milton had talked to Sarah about the shower, he didn't think that she sounded real enthused with the idea. Milton shrugged it off. It was probably just him. Carlisle stopped eating his hamburger and tilted his head so that he could listen to his radio. Milton couldn't make out the call because of the truck idling beside them.

Carlisle picked up the microphone. "Ten-four, I'll be seventy-six," he spoke into the mic. When he put it back into its holder, he looked over at Milton.

"You two both need to lighten up," Carlisle said. "She's gonna be just fine. Everyone is going to like her.

She isn't any different from any other new wife coming in, it takes a while for the other wives to get to know her. Don't make problems when there ain't any problem."

"You're right," Milton said. "I don't know why we get so defensive about everything."

"You both get defensive about her having been a dancer," Carlisle said pointedly. "Just get it out in the open. But nobody cares," he emphasized. "So let it go."

Milton didn't reply. Carlisle was right. Carlisle was his best friend and not afraid to tell him what he needed to hear. Milton just raised his eyebrows a bit, sighed and said nothing.

"That's my Boone County deputy," Carlisle said to Milton. "Gotta go."

"Catch you later," Milton replied. "Let me know what he says. I'm curious, now."

"Will do," Carlisle shouted through the open window as he put his car in gear and drove off.

Milton put his car into drive and followed Carlisle out of the lot to the street. Carlisle crossed the intersection and took the westbound ramp onto the four lane highway. Milton took South Sixteenth Street, which ran parallel across town toward the agency. Drugs, gambling and prostitution, those three were Max's specialty when he was a cop. Milton would have to tell him about this house north of Boone.

Chapter 12

Wednesday

Billy found a single egg in the refrigerator, so he scrambled it and sat at the kitchen table to eat it. Grubber had gotten a call Monday night from the owner at the junkyard where he worked part time, telling him that they had work for him the rest of the week, so he had left the trailer early both Tuesday and today. That was fine with Billy. Grubber had been acting hinky the last two days. He was avoiding him, which just caused a lot of tension in the close quarters of the mobile home.

Billy didn't know what the burr was under Grubber's saddle, but he was getting tired of it. Maybe Grubber had found out that there was a warrant out for him. That would certainly make Grubber nervous. When he had been a Hell Fighter the cops would write him a ticket for anything and everything they could pin on him, wait for it to go to warrant, then follow him to the clubhouse and use it as an excuse to kick the door in. That probably made Grubber a little gun shy when it came to the possibility of a warrant. He probably found out about it and was thinking that any second the cops would come busting through the door. Billy needed to find a job and get out of Grubber's place before that really happened.

Billy's cell phone rang, and he slid it around on the table where it sat so that he could see who was calling. There was no name and he didn't recognize the number. He was going to just let it ring, but decided to answer just before it went to voicemail.

"What?" Billy answered the phone.

"This Billy?" came the response.

"Who wants to know?" Billy asked.

Whoever was on the other end evidently didn't want to play the game.

"Listen, there were some people at the bar this morning asking about you. Two guys who said they were private detectives, and a stripper."

"What the fuck?" Billy exclaimed. "Two private detectives and a stripper?"

"Yeah, two private detectives," the voice on the phone replied. "The stripper was saying that she was a private detective too, but I recognized her. She used to strip over at that club in Ames."

Billy thought about it for a moment. He was confused.

"Why the fuck were they asking about me?" he asked.

"Said that they were working for some lawyers who are representing Union Pacific workers in some lawsuit. They said they was looking for you so that they could give you some money."

"I never worked for Union Pacific," Billy answered. "Sounds like bullshit to me."

"Yeah, well, I thought the story was bullshit, too," the voice agreed. "I didn't say anything to them. I thought maybe they were bounty hunters or something, looking to serve that warrant on you."

Billy was taken aback. "What warrant?"

"That probation violation warrant on you," the voice on the phone answered him.

Billy quickly touched the end call icon on his phone. He felt his chest tighten. Who the fuck would know about the warrant? Who the fuck with his cell number would know about the warrant?

Billy's phone rang again. It was the same number. Billy waited, and just before it went to voicemail, he answered.

"Yeah," Billy spoke into the phone.

"We got cut off," the voice on the other end replied. "They gave me a number for you to call if you want to talk to them. You want it?"

Billy looked around for something to write on. He found a notebook and a pen by Grubber's landline telephone and retrieved it.

"Give it to me," Billy instructed.

"Gee and Bee Detective Agency," the voice replied.

Billy wrote down the name of the detective agency and the number, then quickly ended the call. He waited a moment. The phone rang. It was the same number. He let it ring until it went to his voicemail. He waited a couple minutes more, but no message showed up. He sat thinking about the information that he had just received. His first thought went to Grubber. Had Grubber been jacking his jaws around town? Billy was furious. He sat steaming for a few minutes, thinking about his next move. He looked at the number that he had jotted down in the notebook. He picked up his phone, checked to make sure that it was set to hide his own number, and dialed the number on the piece of paper. He walked to the window and looked out at the street that ran in front of the mobile home while the phone was ringing. He saw nothing out of the ordinary. The whole mobile home court was quiet. He was tempted to go outside, where he could get a better look around, but he decided not to chance it. If anyone was watching, they would expect that. It could be a trap. Whoever called him might be out there waiting for him to make his move. He moved away from the window just as the phone rolled over to voicemail.

"G and B Detective Agency," a recording of a woman's voice answered. "We are not taking any cases at this time. If you would still like to leave a message, please do so at the tone."

Billy waited for the tone.

"Yeah, I think that you guys need to leave me alone. I ain't done nothin' to you guys, and you got no reason to be looking for me. So quit asking around about me." He ended the call and wondered what to do next. He felt like he needed to talk to someone, so he started going through his contacts on his phone. He found the one that he was looking for and touched the call button. It rang several times before it was picked up.

"Hello, Billy" the voice on the other end answered.

"Hi, James," Billy replied.

"To what do I owe the pleasure?"

"I'm back in the area, and I'm looking for some work," Billy replied. "I was wondering if you got anything that I could do."

"I thought that you were going to Texas."

"I was going to go to Texas," Billy explained. "But I ain't got no money, so I came up here and I'm crashed at a guy's place that I know. Anyway, I want to get out of this fucking state but I need to come up with some cash. You got anything for me?"

James thought for a moment. "Let me have some time to think about it," he responded.

"That would be greatly appreciated," Billy answered.

"Anything else?" James asked.

Billy paused for a moment. "That girl, Angie. You still got her?"

"No," James answered without hesitation. "Matter of fact, a fellow I knew wanted to take her down to Mexico to do some cinematic art. I don't expect to see her again."

"Wow," Billy remarked. "She didn't stay with you long."

"It was a good career move on her part, and it worked out well for me," James chuckled. "Look, Billy, give me some time to check around and see if I have any work. I'll get back to you."

"Sure, the sooner the better," Billy replied, but before he got it out James ended the call.

James sat back at his desk, wondering what he was going to do about Billy. He had not expected to hear from him this soon. He had not expected to hear from him at all. James did not like connections. Connections were what brought people down. He had expected Billy to leave town and disappear, taking the connection between him and James with him. But instead, he had apparently followed James to Boone. This was not a good situation and he needed to break the connection before it came back to bite him.

James's first inclination was to just eliminate Billy, but on second thought that might prove to be difficult. Billy was a hard nut. He was tough. He was a veteran of many wars between the Hell Fighters and bigger motorcycle gangs that had tried to muscle into Hell Fighter turf. He was a part of that uneasy co-existence with the Sons. Who would Billy be staying with? He went through the list in his head of bikers affiliated with both gangs who might still be in the area.

James took his phone and went through his contacts. He found the name that he was looking for and called it. The phone rang twice before a voice came over the phone.

"What's up James?"

"Byron, my man," James addressed him. "When's the last time you saw Billy Bonney?"

Grubber hesitated for a moment.

"He shacked up with you?" James reacted to the hesitation.

Grubber hesitated a moment longer. "Yeah, he is, matter of fact."

"Were you keeping it a secret from me?" James accused Grubber.

"No, no, not at all," Grubber answered. "It never occurred to me that you would be interested in Billy Bonney, that's all."

"Why don't you let me decide what I'm interested in?" James asked.

"Well," Grubber started, "Billy showed up at my door last week looking for a place to crash. Told me he didn't have any money. Told me that he was gonna go looking for a job. That's all there is to tell about it."

"That's it?" James challenged him.

"Yep," Grubber replied. "He don't like me all that much, James. I don't like him. He's just staying there until he finds some work. We don't sit around chatting."

"You know anything else that I might find interesting?" James asked. "Considering we are just sitting here chatting."

Grubber hesitated again.

"Well?" James prodded.

"Well," Grubber continued. "There's a warrant out for his arrest from Fayette County for probation violation on a drug possession charge."

"So you're harboring a fugitive?" James remarked.

"One other thing," Grubber added. "Yesterday there was a couple of private detectives looking for him."

James hid his exasperation with Grubber. "How do you know this?" he asked calmly.

"Well, they were asking me about him on Monday," Grubber gave it up.

"You've been talking to private detectives, and I gotta call you up to hear about it? You are supposed to be calling me up when you got intel that I might be interested in." James responded. "They skip tracers?"

"No. I don't think so, anyway," Grubber was feeling a bit more comfortable talking to James. "They were asking about a stripper that went missing. They was saying that they got hired to look for her. They're ex-cops."

"So what did you tell them?" James asked.

"Told them that the last I had heard, Billy and her went to Oelwein," Grubber answered.

"Why Oelwein?" James asked him. "Why didn't you tell them that he went to Texas, or Chicago, or fucking Alaska? Why did you tell them that they went to Oelwein?"

"It just came to me," Grubber defended himself. "I figured that if they went to Oelwein looking for him, it would keep them busy for a while. If I told them anything else they would figure out pretty quick that it was bullshit and just come back with more questions. At least Oelwein wasn't bullshit. That's where he was. He's not there, anymore. I sent them on a goose chase."

James thought about it for a moment. There wasn't any profit for him in pursuing it any farther.

"Why didn't you tell them to fuck off?" James asked.

"I know these guys from their cop days," Grubber replied. "They aren't going to settle for fuck off. They are not nice guys."

"What's their names?" James asked.

"Mosbey and Murray," Grubber replied.

"Have you been talking to Billy about this woman that these detectives are asking about?" James asked.

"Nope," Grubber answered. "Haven't said a word about it."

"Nope?" James said. "Billy is living with you and you don't mention to him that there are some detectives asking you about him and some woman that he is supposed to be with?"

"Okay," Grubber replied with a bit of wavering in his voice. "Here's the lowdown on that. This woman that they are asking about used to be my brother's woman. Then, when my brother died in prison, she got passed on to Billy. So I felt like I needed to look after her for my brother's sake. I started doing just that. But Billy didn't take too well to me meddling in his affairs and threatened to slit my throat and throw me down a coal shaft if I didn't mind my own business. I took him for his word. I don't question him about her anymore." Grubber stopped for a second to catch his breath. "One day I asked him, real causal like, whatever happened to her, and he said that he got rid of her. That's enough for me."

"Got rid of her?" James repeated.

"Yep, and the way he said it sounded to me like that's all he had to say on the subject," Grubber replied. "I didn't press him about it."

"You say you don't talk to him about her, but you do happen to mention something about her? How does that work?" James waited to see if he had anything else to say. When Grubber didn't go on, James spoke into the phone. "Listen up: you stay close to Billy, and I want to know what that asshole is up to every second of the day."

"I gotta work," Grubber complained.

"Who you more scared of, Grubber? Me or Billy Bonney?"

"I'm scared of both of you," Grubber replied.

"I want to know what he is doing every second," James threatened, ending the call.

James sat back and thought about the conversation. Grubber was one more connection. For a moment, early in the conversation, he had thought that he might try to get Grubber to eliminate Billy, but he realized that wouldn't work. Even if Grubber was willing, James didn't think he was able. And even if he could, that would give Grubber a hole card that James couldn't afford to let him have. James thought some more.

Angie had to go. James couldn't see any other way out. As far as Billy knew, he had already gotten rid of her. She was gone. She was in Mexico. As far as Grubber was concerned, Billy had gotten rid of her. That was all Grubber knew or wanted to know. So Angie had to go. She was the hinge pin. But how? That was the question. Ship her out or eliminate her? He hated to think about it, but he was going to have to eliminate her. If he didn't, if he sent her away, first chance she got she would come back and fuck everything up. That's how she was. She would always come back. He couldn't have any witnesses. As much as he would like to put it on someone else, he had to do it himself if he wanted to sever the connection.

James felt like a big load had come off his shoulders. He knew what he had to do. Eliminate Angie and those two detectives would go around in circles forever looking at Billy and Grubber, wondering which one was responsible for her disappearing. Then, if he could get Billy out of the picture for a while, even better. It might be worth funding Billy's departure to parts unknown. That would leave Grubber with nowhere to go, and the shit would end up in his lap.

Chapter 13

Wednesday

Skip proceeded west on Mamie Eisenhower toward the Boone County Courthouse.

"Check it out on the right," Max told Skip as they came up to a small bar and grill tucked between the seedy looking attorneys' offices that occupied the blocks surrounding the courthouse. Skip pulled in and parked the car. The place looked abandoned.

"I don't think it is open," Skip remarked.

Max tried the door and it came open. Skip and Monica followed him into the dark bar. There was no one in sight as their eyes became accustomed to the darkness.

"You think they just forgot to lock the door last night?" Skip asked.

As soon as he said it they heard a voice from the back call out, "Be right with you."

They stood facing the bar as a middle-aged man of medium height and build, medium complexion, with a full head of brown hair cut medium length, came from the kitchen behind the bar. The first thing that came to Max's mind was that it would be almost impossible to describe the man.

"What'll you have?" he asked.

"Miller Lite," Max piped up, taking a stool at the bar.

"Actually," Skip said before the bartender could get a glass for the beer, "we're mostly looking for information." Skip handed the bartender his G&B Detective Agency business card across the bar.

"Sure," said the bartender. "You still want a beer?" he asked Max.

"Might as well," Max said as the man turned and filled a glass from the Miller Lite tap behind the bar. Skip gave Max a look and Max shrugged his shoulders. He looked toward Monica. She shook her head no and took a seat on one of the bar stools.

"What kind of information you looking for?" asked the bartender over his shoulder.

"We are looking for a fellow named William Bonney. We were wondering if you know him and if he has been in recently," Skip replied.

"I know him, haven't seen him for a long time, and he don't regularly hang out here," the bartender replied.

"You're not much help," Max chided the man good-naturedly.

"I'm right here a block from the courthouse, a block from the sheriff's office and two blocks from the probation offices. I cater to lawyers, deputies, county attorneys, city cops and probation officers. The likes of Billy Bonney come in here if they have to go to court for something. Otherwise they stay away."

"Makes sense," Max agreed, taking a sip from the glass of beer that the bartender had just put in front of him. "What's your clientele look like at night?"

"We do karaoke on Thursday and Friday evenings," the bartender said. "We get a pretty good crowd for that. I'm closed Sunday, Monday and Tuesday nights. Wednesdays are dead; Saturdays I try to get some live music in if I can. I get mostly people from the neighborhood in here Saturday nights. Honestly, since they put in that new Boone County Law Enforcement Center down the block, people don't come in here and drink a lot in the evenings."

"Sounds like business is slow, then," Skip observed.

"I make my money on the grill part of 'bar and grill,'" the bartender explained. "It suits me fine. I'm the neighborhood bar and grill. I like to close early and go home when I can. Business is just fine."

"So Billy Bonney," Skip changed the subject. "What do you know about him?"

The bartender thought for a moment. "Biker type, gets in trouble a lot for minor things. I think he got picked up for DUI a few years ago, for possession of weed one time. Disorderly conduct for fighting up in Pilot Mound a year or so ago. Nothing to do time over. Just misdemeanor stuff. He's no secret. He's been around for a long time. He hardly ever comes in here, but I would see him once in a great while, more around town."

"Where is he now?" Skip asked.

"No idea," the bartender replied.

"He was with a woman, maybe still is," Skip continued. "A gal named Angie, you know anything about her?"

The bartender thought for a moment. "Nope, I don't think that I ever saw him with a woman. But then, I don't socialize a lot with biker gangs, so I don't know who he takes up with." The bartender was starting to become defensive with the line of questioning. He looked over at Monica, who was sitting on the stool next to Skip.

"Ma'am, can I get you a drink, a glass of water?"

"I'm good," Monica answered. "Thank you, though." She gave the bartender a smile. He grinned back, giving her his attention, dismissing any more conversation from the two detectives. He was looking her up and down when he noticed her playing with the big diamond engagement ring on her left hand. He turned his attention back to the detectives.

"What do we owe ya?" Max asked.

"Two-fifty," the bartender replied.

Skip got out his billfold and placed a five dollar bill on the counter.

"We're good," he said to the bartender as the three stood up.

"You have our card there," Skip said. "If you hear anything about Bonney or that woman that he might be with, a call would be greatly appreciated."

The bartender had the card in his hand. He looked down at it. "Will do," he replied as the three made their way to the door and out into the sunlight.

"You turning into teetotalers?" Max asked as soon as the door closed behind them. "I mean, walk into the guy's business and ask a bunch of questions, then don't buy anything, that's not good."

"You gonna have a beer every place we go today?" Skip asked.

Max shrugged his shoulders. "I'm a grownup."

"I don't care," Skip replied, "I was just wondering."

When they got to Skip's car, Max got in the back again. Monica climbed in on the passenger side. "What now?" she asked.

"You know of any other bars in town here that are open this time of day?" Skip asked over his shoulder.

"Not really," Max replied. "Wanna go back up where we started, that bar in Pilot Mound?"

"Might as well," Skip replied.

The drive to Pilot Mound was uneventful. Monica seemed lost in thought. Max and Skip could see that she had something on her mind, so they let it go. Max sat in silence in the back seat, surfing the net on his phone. Skip just drove, engaged in his own thoughts. He wondered if Monica was thinking about Angie, or if she was thinking about the guy in the bar who had called her out. Either way, he was content to just drive.

As Skip drove into Pilot Mound, Max leaned forward between the front seats and looked out the windshield. "See Grubber's car there?" he asked.

"Nope," Skip answered.

Max did see an older Chevy pickup truck parked by the front door. It looked like it had a motorcycle in the back, covered up with a tarp.

"Bikers?" Max asked.

"Probably," Skip replied. "'If they can't ride 'em, they haul 'em.' *Easy Rider*," Skip remarked.

"That where that came from?" Max asked.

Skip parked the car and the three got out. Max peeked under the tarp as he walked past.

"Shovelhead," Max observed. "I'm impressed. I used to have an old Electroglide."

When they went into the bar they recognized the bartender as the same one that they had talked to on Monday. Off to the side were two bikers wearing their colors and shooting pool. One had his back to the three, and it was clear from his motorcycle jacket that he was a Hell Fighter.

"*Interestante*," Max said under his breath just loud enough for Skip to hear.

"Yep," Skip replied. "Hell Fighters."

The three took stools at the bar where the bartender was sitting on a beer cooler watching them come across the room.

"What's up?" Max asked. "Remember us? We were here the other day."

"I remember you guys," the bartender replied. He looked over at Monica. "I don't remember the lovely lady being with you, though."

Monica gave him her charming smile, flashing a row of perfect white teeth that were guaranteed to keep his attention.

"So anything new been happening around here since we last spoke?" Skip asked.

"Nope," the bartender replied without looking away from Monica.

"Well, you got some Hell Fighters, I see," Skip replied. "You said the other day that you don't get any of them in here anymore."

"Don't usually," the bartender turned back to Skip. "But I got a few today."

"What are they up to?" Skip asked.

"Looks like they're shooting pool," the bartender came back.

Skip could see that they weren't going to get anywhere with the bartender.

"You got anything to eat here?" Max asked.

"Pizza, burgers and burritos," the bartender answered, tilting his head toward the menu on the wall behind the bar. "Out of chicken nuggets."

"How long does it take for a pepperoni?" Max asked.

"Twenty minutes," the bartender answered.

"We'll take a pepperoni and I'll have a Miller Lite in a bottle," Max said.

"Make it two," Skip added.

"Ma'am?" the bartender looked at Monica.

"Sure," Monica replied. "I'll do a Miller Lite."

The bartender got up from the cooler and opened it, pulling three bottles of Miller Lite out between the fingers of one hand. He deftly popped the tops off of them and placed them in front of his customers, then turned to go back to the kitchen.

"Got any quarters?" Max asked Skip and Monica. Skip searched his pockets while Monica looked in her purse. Max already had two quarters in his hand. Monica found four and gave them to Max. Skip came up with two more.

Max and Skip watched the bartender through the window to the kitchen from their stools. When he got the frozen pizza unwrapped and into the oven, Max stood up and started toward the pool table.

"Talk to him," Skip said quietly to Monica, nodding toward the bartender coming out of the kitchen.

Max crossed the room to the pool table with Skip right behind him. He placed four quarters on the rail. The two bikers stopped shooting pool.

"Private game, or you fellows want a little competition?" Max asked.

"What you thinking?" the taller biker asked.

"Ten bucks a game," Max suggested.

The biker glanced at the shorter one, who gave him a slight nod. With his cue, he raked the balls off the table and into the corner pockets. When they had settled, Max stuck his four quarters into the machine. The balls rolled to the end of the table where the shorter of the two bikers racked them.

"Wanna lag for first shot?" Max asked.

"You're good," the taller biker replied.

Monica watched the pool table while the biker racked the balls and Max broke them. She watched two stripes go in on the break. Monica could sense the bartender standing over her. She turned.

"Those boys like to play pool," she said.

"Yeah, well, those two bikers like to play pool, too," the bartender replied. "And they're pretty good."

"I guess the guys were up here snooping around the other day," Monica remarked casually. "They said that they came up here looking for some biker named Gonad. I mean, who names their kid Gonad?" Monica giggled.

The bartender laughed a little harder than he needed to. "Yeah, Gonad Grubber. They talked to him a little bit. I don't think that they got much from him, though."

The bartender watched the pool game for a while.

"What's your connection with those guys?" he asked.

"That one that broke is my stepdad," Monica answered. "I go to college and I'm on spring break, so I just came along for the ride."

Monica noticed the bartender raise his eyebrows a bit when she said that Max was her stepdad. She didn't even know why she said it. It just came to her. She felt pretty good that she could play this game.

"Yeah, he and my mom hit it off probably twenty years ago," Monica continued. "Couple of little love birds."

The bartender didn't respond. He looked at her with a curious expression, like he wasn't sure where she was going with the conversation. Monica didn't know, either.

"You know those two that the guys are playing pool with?" she asked. "They don't look like the friendly kind."

"They've been coming in pretty regular, recently," the bartender answered. "They work for some fellow down south of here. They're in the security business." He stopped short there.

"Like that concert?" Monica asked.

"What concert?" the bartender asked.

"The one the Stones did way back in the early days. The Hells Angels were doing security for the Stones concert and they stabbed someone."

"I never heard of that concert," the bartender replied.

"Yeah, I read it on the internet one time. Like one of those clickbait things." Monica crossed her legs and jiggled her foot.

The bartender was confused. He had no idea what she was talking about. She was cute. Kind of an airhead, though. He wondered what she was studying in college.

"It's nothing," Monica continued. "Just bikers working security, just made me think of that. I mean, who hires bikers for security?"

The bartender decided not to respond. Monica looked at him across the bar and smiled.

The bartender realized that she was waiting for an answer. "I don't know," he finally said. "Someone who don't want people nosing around, I guess."

"Yeah, I suppose so," Monica agreed. "I'm guessing those guys are pretty tight lipped about it, especially around people like you and me."

The bartender didn't respond.

"I'm guessing a pot grow, or maybe a meth lab?" Monica leaned over the bar and whispered. "What do you think?"

The bartender stood up and shuffled his feet a bit. This woman was making him nervous. He was just trying to have a nice conversation with her and she was taking it in a direction that could get him in trouble.

"Well, I never said anything about drugs," the bartender replied defensively. "I don't want anyone thinking that I said that they was involved with drugs."

"I didn't say that you thought they were involved with drugs," Monica replied. "I'm just speculating." She paused for a moment. "That's the problem with speculation: people speculate, and then they start believing their speculations. If you know what I mean. I'm not saying to anyone that you said that they were involved with drugs, but I don't know what else it would be, do you? I mean, you know them better than I do. I'm just saying what it sounds like to me." She paused again. "From what you've said, I mean, what else would someone up here be doing that they needed to hire bikers for security?"

The bartender wanted to end the discussion, but he didn't want to leave her thinking that he thought those two Hell Fighters were involved with trafficking drugs. "I've heard that it's for some kind of private club, that's what I heard."

Monica frowned. "Private club? What kind of private club? Like a country club? Do they have a golf course? Who hires bikers for security at a country club?"

The bartender didn't know how to answer. He really just wanted to walk away, but he couldn't seem to move.

"I really don't know nothing about it," he said, exaggerating the exasperation in his voice. "Just a club. A gentleman's club. That's all there is to it."

Monica started to speak.

"That's all I know," the bartender said, and finally walked away toward the kitchen.

Monica watched him leave, then turned back to watch the pool game.

Max was talking away to the two bikers, who seemed not to be engaging with him. Max was talking, anyway. He would run three or four balls at a time, and just when it looked like he and Skip were going to win, Skip would knock the eight ball into a pocket and lose the game. They were on their third game, and Max had cleared most of the table. Only the eight ball remained. The taller biker sank two balls. The next shot missed the pocket, but the cue ball struck the eight, propelling it up against the cushion, before falling into the pocket to scratch. Monica saw Max wink at Skip. Skip retrieved the cue ball and placed it just behind the markers.

"Corner pocket," Skip mumbled, pointing his cue stick toward the pocket to the left of the eight. He carefully lined it up and tapped it lightly with plenty of right English on it. The ball ever so slowly bounced off the side cushion and proceeded at an angle, hitting just the outside of the eight ball, and just as slowly, the eight ball began its journey along the cushion and into the corner pocket.

"Sweet," Max remarked as the eight ball fell into the corner pocket. "You guys want to do one more, maybe even it up?"

"Gotta go," the taller biker replied, as he put his cue stick into the rack on the wall.

As he was doing so, the bartender was delivering the pizza that Max and Skip had ordered. He placed it in front of Monica.

"If I were your stepdaddy and his partner," the bartender said, "I wouldn't be pushing those two Hell Fighters too hard. They might just find them waiting outside when they leave."

Monica smiled serenely at the bartender and wrinkled her nose.

"If I were those two Hell Fighters, I wouldn't want to be out there in the parking lot when my stepdaddy and his partner go outside," she replied in a low voice. "They might just want to push them a little harder, and I'm sure it wouldn't be a pleasant experience."

The bartender stood looking back at her. Max and Skip were laughing at something Max had said as they walked to the bar.

"Pizza looks good," Max observed. He smiled at the bartender. "Don't you just hate having to let dumb shits like that win?" He laughed.

Chapter 14

Wednesday

The three detectives walked outside to Skip's car. The pickup with the motorcycle in the back was gone. As Max walked around to the passenger side of the car to get in the back, he saw that the whole length of Skip's car had been keyed.

"Assholes," Max exclaimed.

Monica was coming around to the passenger side of the car as well. She stopped and looked.

"What?" Skip asked.

"Come over here," Max said. Skip was already coming around the front of the car.

"God damn it," Skip exclaimed as he came around to the passenger side with Monica and Max. "Why did they have to do that?"

"I think it was that last shot on the eight ball, actually," Max observed.

"Damned assholes," Skip replied.

"Wanna go hunt 'em down?" Max asked.

"Yes, I do," Skip replied in anger. "But right now we better just stay on the case. We're looking for Angie. That's more important, and I can get the car repainted. I don't want to fuck up this case just to get even with a couple of asshole bikers."

Max shrugged his shoulders. "We can get them later. No hurry."

Skip nodded and went around to the driver's door and got in. Max and Monica climbed in as well, and Skip backed out of the parking spot and onto the street.

Monica was as angry as Skip and Max. "You need to report this," she said.

"Ain't the first time I've been keyed," Skip said. "They used to get my patrol car regularly. I can get it fixed. Ogden, look for Grubber?" he asked, already not concerned with the keyed doors.

"Sure," Max responded. "So, Junior Detective Monica Benson, soon to be Jackson, did you get the bartender to spill his guts?"

"I wouldn't say that he spilled his guts," Monica replied. "But he did tell me a couple of things that might help."

"Let's hear it," Max said.

"Okay," Monica began. "First off, those two bikers work security at some place south of town. Second, it is some sort of private club." She let that sink in.

"What kind of private club?" Skip asked.

"He called it a gentleman's club," Monica replied.

"Interesting," Skip responded. "What exactly is a gentleman's club?" He pondered. "Would that be a bordello?"

"No idea," Max replied. "You ever hear of a gentleman's club around here?" he asked Monica.

"Nope," said Monica. "But I didn't get around a lot. I stayed in Ames." She thought for a moment. "But still, I've never heard about any gentleman's club, or anything like that. The closest thing was a strip club down by Des Moines that was named The Gentleman's Club. But it wasn't any kind of club, it was just a strip bar."

"You ever work there?" Max asked.

"No," Monica replied with a bit of bluntness in her voice. "I just told you that I stayed close to home."

"Don't get touchy," he replied.

"I'm not touchy," Monica retorted.

"Okay," Skip stepped into the conversation. "Let's not talk about gentleman's clubs right now. Let's save that until later. Let's go to Ogden and see if we can find Byron."

"What did the two bikers have to say?" Monica asked.

"We didn't really talk to them about much," Skip replied. "First off, we didn't want to tip our hand while you were talking to the bartender. Second, we didn't want to tip our hand to a couple of guys who probably weren't going to talk to us, anyway. Also, we didn't want them running off and telling anyone else that we were nosing around until we are ready for them to do that. So short answer, we didn't ask them anything."

"We should have tailed them," Monica said, using her detective vernacular.

"Tail them where?" Skip asked. "To the next bar? Home? What would we gain by that? That's just a big gamble when it comes to investigation. We know that they are out there. Maybe we find them doing something other than shooting pool in a bar at noon, something that connects them to Billy, then we'll tail them. Or we make it a point to run into them another time and plant some seeds. See how they grow. Being strategic is the name of the game. We got to figure out the best way to use those guys."

The three didn't talk much more on the way. Each was thinking about the gentleman's club, and how it may or may not be connected. But at the moment it was a subject that everyone was shying away from for some reason. Actually, they each knew the reason, but it would have to wait. Skip pulled up in front of Temple's and parked.

"Don't see Grubber's car," Skip observed. "Wanna go in anyway?"

Max was already getting out of the car.

"Guess so," Skip mumbled to himself.

The three went into the bar and took up stools. The same bartender that had been there when they had talked to Byron was behind the bar.

"Hey, how's it going?" Max asked. "We were in here the other day with Byron Grubber. We're looking for him again, you seen him?"

"You just missed him," replied the bartender.

"Got any idea where we might find him?" Max asked.

"You guys need a drink?" the bartender asked.

Max looked at Skip. "Miller Lite?"

Skip nodded. Max looked at Monica.

"Why not?" she replied.

"Three Miller Lite draws," Max told the bartender.

The bartender turned away to get their drinks.

"You guys drink a lot of beer," Monica said.

"Well, we're in bars, and when you're in bars you need to drink if you want people to talk to you. I mean, you can put down a lot of Miller Lite if you have to," Max explained. "People trust you better if you're drinking with them."

"Why did you guys get bottles at the other bar, instead of draws?" Monica asked.

"When you're shooting pool with a couple of hard cases like that, a bottle hits harder than a glass," Max replied.

"You were going to hit those guys with a bottle?" Monica asked.

"If we got pushed into it," Max shrugged. "Those guys like that are unpredictable."

"Geesh, you guys take the cake," Monica replied.

The bartender brought their beers.

"Question," Skip said. "You ever heard of a biker called Billy the Kid, or one called Snake Eyes, or more importantly, a woman named Angie Williamson?"

The bartender thought a moment.

"I heard of Billy the Kid, and Snake Eyes is Byron Grubber's brother, but I never heard of the woman."

"When's the last time you heard about Billy the Kid?" Skip asked.

"Just a little while ago. Grubber was talking to someone about him," the bartender volunteered.

"Not to us?" Max asked. "'Cause we were asking him about Billy the Kid when we were here the other day."

"No," replied the bartender. "He was talking to someone today, when he was in here for lunch."

"You know who it was?" Skip asked.

The bartender paused for a moment in thought. "Actually, he was talking to someone on the phone about him. I heard the conversation."

"How did the conversation go?" Skip asked.

"You know," the bartender replied. "I didn't listen that close. I just remember him saying the name."

The three sat looking at the bartender, waiting for more, but there wasn't anything else. The bartender shrugged his shoulders and walked down the bar, busying himself by looking at a note that was next to the cash register. He looked toward the three detectives down the bar, but quickly went back to the note.

Max and Skip finished their beers. Monica had hardly drank hers.

"Drink up," Max told her.

"I'm done," Monica replied.

Skip stood up and the other two followed. They went out to the parking lot and got into the car. As Skip headed out of town and onto Highway 30 to go back toward Ames, Max spoke up. "So I'm starting to think that Billy the Kid is around here somewhere, holed up because there's a warrant out for his arrest."

The other two nodded in agreement.

"But there's no indication that Angie is with him," Max continued.

"No indication that she isn't," Monica interjected.

"Yes," Max agreed. "But I think that we still need to recognize that finding Angie is our focus, not finding Billy. I just feel like we keep pinning this investigation on finding Billy."

"That's because he's the only connection that we have to Angie," Skip remarked.

"But we haven't looked for any other connection," Max argued. "Just take Billy out of the equation. Grubber knows her, has a history with her, Grubber could be a connection."

"Those two bikers are in the same motorcycle gang as Angie's boyfriend and her other, dead boyfriend," Monica added. "That's a connection."

"That is," Max agreed. "This is Angie's old stomping grounds, she probably has her own connections up here. You're a connection, Monica: she called you and that started this investigation. That's a huge connection."

"That one doesn't really take us anywhere, though," Monica argued. "Agreed. It started the investigation, but it hasn't gone anywhere from there."

"It's gone a lot of places," Skip observed. "Everything we have came from that connection. So it is significant, we just can't see why yet. Why call you?"

Monica thought about that. "Because she knows me, because she knows that I work for a detective agency, because she knows that I'll try to help her," Monica paused.

"She knows your phone number, because she called it from someone else's phone, someone you don't have in your contacts. She could dial your number off the top of her head," Skip observed.

"So we also have the guy who answered the phone when we called back," Monica added. "He is connected in some way. Maybe if we can get a little more on him?"

"I think that would be a path to follow some more," Skip agreed.

Skip drove into the parking lot at the G&B Detective Agency and parked next to Monica's car. They got out and went inside.

Max and Skip took their seats across from Monica's desk. "Let's just talk about this gentleman's club." Skip suggested. "What exactly is a gentleman's club? Is it a bordello?"

No one answered for a moment. Monica finally decided to broach the subject.

"We're talking connections here, and you're wondering if there is a connection with the gentleman's club and Angie." Monica said. "You guys are wondering if it is possible that Angie is a prostitute at this gentleman's club, right? That's what you want to know?"

"Or a waitress," Max replied. "Or an entertainer, or a bartender, or a bus girl, or a door girl, or…" Max tapered off. "We're not calling Angie a prostitute."

"It's possible," Monica replied. "She could be any of those things, but truth is, prostitute would probably be more in her skill set. When we were stripping, she used to pick up extra money in the parking lot giving blowjobs, so yes, she could be prostituting at a gentleman's club."

Max was staring at Monica.

"What?" she asked.

Max didn't reply.

"Don't look at me that way, there's no profit in tip-toeing around it for my sake. I didn't give blowjobs out in the parking lot, or anywhere else," Monica directed her point straight at Max. "But let's just say it: a lot of dancers do, and I think that is a consideration that we need to explore. So a prostitute at the gentleman's club is a good connection, I think."

"I think so, too," Max replied, agreeing with her. "And by the way, on Monday the bartender said that he hadn't seen any Hell Fighters for a long time, and lo and behold we show up two days later and there are two Hell Fighters shooting pool in his bar."

Max paused for a moment for effect.

"And he tells Monica that the two bikers come in regularly, and that they work security at a gentleman's club somewhere out there in the boonies, but close enough that they come to Pilot Mound at lunch time instead of Boone or Ogden," Max stated. "So that is a contradiction to think about. That bartender probably knows a lot more than he's telling. Even if he doesn't know specifics, which I would be surprised if he didn't, he's got some suspicions."

Everyone sat quietly for a moment.

"We have some connections," Monica announced as she was picking up the phone. "We have a message," she said, turning her attention to it.

Monica held the receiver to her ear while she punched the numbers on the phone. She listened for a moment, frowned, and held up her hand for silence, even though neither Skip nor Max were speaking.

"Listen here," she said, placing the phone on speaker and pushing buttons to replay the message.

"Yeah, I think that you guys need to leave me alone. I ain't done nothin' to you guys and you got no reason to be looking for me. So quit asking around about me."

The message ended. The three looked at each other. "Again," instructed Skip.

"Yeah, I think that you guys need to leave me alone. I ain't done nothin' to you guys and you got no reason to be looking for me. So quit asking around about me."

"Billy the Kid," Max said. "And somebody we talked to talked to him."

"Guessing the guy this morning," Skip replied.

"Could be," Max agreed. "So, Billy knows we're looking for him and he doesn't want to talk to us."

"Now we have another connection to Billy," Monica observed. "Is that how it's done?"

Skip went back to his office, leaving Monica and Max in the reception area. He returned with a legal pad and began making notes.

"Connections?" Max asked.

"Trying to map them out here," Skip replied. "Who we got?"

"Start with Angie," Max suggested. "Both Grubbers, though we won't get much out of Snake Eyes, Billy the Kid, this gentleman's club, two Hell Fighters up in Pilot Mound, Pilot Mound bartender, shithead in the bar this morning, bartender in Ogden who heard Grubber talking about Billy," Max stopped to think. "Add the three of us, Kind and Duffy.

Skip looked up from his legal pad.

"Might as well put them down," Max suggested. "I have a feeling that those two know something that they aren't telling us."

"To the conference room," Skip suddenly said. "Let's put this all up on the whiteboard where we can see it."

The three jumped up and went into the conference room which was located in the room behind Monica's desk. Skip wiped off the scribbling that Essie had done on the board while playing in there and then copied what he had written on his notepad.

"Who else?" Max asked.

Skip shrugged his shoulders. "How about the probation officer, Robinson, and that cute little deputy down in Fayette County who was asking about Milton?"

"What deputy?" Monica asked, glaring at Skip.

"Just a nice little gal down there that had run into Milton a time or two and was interested in how he was getting along," Skip teased.

"We told her that he was tooken'," Max said. "She looked a bit heartbroken, if you ask me."

"Tooken'?" Skip asked.

"'No more lookin', I know I been tooken'," Max recited a line in the song "Hey Good Lookin'."

"Sometimes you are weird," Skip replied.

The three looked at each other.

"Anyone else?" he asked.

"Can't think of anyone," Max said after a moment.

"I have to pick up Essie pretty soon, and Milton's coming over for supper tonight," Monica replied. "I gotta get going."

"A special occasion?" Skip asked.

"No," Monica answered. "Mom makes supper for him every Wednesday. Then we put Essie to bed and leave her with Mom while we go out for two-dollar draws."

"Shawna makes Milton supper every Wednesday?" Skip asked incredulously.

"Yes," Monica replied. "I told you that she and Milton are getting along better. She's making him meatloaf, baked potatoes, cornbread and green beans tonight."

"You know," Skip looked over at Max and winked. "I think this whole thing might work out. I mean Milton, Monica and Shawna."

"Jesus, just the thought of those three living together in marital bliss scares me a little," Max teased.

Monica picked up her purse from her desk and was digging out her keys.

"You guys have your fun," she said as she walked out the door. "Lock up," she called over her shoulder.

Max turned to Skip. "Will you take me home?" he asked.

"Take you home to my home?" Skip answered. "Or take you to your own home, which is the other direction from my home?"

"Take me to my home," Max replied, narrowing his eyes as he said it, knowing quite well that Skip knew what he was talking about.

Chapter 15

Wednesday

Byron Grubber pulled his Saturn into a space next to a pickup with a motorcycle in the back that was parked in front of the bar in Pilot Mound. There was one other car, parked on the other side of the truck. The boss had been working him hard all morning and he was glad to get out of there for lunch. He had an hour. The other guys at the junkyard had brought their lunches, but Byron had not. There was nothing in his house to bring. Billy was eating him out of house and home. It was starting to wear on him. Just before he had left for work, Billy had told him to stop by the grocery store on the way home and bring back something to eat, but Byron wasn't going to buy any more groceries until Billy either offered to pony up some cash or found somewhere else to live.

Byron got out of his car. He recognized the pickup as belonging to a couple of Hell Fighters from Omaha who had been hanging around for a couple of weeks. He hadn't talked to them, in fact he was avoiding talking to them, and they didn't seem to be interested in talking to him. The bartender had told him that James had brought them in from Omaha to do some security work for him over at his place. Byron would like to know just exactly what James did at his place, but he was afraid of James. James got information from people, he didn't give it out. Whatever it was that James was doing, Byron was quite sure that it would not pass close inspection by the authorities, and Byron was still being blamed for the big drug bust. He sure as hell didn't want anything to come down on James that he could be blamed for as well. Byron wasn't sure how James had gotten his hooks into him, but Byron gave him just enough information to keep James off his ass, and beyond that he minded his own business. Byron sighed. He was getting sick of riding the fence all the time.

As Byron came around the front of the pickup, he took a look at the brand new Audi sitting on the other side of it and immediately recognized it as the one that Skip Murray was driving the other day.

"Shit," Byron said out loud. "Fuck me."

Byron did not want to talk to those two again. He turned and walked between the Audi and the pickup truck. "Fucking assholes," he said to himself under his breath.

His car keys were still in his right hand. He dragged them along the length of the passenger side of the car, gouging the paint as he went. When he got to the rear of the car, he walked around the back of the pickup truck, got into his Saturn and backed out. He looked around to make sure that no one had seen him key the Audi. As he drove away, he watched the door of the bar in his rearview mirror.

Byron drove south, out of town, heading for Temple's in Ogden. He had to stay away from Mosbey and Murray. He wondered why they were back up in Boone County already, and not over in Oelwein. He wondered whether they figured out that he had sent them on a wild goose chase. He wondered if they were looking for him, or if it was just coincidence that they were up there at the bar. Because if they really had figured it out, they were the kind that would come back and take it out on him. Byron was sick. He was getting pushed from every direction.

There was nowhere he could go and not find himself knee deep in shit. Byron wondered if James already knew that the detectives were back. He was sure that Duffy probably did. He wondered if he should call either or both of them, or if he should wait for them to bring it up. James had been pissed off when he had to call Byron to find out about them the last time. It might be wise for him to call James. But fuck Duffy.

Byron ordered a burger at Temple's. He dreaded going back to work. He had spent the whole morning crawling under old cars and cutting catalytic converters out from the exhaust systems with a battery powered saw. It was muddy, cold work and Byron was soaked through his insulated coveralls from his elbows to his knees. Plus, the cold and damp made him want to piss every half hour. He hated it.

Just when he was getting ready to leave, his phone rang. He fished it out of his pocket and looked at the screen. It was James. He wondered what the hell James wanted and how much shit he would have to put up with if he didn't answer. What was his excuse for not answering? Byron knew that he would have to talk to him sooner or later. Just before it went to voicemail, Byron hit the answer icon and swiped it.

"Hello," he answered, trying to keep the frustration out of his voice.

"Byron, my man," James replied. "How are you? Just checking up on Billy. I haven't gotten an update."

"He's probably still at my place," Byron answered, trying to sound like he was confident that Billy was still there.

"Well, he isn't answering his phone, and I need to talk to him," James said. "Where are you?"

"I'm at Temple's in Ogden eating my lunch," Byron answered. "I gotta go back to work in a few minutes."

"You need to go by your place and tell Billy to answer his phone," James instructed.

"I gotta get back to work," Byron replied. "James, I really can't afford to not work. I don't have any control over Billy."

"You can go back to work when you find Billy and I talk to him," James replied. "Tell him I have a business offer for him."

Byron didn't answer.

"You understand me?" James asked.

"Yeah," Byron replied.

"Good," James said, then ended the call.

"Fucking Billy the Kid," Byron said out loud. He paid the bartender and left.

Byron drove south out of town. He held his phone up where he could see it and drive at the same time. He found Billy's number in his contacts and hit it with his thumb. It took several stabs at it before he could get it to call. Finally he heard it ringing.

Byron waited. After six rings it went to voicemail. It told him that Billy's voicemail was not set up. Byron was pissed and panicked at the same time.

"Why can't you fucking pick up, you asshole?" Byron asked under his breath.

"Business offer," Byron thought. "Why don't I ever get a business offer? I have to crawl under cars and cut catalytic converters out of exhaust pipes for minimum wage, while those two Hell Fighters and Billy get business offers."

Byron held his phone up and went through his contacts again. He pushed the call button with his thumb and it immediately began to ring. Someone picked up after two rings and he heard a voice. "Locker's Salvage."

"Hey, this is Byron, here. I just got a call that my dog got out and somebody ran over him. I gotta go home and see how bad he got hit. I should be back, though, this afternoon."

"Okay," said the voice on the phone. "I'll let them know."

"Thanks," said Byron. "It won't take long."

Byron was still fuming when he pulled into the mobile home park where he lived. As he came into sight of his own trailer, he saw that Billy's pickup truck was gone. Byron pulled into the drive, parked his car, got out and took the steps two at a time to the door. As he was finding the house key on the ring he noticed that the door was neither locked nor completely closed. He opened it and went inside. There were dirty dishes on the table and the furnace was running full blast. It pissed him off that there were dirty dishes. Byron was not the best housekeeper, but Billy was a guest in his home. Billy ought to clean up his own dishes.

Byron walked back to the bedroom that Billy was using. All his stuff was still there, strewn about the room. He hadn't moved out. Byron went back to his own room and looked around. It appeared to be the same as when he left it. He peeked into the bathroom on his way back to the living room. Byron didn't know what to do. He could just leave and go back to work, or he could go looking for Billy. He had no idea where to start looking, though. He wondered if he should just call James and get it over with. Byron fished his phone out of his pocket and found James's number. He hesitated, then hit the call button. The phone rang three times before James answered.

"I was expecting a call from Billy, not you," James answered the phone.

"I'm at my place and he's not here," Byron replied. "He left a note saying that he is coming out to your place to talk to you about a job."

There was silence on the other end.

"He's on the way out here?" James asked.

"That's what it says," Byron answered.

"When did he leave?" James asked.

"Don't know," Byron replied.

There was silence over the phone again.

"Okay," replied James, and the call ended.

Byron went out the door smiling. He was feeling good. He had just pulled one over on James. He locked up behind himself, went down the front steps to his car and got in. He looked at his watch. He would only be a half hour late, if that.

As soon as James ended the call, he got up from behind his desk and went to the garage. The last thing he needed right now was for Billy the Kid to show up and by chance to see Angie, or for Angie to see him. Above the garage was a room where his security people had their equipment. One of the two Hell Fighters that he had enlisted from Omaha was considered an expert in electronic surveillance. James only knew him as Joe, and knew that was probably not his real name. The other was the muscle. James just knew him as Hammer. Joe was short, skinny, with black hair. He looked like the devil. Hammer was huge. He looked like one of those MMA fighters. Hammer even made James feel a little nervous being around him. James made his way into the heated four car garage and took the steps to the room above it. He walked through the door unannounced. The two Hell Fighters were in their shirtsleeves, their colors hanging over the back of the two swivel chairs. Near the wall were six TV monitors, and each monitor was divided into four views. There were security cameras for almost every room in the house, one covering the entrances, inside and out, one covering each side of the house, and one on the gate at the road. They were all on.

The two bikers watched the monitors every night, from the time customers started showing up until the last one left. If there were any problems, they responded. Otherwise they stayed up there, out of sight. But there were seldom problems. James vetted every one of his customers thoroughly. James did not want his customers intimidated by those two unless there was something that he couldn't handle himself. At first, Joe had convinced James to put hidden microphones in strategic places through the house so that the two security men could listen in and report back to him what people were saying or talking about, but he soon realized that a lot of what they were listening to was him. He had the microphones removed. Joe liked to wire everything. He bragged about how he had actually wired the office of the Omaha Police Department's Vice Commander. He tried to convince James to record everything that went on, but James had nixed that idea. Joe had even worked up a surveillance plan that he tried to present to James, but James wouldn't even look at it. Joe poked around in the ceiling tiles, in the ducts and the walls, even did sound tests, but as far as James was concerned, it was a wasted effort. Recordings were irrefutable evidence. Recordings eventually brought people down, from Nixon to Trump. James did not trust recordings. They could be copied. They could end up anywhere, and usually they ended up with a jury watching and listening to them. James was smarter than that. Joe tried to argue, tried to defend the idea, but James didn't want to hear it. So Joe removed the microphones and let it drop. Instead, he and Hammer constantly monitored the screens in the room above the garage, watching for trouble.

The two men turned to look at James as he came in, then turned back to what they were doing. They were connecting a black and silver box to one of the computers that was connected to something else, that was in some way connected to the monitors and the cameras. James had no idea what it all did. It didn't matter, the Hell Fighters knew. That's what he was paying them for. Still, James wondered what they were up to.

"What's that?" he asked.

"Triplicator," Joe answered without hesitation, and without looking up.

"Looks kind of big, what does it do?" James asked.

"Triplicates the omnience of everything," Joe replied.

"What does that mean?" James asked, looking at the black box with cables coming out of it.

"Makes everything come out triple better," Joe explained. "Gives us a three times better picture. Allows us to see exactly what every customer is up too. We can see if they are professional card sharks. It makes everything three times faster, makes everything work three times better," Joe looked up and smiled. "State of the art."

James watched Joe connecting up the box for a moment, then spoke up.

"You guys know Billy the Kid?" he asked.

"You mean Billy the Kid, the Old West outlaw?" Hammer asked.

"No, Billy the Kid, the Hell Fighter," James replied.

"Yeah, I know him," Hammer answered. "What about him?"

"I think that he might be on the way out here. I need you, Hammer, to take the town car out to the gate and turn him around if he shows up," James instructed.

"How about we just don't open the gate," Hammer responded.

"He'll ram it and drive in anyway, or he'll just leave his car sitting in the middle of the drive, jump the gate and hoof it," James replied. He was getting tired of arguing about it. "Simple. I want you out there and when he shows up, I want you to make it clear that he is not to come out here again under any circumstances, and make sure he listens."

Hammer shrugged his shoulders. "I can do that," he replied.

"Good," said James as he turned to the door and walked out.

The two Hell Fighters listened to his footsteps as he went down the stairs and across the garage. They heard the door close between it and the house. Hammer went to the stairs to make sure James was gone.

"He's so fucking stupid," Hammer remarked.

"Triplicator," Joe laughed. "So Billy is coming over. I didn't think he was around these parts anymore."

"I didn't, either," Hammer agreed. "I better get out there and head him off at the gate. We really don't want Billy around. That would not be good."

"I got this new hard drive almost hooked up. It should work better than the old one," Joe said.

"I thought that the old one was fine," Hammer replied.

"I didn't," Joe remarked

"Whatever," Hammer replied. "I don't think it is a hardware problem."

Hammer left the room and went down the stairs. Joe heard the garage door open, the car start, then the garage door come down again. Joe watched the monitor and a few minutes later saw the town car park at the gate. Hammer's colors were still on the chair in the office. Smart move on Hammer's part, Joe thought. He wouldn't have thought of that.

It was 2:30 in the morning when Billy finally came back to the trailer. Byron was awakened by him banging on the door and yelling for Gonad to let him in. Byron got up and opened the door.

"Where's your key?" Byron asked tiredly.

"I don't know," grumped Billy. "Fuck you."

"Where you been?" Byron asked as he started back to his room.

"I went out to James's place," Billy replied.

"James's place?" Byron stopped and asked.

"Yeah," Billy answered. "He said that he would give me a job the other day, and I went out there to see what the fuck is the holdup."

"You went out to James's place," Byron said in wonderment, laughing out loud at the coincidence of it all. "So you been out there all night?"

"No," Billy said angrily. "Some big red-haired ape was at the gate and he wouldn't let me in. In fact, when I started to get out of my truck the big fuck grabbed me by the front of my coat and threw me back in it."

"A Hell Fighter?" Byron asked in surprise.

"No," Billy said. "He wasn't a Hell Fighter. I never seen him before. He was just a big red-headed guy with a beard and muscles coming out of his ears. I would have kicked his ass if he wasn't so damned big."

"Interesting," Byron said. "So then what?"

I went to the bar in Pilot Mound and got drunk," Billy replied.

"Holy fuck," Byron snorted as he left Billy and went back to his room.

Chapter 16

Wednesday

Milton showed up right on time for supper. Monica was setting the table, while Shawna was putting the last touches on the food coming out of the oven. Milton loved anything that came out of an oven. He could smell the aroma as soon as he came in the house. Essie ran up to him as he came through the door. She was always so glad to see him. She squealed and tried to punch him in the leg.

"You wanna fight?" he asked as he grabbed for her.

She dodged his grab and ran in the kitchen with Shawna.

"No punching and no fighting," Monica called out. "We don't punch people in this house."

"Who doesn't punch people?" Milton asked as he came into the dining room.

"We don't punch people," Monica repeated. "Okay?"

Milton pulled out a chair and sat down. "Have fun playing detective today?" he asked.

"I take offense to that question," Monica said sternly. "I *was* a detective today, I was not *playing* detective today."

Milton reached out and pulled her to his chair. "Just funning you," he said.

"People don't say 'funning you' anymore," Monica replied. "That's kind of old hick talk."

"So how did it go?" Milton asked, ignoring her chastising.

"Pretty good," Monica went on. "Kind of slow, actually. We talked to an ISU DPS officer who lives over in Boone, and he didn't know anything. Then we went to some bars in Boone and asked people if they knew this guy, Billy the Kid. Then we went to a bar in Pilot Mound and I tried to get some info from a bartender by batting my eyes at him and smiling, while the guys played pool with some bikers." Monica paused for a moment. "Then we went to a bar in Ogden and talked to another bartender, then we came back and talked about what we found out and how it all fit into the case."

"Sounds like how investigations go," Milton remarked. "Going around talking to people and getting a lot of nothing."

Shawna came in with the meatloaf and put it on the table. She frowned at Milton, who was sitting spread-legged in his chair with his arms around Monica's rear, pulling her into him.

"Christ," Shawna said, "Why don't you two get a hotel room? We got a child in this house."

"Gonna be more of it in a few months," Milton shot back. "When we're living in the same house."

"God forbid when that day comes," Shawna said as she walked back out to the kitchen.

Milton let Monica go.

"It wasn't all nothing. We got a little to work on," Monica said. "The bartender up in Pilot Mound let slip a little info that might be worth following up on."

"What's that?" Milton asked.

"Something about a gentleman's club somewhere up in Boone County on the river," Monica said with a lilt in her voice. "Plus, we caught the bartender making some contradictory statements."

Milton raised his eyebrows. "Sounds like you are quite the interrogator."

"Yes, I am," Monica replied. "I'll bet that if I tried, I could get you to tell me everything you know, even stuff that you aren't supposed to tell anyone. I could pry all of your secrets out of you."

"Sure you want to do that?" Milton laughed.

"Come on," Shawna said to Milton as she came in with a plate of baked potatoes. "You two are sickening with all this sweetie talking." Shawna turned to Monica. "Would you please help me get stuff on the table?"

Essie came into the room. "So what did you do today?" Milton asked her. "You got a boyfriend yet?"

"No," Essie laughed.

"You got any boys that might be a boyfriend someday?" Milton asked.

"No," Essie stood looking up at Milton. "Maybe," she said.

"Oh," said Milton. "You give me a name and I might go have a talk with him."

Shawna and Monica were bringing the last platters of food to the table.

"Maybe someone should have had a talk with you as soon as you started making eyes at my little girl," Shawna commented as she walked by.

"I'm waiting for the day you come up to me all humble pie and tell me that I'm the best son-in-law that there ever was," Milton replied.

"That will be the day," Shawna shot back.

Milton opened his mouth like he was going to say something.

"Stop," Monica admonished him. "Do we have to do this all night?"

Milton turned his chair toward the table and reached for the serving fork stuck in the pan of meatloaf.

"Grace," Monica said.

Milton put his hands in his lap and bowed his head.

"Thank you Lord for this bounty which we are about to receive," Monica said.

As everyone said "Amen," Monica beat Milton to the fork and started to dig out a serving of meatloaf.

"I like the ends," Milton said. "They're crispy."

"There's two of them," Monica replied.

The supper was delicious. Milton had to admit that Shawna was about the best cook that he had ever seen. She was even better than his mother, and his mother was a good cook. Milton was about to take his third portion of meatloaf when he stopped.

"Are we having dessert?" he asked.

"I didn't make anything," Shawna replied. "Did you bring dessert?"

Milton didn't answer. He was already digging another slice of meatloaf out of the pan and putting it on his plate.

"This is really good," he said to Shawna.

"I'm glad you like it," she replied, giving Monica a bit of a smile.

When they were done, Milton helped Monica clear the table and wash the dishes while Shawna cleaned up Essie and kept her occupied. Shawna would have liked to get Essie ready for bed and try to get her to go to sleep, but she knew that wasn't happening as long as Essie thought she might get to play with Milton before he left. Finally, Monica and Milton came out from the kitchen and started putting on their jackets.

"Okay," Monica said. "We're going out for two-dollar draws, and we'll be back later. Give Milton a hug, Essie."

Milton bent down and Essie ran to him, wrapping her arms around his neck. He stood up, and she hung on, her feet dangling.

"Okay," said Milton. "Let's go."

Essie was giggling. Milton bent over until her feet were back on the ground and Essie let him go. Monica got down and gave her a kiss.

"You be good," she said.

Milton and Monica went out the door to Milton's Jeep.

"Well, that was pretty good," Milton observed. "Supper, I mean."

"She likes you, you know," Monica said.

"Essie?" Milton asked.

"Shawna," Monica replied.

Milton parked the Jeep on Main Street in front of their favorite bar. The two went inside and miraculously found an empty booth. They sat down and waited for the waitress to come. As soon as they got comfortable, a fellow walked up to the table and addressed Milton in a jocular voice. "Hey man, how's it goin'?" he asked.

Milton sort of recognized the man from somewhere. He was about six feet tall and thin. Middle aged. "Fine," Milton replied, trying to place him. "How's it going with you?"

"Pretty good," he replied good-naturedly. "Hey, man, I'm just having a couple of beers, don't call me in when I leave." He chuckled at his own joke.

"I won't," Milton replied in a deadpan voice. "Look, man, nice to talk to you, but I'm here with my lady and we kind of want to be alone."

"No problem." The guy winked at Monica and staggered away, feeling like all eyes were on him, talking to the cop and his girlfriend.

"How do you take it?" Monica asked. "I mean, you never get a moment in a bar where someone doesn't come up and try to make a joke."

"He was just funning us," Milton joked.

"Cut it out," Monica replied. "I mean it, we never go out where someone doesn't come up and try to be funny."

"I don't know," Milton answered. "It isn't ever going to go away. I go out for beers with Max and Skip sometimes, and people still come up to them and try to joke around. They've been gone a long time, but people still come up and call them 'ossifer.' It just comes with the territory. I just tell myself that I'm glad that I'm not that stupid. It makes me feel superior." He chuckled.

Monica sat for a moment, looking down at her hands. "I was in a bar in Boone this morning with the guys, talking to the night shift crowd, and someone there recognized me."

"Well," Milton smiled. "You're kind of hard to forget."

"He called me a stripper," she said seriously. "He said, 'You're a stripper. I saw you stripping.'"

"Okay," Milton said in a more serious tone. "We've been over this before. It is something we are going to deal with for a long time. We have to deal with me being a cop, we have to deal with you having been a dancer, we have to deal with the fact that we're a mixed-race couple. We have a lot of things that we are going to have to learn to let go."

"I cried," Monica said.

"Why?" Milton asked right back.

"Because it made me feel bad. It made me feel like I wasn't good enough," she answered.

"You are good," Milton assured her. "You are very good. Just let it go. Hasn't anyone ever picked on you before?"

"Yes," Monica replied. "I've been picked on a lot, and I don't like it."

"Don't let them take it away from us," Milton said. "It is your happiness, it is our happiness, don't let people take it away. We never get it back if you let them take it. Fuck 'em; we don't care about them."

Monica smiled at Milton and took his hand across the table. The waitress came up while they were doing their googly eyes and asked them what they would have. They each ordered a two-dollar draw. She took the order and left.

"Hey," said Milton, as an earlier conversation clicked in his mind. "You were talking about the bartender up in Pilot Mound saying something about a gentleman's club. I was going to tell you something about that before we were so rudely interrupted by meatloaf and baked potatoes."

"What?" Monica asked, leaning forward.

"Okay," Milton began. "So I was talking to Carlisle at the truck stop, and he was waiting to twenty-five with a Boone County deputy. Apparently, Carlisle was at a Casey's store in Huxley or Slater or somewhere this morning, and some mope was telling him about a big gambling house up north of Boone. Carlisle was going to pass on the info to Boone County. I'm just wondering if we're talking about the same place."

Monica was almost jumping up and down in her seat. "I'll bet it is the same place. It's got to be the same place. We should call up Skip and tell him."

"You can tell him in the morning," Milton said, squeezing her hand. "Calm down, were out having beers."

Monica was finding her phone with her free hand while Milton was talking.

"Stop," he told her. "You're off duty. Skip isn't going to jump up and go looking for it tonight. You can talk about it tomorrow. If you're going to be a detective, you have to learn that you don't work twenty-four hours a day. You don't just run around in circles for no reason. You can talk about it tomorrow and decide what is the best way to proceed."

Monica frowned at Milton. "This is pretty good info. Angie is missing, and every minute that we wait is another minute that she is in need."

"You're absolutely right," Milton replied. "But running around Boone County looking for a gentleman's club or a gambling den at eight o'clock at night with nothing more to go on than some rumors is a waste of good time. Wait until tomorrow."

Monica sighed. Milton could see that she was itching to make the call.

"Go ahead," he said. "Call him up."

Monica had already found him in her contacts. She hit call and waited. After two rings, Skip's voice came on the line.

"What's up?" Skip asked.

"Milton was talking to Carlisle this morning, and he had someone at a Casey's tell him that there is a big gambling house north of Boone. Carlisle was going to tell a Boone County deputy about it. Milton and I think that our gentleman's club and this gambling house might be one and the same."

"Could be," Skip replied. "It sounds like you guys are in a bar," he observed.

"We are," Monica answered. "We're getting our Wednesday night two-dollar draws."

"Well, that's all interesting. Enjoy yourself," Skip said. "We'll have to take a closer look at it in the morning."

There was silence for a moment.

"Do you want to do something tonight?" she asked.

"Nothing we can do tonight," Skip answered. "Good starting point tomorrow, though."

"This is about Angie," Monica argued.

"I know," Skip answered. "We'll get on it tomorrow morning, first thing. It sounds like something we need to follow up on."

"That's it?" Monica asked.

"Good info," Skip replied. "Talk to you in the morning."

Monica ended the call.

"You guys are really cold," Monica admonished Milton. "We have a missing person here, a human being who needs help, and you guys don't even want to follow up a lead."

"What lead?" Milton asked.

"That there is a gambling house up in Boone County and Angie might be there," she replied.

"There might be a gambling house up in Boone County, but we have no idea where it is at, and we have no reason to believe that if there is a gambling house in Boone County, that Angie is there and in some kind of trouble."

"But she could be," Monica argued.

"Yes, she could," Milton agreed.

Monica didn't feel like a beer anymore, or feel like talking to Milton. All she could think of was the gentleman's club, the gambling house and Angie. Milton tried to talk, but gave up after a while. He could see that Monica was worried about Angie, and there was nothing he could do at the moment to help her. As soon as he was done with his beer he got the attention of the waitress and paid the bill in cash, giving her a three-dollar tip for the four-dollar bill. Monica left most of her beer on the table.

Milton and Monica got up and left the bar. On the way to Monica's townhouse, Milton listened to the radio. When they pulled into the parking space by her garage, Milton reached over and took her chin. He turned her face toward him and gave her a kiss.

"I'm going to go ahead and go home," he said. "What time are you going in tomorrow?"

"Six-thirty," Monica replied. "A little after. I'm going to drop off Essie at daycare and then go straight to the office."

"What time are the guys coming in?" Milton asked.

"I don't know," Monica replied. "When they get there. Probably early."

"When they get there, give me a call," Milton said. "I'll come on over and let them know what Carlisle told me. Maybe I have some contacts or resources at the PD that could help us out. I'll do what I can."

Monica gave Milton another kiss on the lips and got out.

"See you tomorrow," she said.

Chapter 17

Thursday

Monica was sitting out front of the daycare center ten minutes before it opened at six-thirty. She got Essie out of her child seat as soon as she saw the woman who owned the daycare unlocking the glass door. The woman held the door open for Monica and Essie to come in.

"You're early, Monica," the woman said as they passed through the door.

"I'm helping the guys work a case," Monica responded. "I don't know how late I will be tonight, but if I'm not going to be able to pick her up before six, I'll let you know and have Milton do it."

"The woman was helping Monica get Essie's coat and mittens off. Even though it was the first days of spring and the weather was warming a little during the day, Monica still layered Essie when she took her outside. When her stocking cap came off, her sweat-soaked curls cascaded from under it.

"I think I dressed her up too warm," Monica remarked.

"The first one is always like that," the woman answered. "After three or four you don't worry about them as much."

"I'm not planning three or four at this point in my life," Monica laughed.

"You know," the woman said seriously. "They aren't always planned."

"Don't I know that," Monica said as she kissed Essie on the cheek and left her in the care of the woman.

Monica went back outside and got into her car to head toward the agency. The drive was only five minutes, and she looked at the clock on the dash as she pulled into the parking lot. It was six-thirty-six. Neither Max nor Skip were at the office. Skip seldom showed up before seven. She had hoped that the urgency of the information that she had given him the night before might prompt him to come in earlier. Max seldom came in until after eight. She wondered if Skip had called him and told him not to lollygag around this morning. Regardless, neither were there yet. Monica got out of her car and went to the door, unlocked it and took a seat at her desk. She started her computer and impatiently waited for it to boot up. She had no idea what she was going to search for when it did, but she had to do something.

At seven o'clock on the nose, Skip came wheeling into the parking lot, with Max's Camaro right behind him. Monica had spent almost a half hour on her computer searching everything from "gentleman's clubs Boone County, Iowa," to "gambling dens central Iowa." She had checked Craigslist personals and all the social media that she could think of for any hint of gambling or prostitution activities that could be connected to anyone or any place in Boone, Story or Fayette counties, and came up with little. She had jotted down a few notes, but she knew that they were long shots.

Monica picked up her phone and found Milton in her contacts. She punched him in, and he answered on the first ring. "Just down the street," he said.

"See you in a few," she replied, and ended the call.

Both Max and Skip were coming through the door. Max was complaining about the early hour and how work ethic was a propaganda scheme invented by the world industrial complex to brainwash people into thinking that hard work and long hours made them noble and better than slackers such as himself. Max said that he wasn't buying it. Skip wasn't commenting either way.

"What's up?" Max asked as he came through the door. "Solved the case yet?"

Monica looked at Skip. "Did you tell him what Milton said last night?" she asked him.

"I just got here," Skip said defensively.

Milton was pulling up and parking his patrol car beside Monica's car. She could see that he had the radio microphone to his mouth and was calling out. He seemed to be taking an inordinate amount of time doing it. All three were watching out the window, waiting for him to come in before they discussed anything. Monica went around her desk and tapped on the window. Milton was looking up at her while she motioned for him to come in. Finally, he put the microphone down and got out of the car.

"About time," she mumbled as she went back to her desk.

When Milton came in he was met by Monica's frown. "What?" he asked.

"Nothing," Monica replied.

"So, tell us," Skip said. "Just what exactly did this goofball in Huxley, or wherever, tell Carlisle about a gambling concern operating up in Boone County?"

"That's about it," Milton answered. "Just that the guy wanted to let Carlisle know about it. Nothing else that he mentioned anyway." Milton was pulling his phone out of his pocket as he spoke. He held it out to Skip. It was Carlisle's cell number.

"Give him a call," Milton said. "He talked to a Boone County deputy about it yesterday. Maybe the Boone County deputy already knew about it."

Skip got out his own phone and punched in the numbers. It rang a couple of times, then Carlisle picked up.

"Hello," Carlisle answered.

Skip put his phone on speaker. "Carlisle, Skip Murray here," he began. "So according to a confidential somebody, someone reported a gambling den up in Boone County to you at a convenience store, and you in turn reported it to a Boone County deputy. What can you give us on that?"

"I figured you would be calling," Carlisle replied. "That's about it, except that it's supposed to be a pretty big setup. Tables, big screen TVs, poker, roulette wheels, sports betting. Sounds like it isn't just a few guys getting together to play a little Texas Hold 'Em. According to the guy I talked to, anyway."

"Any specific location?" Skip asked.

"No," Carlisle replied. "I don't think he had been there himself, he just heard about it and wanted to tell me. You know how it is, someone sees you and they just want to come up and talk to you. This guy was like that. Like he just wanted an excuse to talk. But what the hell, I thought that I might as well pass it on. It isn't like I was doing something else. Besides, sometimes a tip like that pans out."

"I hear you. Who did you talk to over in Boone County?" Skip asked. "Did he already have any intel on it?"

"Duffy," Carlisle replied. "He didn't seem to be too concerned about it. I gave him what I had, and he thanked me and left. Said he would look into it. He didn't hang around and shoot the shit or anything. Just thanked me, said that he would pass it on to the rest of the department. Then he said that he was on his way to a call and took off. He seemed like he was in a hurry to go somewhere else."

"Sounds kind of brusque," Skip remarked.

"Yeah, I thought so," Carlisle agreed.

"Do you have a number that I can call Duffy and talk to him about this?" Skip asked.

"Hang on," Carlisle replied. "I got to pull over."

The three detectives waited for Carlisle to pull off the road. They could hear his radio squawking in the background, but couldn't make out the words.

"Ten-four," they heard him say. "En route."

Carlisle came back on the phone with the number. Monica wrote it down on her notepad.

"Anything else you need?" he asked.

"Not at the moment," Skip answered. "If you can get any more info to pass on if you happen to run into that guy again, it would be appreciated."

"I'll keep an eye out for him in my travels," Carlisle replied. "Your unreliable informant there with you?"

"Yep," Skip replied.

"Ask him if he plans on twenty-fiving at the truck stop for lunch."

"Ten-four," Milton shouted toward the phone.

"I'll go down and see if I can find that guy and get anything more out of him," Carlisle said. "I was giving him the bum's rush yesterday, because I thought that he was just jacking his jaws, but I'll see if I can wrangle some more out of him."

"Greatly appreciated," Skip replied again.

Skip ended the call. He pointed at the number on Monica's desk and she handed it to him. He dialed the number into his phone and waited. The phone rang several times before Duffy picked up.

"Hello," he answered.

"Duffy, this is Skip Murray, G and B Detective Agency. We talked to you the other day up at your place," Skip replied.

"What do you need?" Duffy asked easily.

"We heard that Story County Deputy Carlisle talked to you about some information that he got on a large scale gambling operation up north of Boone somewhere, and we were wondering if you did any follow up on it, and if so, do you have any info you could share?" Skip asked.

"Yeah," Duffy replied. "I talked to him and passed the word around. I'm heading into briefing right now, and I was going to have them put it out this morning as well so that all the shifts get it."

"Did you happen to look into it yourself yesterday?" Skip asked.

"Busy day yesterday," Duffy replied. "I didn't get to it, maybe today."

"Do you think that you could keep us up to speed on it?" Skip asked.

"Probably not," Duffy said matter-of-factly. "The word from the top is that we don't share anything that is ongoing and isn't public record with private agencies."

Skip didn't say anything.

"Look, guys," Duffy went on. "Nothing personal on my part, but the sheriff doesn't like people hearing stuff before he does. If I could, I would, but I can't. Sorry."

"It's fine," Skip replied. "We understand. We don't want to compromise you, and we don't want to ruffle Sheriff Kind's feathers, either. We're good."

"Listen," Duffy said. "Honestly, off the record, I think that the guy who talked to Carlisle was just that, talking. If there was something like that going on up there, we would have come across it long before we hear it from some guy at a convenience store in Story County. Something that big doesn't go unnoticed."

"Probably," Skip agreed. "It's just that we're still looking for Angie Williamson and William Bonney, and it sounded like something that they might be involved in. So we were just wondering if there was anything to it."

"I understand," Duffy replied. "But I don't think we are talking about anything big here. Maybe some locals playing a little penny ante poker and fantasy football is my guess. The guy talking to Carlisle was just making it sound bigger than it is. I'm not discounting it, I'm going to look into it, but that is what I think we got here."

"One thing," Skip added before Duffy got off the phone. "We think that William Bonney is back up there around Pilot Mound and Fraser. We talked to a guy yesterday that seemed to be in contact with him, and just a little later Bonney left a phone message on our answering machine that we didn't have any reason to be looking for him and that we need to leave him alone."

Duffy paused for a moment. "Did he say anything else?"

"Nope, that's it," Skip answered. "But I think that it is a pretty good indication that he's around there somewhere, and I also happen to know that there is an arrest warrant out on him for probation violation in Fayette County."

"Thanks for the info. I'll pass that on at briefing, too," Duffy replied. "Anything else you got for me, or I can help you with?"

"Nope," answered Skip.

Duffy ended the call.

"What do you think?" Max asked as soon as the call was over.

"Not much to go on," Skip responded. "He seemed a bit taken aback when I mentioned Bonney. I wonder what's up with that. But I think that we pull up Google maps and get the satellite images up there along the river near Pilot Mound, and go down river frame by frame to Highway 30. See if we see anything big enough and far enough off the road to support a big gambling setup. That seems like a start."

"It would eliminate a lot of shacks up there," Max observed. "At least narrow down the places we want to look at closer."

"I'll do that," Monica volunteered. "I got good at it last fall when we were looking for the source of that fish kill."

"Go for it, then," Skip replied. "I'm going back to my office. If you come across anything that looks promising, give us a holler and we'll come up and look at it together."

"I'm going to get ahold of Langston again," Max replied. "See if he can come up with anything from the new info. If he can't, maybe he can point me toward someone who can."

Skip was already down the hall. Max followed. Monica was on her computer. Milton just stood for a moment in silence.

"Okay," he said. "I guess that I'll go back on patrol."

"See ya later," Monica replied, not looking up from her computer screen.

Milton went outside and got into his patrol car. He picked up the mic and called ten-eight, back in service. As he pulled out of the parking lot and onto the street, he felt a little left out. He started racking his brain for someone he could talk to that might help with the case. Milton knew a lot of mopes.

Chapter 18

Thursday

Duffy got to the Boone County Law Enforcement Center late. He walked past the briefing room and down the hall to the sheriff's office. The door was open when he got there, and Sheriff Kind was sitting at his desk going over some papers. Duffy knocked on the door frame and the sheriff looked up.

"Duffy," the sheriff said. "What do you need?"

"You know those two detectives snooping around looking for the woman?" Duffy asked. "Well, I just got off the phone with them and they got wind of James's place. They don't know where it is or what it is, but they were asking questions about it."

"Well, that's fucking fantastic," the sheriff replied. "How did they find out about that?"

"Yesterday, a Story County deputy got some info on it from some citizen out in the county," Duffy explained. "So he twenty-fives me to pass it on. He doesn't think that there's anything to it, but he passes it on, anyway. He was bored. But somehow the Story County deputy must have told someone else about it, who must have told those two detectives, and they called me up this morning to see if I had followed up on it."

"So what did you tell them?" the sheriff asked.

"I told them that it was probably some hicks playing poker and fantasy football or something," Duffy answered. "I played it down."

"They buy it?"

"I don't think so," Duffy answered. "I think this is the first lead that they've gotten that has any promise, and I think they are going to follow it up. I'm guessing that they are going to go looking today, this morning."

"Any way to persuade them that it would be in their best interests if they just let it go?" the sheriff asked.

Duffy paused for a moment. "I don't think so. I know these guys, at least by reputation, and they aren't going to be easily dissuaded. There is a line with those two. I don't think it is wise to go past it."

"I'm afraid you're right," the sheriff agreed. "We can probably misdirect them for a while at least, until we can figure something out."

The two were silent for a moment, lost in thought.

"Any chance that woman they are looking for is out there?" the sheriff asked.

"That reminds me," Duffy replied without answering the question. "They were asking about William Bonney again. Seems he contacted them. Left them a phone message. They think he is back up here."

"Interesting," the sheriff responded. "I think you need to talk with your two guys out there, tell them what the hell is going on and see what they think. Because there is only so much we can do for them." The sheriff paused. "This whole thing is about to get messy, and if that woman is out there, it is going to get even messier. You better give them a heads up on Bonney, too."

"I'll call them right now," Duffy replied.

"Let me know what they say."

Duffy left the sheriff's office and went down the hall to the briefing room. Shift briefing was over, so the room was empty. He sat down at the table and got out his phone. He looked through the contacts until he found the one that he wanted, and punched call. It rang twice before someone picked up.

"Hello," the voice answered.

"Duffy here," the deputy replied. "Got some info for you, is it a good time?"

"Shoot," said the voice on the phone.

"A couple of private eyes are looking for a missing woman. She's a stripper," Duffy started. "She is supposed to be the woman of a Hell Fighter named William Bonney. Like, I mean, Billy the Kid, and that's what they call him: Billy the Kid. Anyways, they've been nosing around and they got a whiff of James's setup out there, and they are chasing it down. We think it's just a matter of time before they get the scent."

There was silence on the other end of the phone. Duffy got the impression that the person on the other side was talking to someone else. After a few moments, the voice came back over the phone. "All right, I was talking to Hammer. Who are these detectives?"

"Mosbey and Murray," Duffy replied. "Ex-Ames cops."

There was silence again.

"They're just looking for the woman," Duffy added, breaking the silence. "That's it. Woman named Angie Williamson. Blonde. Five-four, slim build. Is she there?"

"He's got some women out here," the voice answered. "But I don't know who they are. They all got fake names, and besides, we don't get near the merchandise. But they are all blonde, five-foot-four and slim. Maybe there is a brunette in the bunch, or a redhead. Hell, I don't know who he has out here. I mean, he has hookers out here. I don't know if any of them are who those guys are looking for. They come and go."

"What about Billy the Kid? Kind wanted me to give you a heads up on him," Duffy replied.

"Yeah, we know about him," the voice answered. "He's all pissed off at James because he says that James was supposed to give him a job and he hasn't heard anything. He came out here yesterday screaming and yelling that he wanted to talk to James. Hammer took care of it."

"There's a warrant on him for probation violation," Duffy informed the person on the other end. "You want us to hunt him down and serve it? That would get him out of your hair."

There was silence again. "No, let it slide. We can take care of him if he comes back. We don't want him getting picked up and talking. As long as he thinks that he's on the run, he'll lay low."

"Anything you want me to tell Kind, then?" Duffy asked.

"Nope, not at the moment," the voice on the other end replied. "Thanks for the info. We'll get back to you if there is anything we need from you."

"Okay," Duffy replied, "What about the detectives, what do you want to do with them? We could probably start leaking some bullshit to them and see if we can get them off track."

"No, but keep an eye on them if you can," the voice replied. "If they start getting close, let us know and we'll deal with them."

Joe put down his phone and looked at Hammer. "What the hell? Business was going so smooth, and now we got these two detectives screwing around."

"Those two shooting pool yesterday," Hammer replied. "Gotta be them. Maybe we just have a little talk with them."

"Ex-cops," Joe remarked.

"Maybe we just have a talk with them," Hammer repeated.

"Yeah, they're ex-cops. Emphasis on the 'ex.' I don't know," Joe replied. "I just don't know. They're looking for some woman. If we try to make a deal with them and they don't go for it, we're fucked."

"What's her name? Maybe we drop a hint to James. If she is in his stable, maybe he should kick her back out on the street." Hammer suggested. "We give them detectives a call and tell them what corner to find her on, end of case."

Joe thought for a moment. "That would just make him nervous. Besides, if she is here and James kicks her out, she's going to start talking. I mean, we can't afford to have her out there talking. I don't even know how to approach James about it without him getting all goofy."

The two sat for few minutes, thinking.

"Let's just keep it under our hats and deal with things as they happen," Joe finally said. "I think going proactive with this gal is just going to confuse things. We don't even know that she's here. I say that getting James all worked up is not good for business. Let's just wait and see where this all goes."

Hammer nodded his head in agreement.

Duffy went back to the sheriff's office and knocked on the door frame to get his attention again.

"What's up?" Kind asked.

"I told Joe," Duffy replied. "And they're going to take care of it."

"What about the woman?" Kind asked.

"He said that they got some women up there, but he don't know their names," Duffy answered. "Anyway, I told him, and he said that they would take care of it, and that's all."

"Okay," replied Kind. "We held up our end."

James looked at the alarm clock in his room. It showed a little after nine. He got out of bed, brushed his teeth and showered in the bathroom connected to his bedroom. There was no indication than anyone else upstairs was moving. James got dressed, left his room and went down the stairs. The downstairs was still a mess from the night before. Half-empty glasses of beer sat on the end tables and on the mantle over the fireplace. It smelled bad. James knew that the cleaning crew would start putting things back in shape in an hour.

James walked into the kitchen, where he found Jean.

"How about some breakfast?" he asked her.

"Coming up," she replied, opening the refrigerator and taking out a pound of bacon and a carton of eggs.

"I got a business deal with someone down south, and they want Angie," James said. "I'm arranging transportation. Anyway, you need to keep her busy tonight and get her ready to leave tomorrow evening early, before the rush."

"So we'll be short for the weekend?" Jean asked.

"Until I can get someone else in here," James replied.

Jean knew not to ask questions. She was surprised that James would move a girl out before he had one coming in to take her place, so she wondered why he was moving her. The whole enterprise was just getting started up. James usually didn't like to shake the basket, as he liked to say, until things were going strong. But it was not her business, so she put it out of her mind. It was better that way. She busied herself frying up James's bacon and eggs. She poured him a glass of orange juice and placed it on the table in front of him.

James watched Jean as she cooked his breakfast. She wasn't bad. A little past her prime, but she could probably pick up the slack if need be. James wasn't sure if he wanted to do that, though. Jean was under the impression that she could come and go if she wanted. She got to go to the grocery store. She went shopping for clothes for the girls. James could trust her out of his sight for a few hours in the afternoon while she went off to take care of her duties. She had been with him for a long time. Putting her up in one of the rooms for the clients might not be good business. He couldn't afford to put her in a position where she might want to leave. He didn't want to deal with that. But then, maybe he could talk to her about it. Maybe she would do it willingly, to help out. Maybe it would even be a nice change for her. He made a mental note to talk to her about it later. He would throw it out there and see how she reacted. The more he looked at her, the more he thought that it just might work, for both of them.

Jean put James's breakfast in front of him. He thanked her. She fixed three more plates of bacon and eggs and put them on a tray to take upstairs to the women in their rooms.

"Don't say anything to Angie right now," James instructed her. "I haven't told her that she's leaving, and I don't want her getting all upset about it tonight. We'll tell her tomorrow."

Jean nodded as she put three glasses of orange juice on the tray and left the room.

James sat finishing his breakfast. He wondered how in the hell he had gotten himself into this business in the first place. Like so many, he wondered where he would be if he had gone a different direction in life. For James, it had all started in college. James was a big guy. He was a rough guy. He came from a rough neighborhood. He liked to mix it up. So he was a natural as a doorman and bouncer. After a year of not studying for his classes, he dropped out of college, then he started getting in trouble and drawing the attention of the cops. He moved from working college bars to working the downtown bars, then he went to the strip clubs were he could make more money pimping the dancers out.

The girls in the strip clubs were always looking for someone to take care of them. They would split their tips with him if he would make sure no one beat them to a pulp inside or outside the bars. Then he started pimping them out, and if they didn't want to play or pony up, he would beat them himself until they did. And so it went. Ten years of that and now he owned the girls, whether they knew that they were owned or not. He owned them all. Drinking, drugs, prostitution and gambling: they went together like caramel and nuts on a chocolate sundae. It was just too delicious for people to pass up. That's how he made his living, selling highs. And now he was going to have to take it up a notch. He had never had to actually get rid of someone. He had never had to make someone just cease to be anymore. But he would do it. There was no alternative. It was okay. He remembered the first girl he had beaten. It was hard, those first few times, but after a while he got used to it. He stopped looking at them as girls and realized that they were just a commodity. They came, and they went. But he had never before been in a situation where he stood to lose everything he had built. He told himself that it was just the next step up the ladder. He was up to it. He could do it.

James finished his breakfast and left the empty glass, plate and silverware on the table. He walked out the door and headed to his office. He wanted to talk to Joe and Hammer about Billy Bonney when they came in. He was starting to think that it would be a good idea to have them pay Billy a visit Friday evening and persuade him to leave the state while James was busy taking care of Angie. He didn't want them to put two and two together when he left with her. It would be a good way to get them out of sight for an hour or so while he did what he had to do.

Chapter 19

Thursday

"I got a few for you guys to look at," Monica yelled down the hallway. "Come up here and look."

Skip and Max almost ran into each other coming out of their offices. Skip motioned Max to lead. Both men walked behind Monica's desk and stood on each side of her, looking over her shoulders.

"First one," she said as she zoomed in on a big house set back from the road along the river and surrounded by outbuildings. She kept zooming until it blurred a bit, then she went back to sharpen the image.

"Big enough house," she commented. She let the two study it a moment.

"Looks like a farm to me," Max replied. "Those look like a barn and maybe a feedlot of some kind."

"Maybe," Skip said. "But maybe not. Maybe it is an old farm being used as a gentleman's club."

Max shrugged his shoulders. "We can check it out."

Monica jotted down the coordinates for it and moved downriver to the next one. The two detectives studied it closer.

"Nice big house, looks like a machine shed, maybe a big garage. House looks newer," Max observed. "I wonder if we can get on the Boone County assessor's page and get a better look at it."

"I can try," Monica said. "Wanna do it right now, or keep going?"

"Keep going," Skip replied.

Monica wrote down the coordinates and moved to the next one.

"Problem is," she said as she located the next property, "I can get a coordinate, like a GPS coordinate, but this map thingie is not giving me physical addresses. So I don't know if I can search the assessor's page with GPS coordinates. I might have to try some other map sites. Maybe Yahoo maps or Google maps would give me an actual address."

"What say we go over them here and now, pick the ones we want to get a closer look at, go up there and drive by them and write down the addresses, then come back and look them up?" Max suggested. "Maybe we can get an eyeball on some of them and decide on each one if we want to leave it on the list or if we want to rule it out."

"I think that is a great idea," Skip agreed. "Let's keep going."

"Print 'em out as we go," he told Monica. "Are we looking at both sides of the road?" he asked as an afterthought. "Or are we just looking at the side between the road and the river? Because there isn't anything telling us that this place is actually along the river. Could be either side."

"I was looking at both sides," Monica replied. "There's a few that look promising on the other side of the road. I mean, I started on the west side of the road between there and the river, but there's some down here on the other side that are worth a look."

The three went down the river on Monica's computer screen, commenting on each place that she brought up, trying to determine which places were worth looking at. They were surprised when they were done that they had been bent over her screen for almost an hour. They had identified eighteen places that they wanted to get a closer look at. Monica collected the printouts, paperclipped them together in order and placed them on her desk.

"I think that we have some work ahead of us," she sighed, looking at the stack.

"That's the way it is," Skip remarked. "This isn't as glamorous of a job as they show it in the movies and on TV."

Monica looked up over her shoulder at Skip. She looked like she was going to cry.

"What's wrong?" Skip asked.

"We just aren't getting any closer," she replied in a defeated voice. "It's been four days, and it feels like we are still looking for a needle in a haystack."

"That's exactly what we're doing," Skip remarked. "Needle in a haystack. But that's the way it always is, and we'll find the needle. We can't lose focus on the needle. We will find Angie. We can't put a time limit on it. We have to let the case take its own course. We will find her, trust me."

Max looked up at the wall clock over the windows across from Monica's desk. It was nine forty-five. "Let's take a pee, get our stuff and get going," Max suggested. "Like Monica says, we aren't getting any closer sitting here."

Max and Skip went to their offices to get ready.

"Packing?" Skip called over to Max.

"Of course I'm packing," Max called back. "I'm always packing. You packing?"

"Probably should," Skip remarked.

By the time Max and Skip had gathered their gear and come up to the reception area, Monica was already standing at the door. She went out and held it open for the two detectives.

"Who's driving?" Max asked.

"Well," Skip replied, "I guess I'll drive."

"What is it with you, wanting to drive all the time?" Max exclaimed. "I thought that you were allergic to driving."

"I just feel like driving," Skip replied.

The three got into Skip's Audi. Monica made her way to the back passenger side door and got in, leaving shotgun for Max, who had been stuck folded up in the back most of the day before.

On the way toward Boone, the three chatted. Max asked Monica about her weekly date night with Milton, and she told them how she had been so concerned about everybody's lack of interest in following up Milton's information about the gambling den that Carlisle had reported to the Boone deputy, that the night was not particularly pleasant.

"Poor Milton," Max remarked.

"No, not poor Milton," Monica shot back. "Poor Angie, who is still missing, and poor Monica who couldn't sleep because her friend is in trouble and her other friends don't care."

"Come on," Max replied. "We care. There was nothing to do last night."

"We could have done what we did this morning," Monica countered.

"Don't argue with her, you're not going to win," Skip told Max.

Max started to say that it wasn't him who she called, it was all Skip. "Tut-tut-tut," Skip said, cutting him off. "Let's just let it drop."

Max mumbled something unintelligible and they continued in silence until they reached the Boone city limits.

"Let's just stay on 30 until we get to the river, and start following it north," Skip suggested. Neither of his passengers replied, so Skip drove through the four-way stop at the intersection of Story Street and Highway 30 and continued until they were looking out over the Des Moines River valley below. Skip made a right-hand turn off the highway and onto a blacktop road that wound north, taking the same course as the river. Monica had her printouts in a folder on her lap, a marker in her hand, calling out each place on her list as they approached. Skip held the speed to forty-five miles an hour, slowing when Monica instructed him so that she could jot down the street numbers as they went. As they passed each place, they commented on whether it seemed worth following up on. Monica jotted down notes so that they could go over them later.

"Remember when county roads weren't streets, they were just county roads?" Max remarked.

"Yep," Skip replied but said nothing more.

"Makes things easier, don't you think?" Max asked.

"It does," Skip was still noncommittal.

Slowly they worked their way up the river.

"Slow down," Monica said. "This place here, it is one of those that we thought was particularly interesting."

Skip slowed as instructed as they drove past the driveway. There were no buildings directly visible from the road, but an ornate gate that appeared to be electrically operated and a callbox on a post stood just off the road. All three examined the gate and the woods around it. As they passed the gate, they could see through the trees that were just starting to bud that the drive wound down toward the river, and they could make out a huge house a hundred yards in the distance.

Skip continued past the house and up the road until he found a place that he could pull off.

"Let me see the printout," he told Monica. She handed it to him, unbuckled her seatbelt and leaned over the back of the seat. Max had done the same and was leaning toward Skip.

"Man," exclaimed Max. "That place really fits, doesn't it?"

"I'm going back by it," Skip replied, checking his rearview mirror and making a bootleg turn to go back south.

Again they strained to get a better look through the trees at the house below. Skip was wandering between the lanes as they went by.

"Keep watching where you're going," Max told him. "I don't want to head-on someone coming north here. It might draw even more attention to us than driving back and forth in front of this place."

Skip got the car back in the lane and found a place a quarter mile down the road where he could do another U turn and go past again. This time Skip drove by at speed, keeping an eye on the winding road while Monica and Max surveyed the property a third time.

"Make that number one on our list," Max commented as they drove by.

Skip continued north. They went by several more places on Monica's list, but the place they had passed earlier became the benchmark, and none of the others came close in potential. Finally they came into the Pilot Mound city limits and drove past the bar. The pickup with the motorcycle under a tarp in the bed was parked in front. Skip looked at his watch.

"Lunch time," he observed.

"I take it you have a plan," Max remarked.

"Yes, I do." Skip pulled in and parked next to the truck, as he had done the day before.

"We looking for trouble, or are we just looking to get your car keyed again?" Max asked.

"Neither one," Skip replied. "Remember that homeless guy that used to hang around that church, and there was a wedding where a diamond necklace that belonged to one of the bridesmaids came up missing and the brother of the bride told you that he saw the homeless guy hanging around the room?"

"Yep," Max replied.

"Remember how you were sure that he did it, and later you found out that the bride's brother gave a necklace exactly like that missing necklace to his new girlfriend a year later?" Skip asked.

"So you're thinking that maybe these shitheads didn't key your car?" Max replied.

"I'm thinking that I didn't see them key my car," Skip answered.

"Who keyed your car, then?" Max asked.

"Someone else," Skip replied.

Max didn't say anything. Skip put the car in park and killed the engine.

"Same as yesterday," Skip said. "If they're shooting pool, we join them like nothing happened, and Monica gets to know the bartender a little better. He seemed to like talking to her yesterday."

"Hang on," Monica said as Skip and Max opened their doors. "That bartender knows you're detectives. I'll bet that he didn't keep it a secret from these guys when they came in today."

"Probably didn't," Skip said as he got out. Max was digging through Skip's console for change.

The three entered the door and let their eyes adjust. It was exactly as it had been the day before. The two bikers were in the corner shooting pool, the bartender was behind the bar. He did not look happy to see the three detectives again. They bellied up to the bar together and ordered drinks and burgers. When Max and Skip got their beers, they sauntered in the direction of the pool table, leaving Monica at the bar.

"How's things going?" Max asked as they got close to the table. The two bikers looked up at him as he put the quarters that he had found in Skip's car on the cushion. "You guys up to taking our money again?"

The bigger biker shrugged his shoulders while the shorter one took a shot.

"Ten bucks a game?" Max asked.

"I think you guys were screwing with us yesterday," the shorter one stood up.

"Five, then," Max suggested. "If you're scared."

The smaller biker pushed the balls toward the holes with his stick. When they had settled, Max inserted the quarters into the machine and let the balls drop into the tray at the end. He rolled the cue ball toward the other end of the table and racked the balls.

"You guys break," he said jovially.

Ten minutes later, the bartender came out of the kitchen with Monica's burger and fries and placed it on the bar in front of her. He went back and came out with two more plates in his hand, carrying them over to where Max and Skip were playing pool and placed them on one of the tables nearby. Then he came back to the bar across from Monica and leaned his arm on it.

"You guys are becoming regulars," he said to Monica.

"Yeah," she replied between bites. "I guess. It's kind of boring, actually. All they do is drive around. I don't see them doing much investigating. I had half a notion not to come along today."

"So not making much progress?" The bartender asked.

"Not that I can see," she replied matter-of-factly.

"That's too bad," the bartender said unconvincingly. "You tell them about our conversation yesterday?"

"What?" Monica asked.

"What we were talking about yesterday. You tell them about it?"

Monica frowned. "What did we talk about yesterday?"

"Nothing important," the bartender replied.

The small talk did not continue between Monica and the bartender while they watched Max, Skip and the two bikers shooting pool. Even from where they stood, they could both see that Max and Skip were purposely missing shots so that the two bikers could win. After three games, they called it quits. The two bikers came to the bar to pay their tab while Max and Skip shot another game between themselves.

The shorter biker gave Monica a smile and winked at her. She laughed out loud when he did, but winked back. After the two left the bar, Max and Skip came up to pay their tab as well.

"Nice talking to you," Monica said to the bartender as she slid off her barstool and Max signed the credit card bill.

"Same," said the bartender.

The three went out the door into the spring sunlight. Skip walked to the passenger side of his car and inspected it, while Max and Monica stood back and watched.

"Nothing new," Skip announced. He came around the front of the car and went to the driver's side to get in. Monica and Skip waited for him to unlock the doors.

"What do you think?" Max asked Skip.

"Either that bartender didn't tell them that they were playing pool with a couple of private eyes asking questions about the whereabouts of another Hell Fighter," Skip observed, "or there is something fishy going on with those two."

"I agree," said Max. "Whether they know who we are or not, when have you ever heard a patched biker say, 'I think you guys were screwing with us yesterday?'"

"I would expect them to tell us to go fuck off when we walked up there in the first place," Skip added. "Any biker that I ever run into would have been right in our faces if they thought that we were dicking with them. They wouldn't say all nice and polite, 'I think you guys were screwing with us,'" Skip said in a falsetto voice.

"Something's up. Those guys were way too well behaved," Max said. "I think that we need to drive back the way we came and see if we can spot that pickup. I'm betting that it is parked down by that big house with the gate."

"Bartender have anything to say?" Skip asked Monica.

"He wanted to know what I told you about our conversation yesterday," Monica answered.

"What did you tell him?" Skip asked.

"I played dumb," Monica answered. "I figured the direction things were going that he wasn't going to be forthcoming, so I thought that I would just play the dumb blonde act, like I didn't know what he was talking about."

"I think that was a good call," Skip replied.

"No doubt, you can pull off that dumb blonde routine, by golly," Max laughed.

"Shut up," Monica retorted.

Skip drove past the house again. He slowed as much as he thought he could without drawing attention, while Max and Monica strained to get a glimpse of the red truck parked somewhere in sight.

"What do you see?" asked Skip.

"Nothing," Max replied. "It's not there."

"I don't see anything, either," Monica said.

"That really surprises me," Max remarked. "I was pretty sure it would be there."

"Maybe they parked it inside." Skip suggested.

"Could be," Max answered. "Would have been nice of them if they just left it sitting out there in the open where we could spot it."

Skip chuckled as he drove on down the road. "Why is it that no one ever wants to make things easy for us?"

Chapter 20

Thursday

Byron drove past the bar in Pilot Mound and spotted Murray's car parked next to the pickup truck that belonged to one of the Hell Fighters from Omaha. He was tempted to stop and key the other side of it, but as he went by the two bikers came out of the bar and got into their truck. Byron didn't want to talk to the two asshole detectives again, so he drove on by.

Joe and Hammer got into Joe's pickup. Joe backed out of the parking space.

"I know those two detectives from somewhere," Hammer said.

"What's with the black girl?" Joe asked.

"I don't know," Hammer replied. "She's with them, that's all."

"You ever see her before?" Joe asked.

"Trying to think, but I don't know," Hammer replied. "She looks familiar, but I'm pretty sure that I've run into those other two. I just can't put a finger on it."

Joe kept his eyes on the rearview mirror as he drove, trying to see if he was being followed.

"See anything?" Hammer asked, turning to look back.

"Yeah, a Harley Davidson motorcycle," Joe answered, shifting his eyes to the driver's side rearview mirror. "Those guys are getting too close. Two days in a row, and I don't think they showed up just so that they could let us hustle them in pool."

"Maybe we need to get Duffy to do something about them." Hammer suggested. "Maybe he needs to step it up a little."

"Not sure that would be a wise thing," Joe replied. "I mean, step it up how? I don't think those two are that easily dissuaded."

"What are you thinking, then?" Hammer asked.

"I don't know," Joe replied. "We need something to throw them off track. We get Duffy involved, and it is just going to make them think that they are on to something."

Joe reached up to the gate opener on the sun visor and pushed the button as he came to the driveway. The gate jerked as it started to open. Joe watched in his rearview mirror as he pulled off the highway and drove through the gate. He watched the gate close behind him as he passed the sensor. Hammer was turned around, trying to see past the motorcycle in the bed of the pickup, looking to see if they were being followed.

"I think it's time to get rid of the Harley," Hammer commented. "Sort of gives us away."

"Maybe so," Joe replied.

Joe drove the pickup past the house, past the spot where he usually parked and behind the shed. It was a little muddy from the spring thaw and Hammer swore a little when he stepped out of the truck and into two inches of muddy leftover winter slime.

Joe was already out of the truck and had reached the corner of the shed, where he stood watching. Hammer walked up beside him. Moments later they saw the silver Audi drive slowly past.

"Fuck me," Joe said.

"Those three are going to be trouble before this is all over," Hammer remarked.

"Call Duffy," Joe replied. "Tell him to do something. I don't know what, but we can't have them nosing around."

"I thought you said that Duffy talking to them would just encourage them," Hammer remarked.

"I know what I said," Joe shot back. "You got a better idea to get them off our asses?"

Joe and Hammer walked out from behind the shed and went to the side door of the garage, tracking mud across the floor and halfway up the stairs before it was all off their shoes. Joe sat down and booted up the computer to the alternate operating system that they used when they didn't want James snooping around. Joe pulled up the recordings and placed a set of headphones over his ears. Hammer took a seat in one of the office chairs where he could watch the sensor that would tell them if James was coming.

After a few minutes Joe took off the headphones and passed them to Hammer.

"Listen to this and tell me what you make of it," Joe said.

Hammer put the headphones on and pressed them to his ears.

"I got a business deal with someone down south, and they want Angie," he heard James say. "I'm arranging transportation. Anyway, you need to keep her busy tonight and get her ready to leave tomorrow evening early, before the rush."

Hammer glanced at Joe.

"So we'll be short for the weekend?" That was a woman's voice.

"Until I can get someone else in here."

Hammer pulled one of the earpieces away. "That's her, the gal those detectives are looking for."

"There's more," Joe said.

Hammer put the earpiece back and listened.

"Don't say anything to Angie right now. I haven't told her that she's leaving, and I don't want her getting all upset about it tonight. We'll tell her tomorrow."

"What do you think?" Joe asked while Hammer took off the earphones and handed them back.

"I think he plans to get her out of here. I think that he got wind of those two detectives on his own. Maybe Grubber said something to him."

"I mean, where?" Joe asked. "Where's he taking her?"

Hammer shrugged his shoulders. "We really need to get a mic in his office."

"I don't think that is going to happen," Joe replied. "I mean, the guy is skittish enough. We're lucky to have bugged the kitchen, the game room and the bathrooms downstairs. We sure as hell aren't going to walk into his office. He knows those damned detectives are looking for her, though. I mean, why else would he be moving one of his girls out like that?"

"I don't know," Hammer replied. "Isn't this what we wanted him to do, though? If she's gone, those detectives don't have a case here. We're back to business as usual."

Joe shrugged his shoulders in resignation. "There's just something about the way he said it. Something just doesn't sound right."

Hammer sat back. He didn't know what Joe thought he was hearing and thinking, but Hammer was glad that James was going to take the woman somewhere else and get her out of their hair. It would make it easier to get rid of those detectives.

"Don't you think that we would make pretty good pimps?" Hammer asked.

Joe pulled the headphones away from his ear. "What?"

"I'm saying, don't you think that you and I would make pretty good pimps?" Hammer repeated.

"I don't think so," Joe responded.

"You know, if we can find out where he's taking her," Hammer began, "maybe we could just get Duffy to tell the detectives, and bingo! They're gone."

"I thought about that," Joe replied, listening to Hammer with one ear and the headphone with the other. "But I only trust Duffy so far. The thing is, things have been going pretty well, and if we want to get our fingers farther into this business, we can't have people getting James all paranoid every time we turn around."

Joe went back to his earphones. Hammer could see that he was watching some video of the game room. Hammer was sitting back, watching the stairs in case James or anyone else came up, and daydreaming about being a pimp.

After almost an hour, Joe took off the headphones and rebooted the computer to the default OS.

"Anything?" Hammer asked.

"Yeah," Joe responded. "There was some shit there that the boss might want to take a look at. I just forwarded it all to him. I think I'm going to call Duffy."

"Change your mind about telling him about the woman?" Hammer asked.

"What's to tell?" Joe answered. "I mean, James is taking a hooker and pimping her somewhere else. What else is new? That's what he does. I don't think that Duffy needs to know."

"I'm still thinking about getting those detectives off of our asses," Hammer replied.

"I don't think that's gonna happen anyway," Joe answered. "We don't even know if we're talking about the same woman."

"Does it matter?" Hammer asked.

Joe thought for a moment. "Maybe not," he replied.

Joe got out his phone. "Keep an eye out," he instructed Hammer while he found Duffy's number in his contacts.

The phone rang four times before Duffy picked up.

"What's up?" he asked. "Two calls in one day. I must be getting popular."

"Those two detectives, or three detectives," Joe said. "Where are they?"

"No idea," Duffy responded.

"I thought that you were supposed to be keeping an eye on them for us." Joe replied.

"I have other things that I need to do," Duffy responded. "Anyway, why are you asking?"

"They were up in Pilot Mound just a little while ago, coincidentally while Hammer and me were there having lunch," Joe said. "And then they did a loose tail on us when we left. They came by nice and slow, checking the place out."

"Okay," Duffy said after a pause. "So that's not good."

"You're damned right that's not good," Joe replied. "You're supposed to be keeping an eye on them and let us know before they are cruising up and down the road in front of here. We're not supposed to be telling you."

"You don't have to get pissy," Duffy said defensively. "What do you mean by three detectives? I only know of those two. Who's the other one?"

"Those two guys," Joe answered. "Then they got a black girl with them. A real knockout. Pretty girl."

"Monica Benson," Duffy responded.

"What do you know about her?" Joe asked.

"Well, first of all, before we talk about Benson, do you happen to know who those two detectives are?" Duffy asked.

"No, not really. They look familiar," Joe replied.

"Okay," Duffy started. "The two detectives are ex-Ames cops. Real hard cases. They won the Powerball a few years back. Two hundred twenty-eight million take-home pay. And they decided for some god-only-knows reason to start a detective agency. The woman is Monica Benson, and she used to be a local stripper. Anyway, they were tight with her when they were cops, and they hired her to be their receptionist when they opened up their agency. The kicker is that she's engaged to a Milton Jackson, APD, and he's just as much of a hard case as those other two, maybe even more so. And he stands about the same size as your buddy Hammer. So that's who's fucking everything up."

"Jesus," exclaimed Joe. "Does this just keep getting worse?"

"Maybe," Duffy said. "It could get worse for everybody if they figure out what's going on."

"Listen," Joe said. "Find them and get an eye on 'em. Just try to keep up with them and let us know where they are at. That's all you need to do."

"I'll try," Duffy replied.

"Listen," Joe said with urgency in his voice. "We got way too much invested in this to have it go sideways. You understand?"

"I said that I'll try," Duffy replied. "Hey, just to let you know," he said with a bit of taunting in his voice, "Jackson's best friend and best man for the wedding is Story County Deputy Carlisle, the guy who wanted to report a possible gambling house up in Boone County to me, and another fucking hard case who is loose on the deck."

Joe ended the call without saying goodbye. Hammer had been listening to Joe's half of the conversation. "What the hell is going on?" he asked.

Joe just stared at him a moment. "This is getting so fucked up," he replied.

Just then the red light that alerted them to someone coming into the garage came on. Hammer pointed toward it. Joe bent over his computer and started typing. Hammer directed his attention to the monitors on the wall. They heard someone coming up the steps, and then James entered the room.

"What are you guys doing?" he asked.

"What we always do, checking equipment and making sure everything is working," Joe responded without looking up.

"Listen," said James. "I got something I need you to do tomorrow night."

Both men stopped what they were doing and looked at him.

"Billy the Kid. I need him to leave. I need him to go somewhere else. Somewhere a long, long ways away. You guys need to take care of that. And I want it made clear that he isn't ever coming back." James replied.

"He's a Hell Fighter," Joe replied. "I mean, he's a brother. A shithead pain in the ass brother, but a brother."

"There's a bonus in it for you guys," James replied.

Hammer spoke up. "Like, we're talking that you want him gone forever? Or are you talking that you want him to leave here forever?"

"I just want him to leave the state," James clarified. "Have a talk with him, explain to him that I don't have any work for him. Tell him that there's no reason for him to stay around, and convince him to leave and never come back. I'm going to give you guys a thousand bucks cash to give him for traveling money. It is up to you how you want to handle that. I don't care. There's a bonus when you get the job done."

"You know where he's at?" Joe asked.

"He's crashing in a trailer that belongs to Byron Grubber, in Ogden," James said. "I'll get the address and trailer number for you before tomorrow. The money, too. But I need you to do it after dark. Leave here at six-thirty tomorrow."

"What's the significance of six-thirty?" Joe asked.

"Just what time I want you to go. I'll make sure that Grubber has him at the trailer when you get there," James said as almost an afterthought.

"Grubber—you talking Snake Eyes?" Joe asked.

"Snake Eyes's brother," James replied.

"Man, I don't like putting the pressure on brother Hell Fighters," Hammer remarked. "It just ain't done. I'm not real comfortable with this."

"I'll make it worth the discomfort," James said.

Joe thought for a moment. "So who'll be keeping an eye on things here while we are gone? Who's opening the gate for customers?"

"I'll do it myself," James replied. "I can do it, and I'll go back down on the floor when you guys get back. No big deal."

Joe looked at Hammer. He nodded.

"Get us the address and trailer number," Joe said.

"Good," James replied. "I'll make it worth your while."

James walked to the door. "Where did you guys park?" he asked. "I didn't see your truck."

"Behind the shed," Joe answered.

"Why did you park behind the shed? Kind of muddy back there, isn't it?" James asked.

"'Cause we didn't want people driving by and seeing our truck sitting there," Joe replied. "And yes, it is muddy back there."

"Who didn't you want to see your truck?" James pushed.

"No one in particular, it's just the way we do things," Joe explained. "We like to keep our movements and whereabouts under the radar. We are security experts, and security starts with us."

James nodded his head, satisfied with the answer.

"That's why we ask you to keep the Escalade in the garage," Joe went on. "Sometimes you like to park it outside, and that isn't a good practice, security-wise."

"Noted," James replied as he went through the door and down the stairs. As soon as they heard the door connecting the house to the garage close, Hammer turned to Joe.

"What is he up to?" Hammer asked.

"I don't know, because he told the gal in the kitchen that he was taking Angie somewhere else tomorrow evening. I don't think he plans to do that and run the gate at the same time," Joe replied. "It's almost like he's trying to get rid of us for some reason. He doesn't want us around when he leaves with her."

Hammer shrugged his shoulders. "I don't know what's going on anymore."

Chapter 21

Thursday

"What now?" Skip asked after they had driven past the house looking for the red pickup.

"Maybe we just try to drive in and see what happens." Max suggested. "Or park somewhere and hike in?"

Max didn't get much of a reaction from the other two. Skip kept driving, past several places in the road that Max thought looked good to pull off on.

"I guess that no one likes my idea," Max said.

"I think that in broad daylight, with a lack of foliage and all, we could get spotted long before we get close enough to investigate anything," Skip suggested.

"I liked it," Monica replied.

"Skip," Max said. "What the heck? What do we have to lose by just jumping the gate and walking in?"

"I got another idea," Skip replied as he pulled off the road and into a drive that looked like it dead-ended fifty yards into the woods.

Max looked around. "This would be a pretty good place to go mushroom hunting," he commented.

"Monica," Skip turned and handed her his phone. "Can you make this block my number if I call someone from it?"

Monica took the phone and started swiping the screen. Max and Skip looked around at the woods. After a few seconds, Monica handed the phone back to Skip.

"Find that number that Angie called you on," Skip instructed her.

Monica found the number and held it up where Skip could see it. He punched it into his phone and pushed call. It rang five times, and just when Skip was expecting it to roll over to voicemail again, a man's voice answered.

"Hello."

"Hey," Skip said in a jovial voice. "Brian Parker here. Been trying to get ahold of you for a couple of days. I got your number from Ben Ralston. He was telling me about that club that you been going to up there north of Boone. He was thinkin' that I might like some of that action, so he gave me your number."

Monica gave Skip a glare when he used the name of her ex-boyfriend and Essie's father. Skip shrugged his shoulders and kept talking.

"Anyways," Skip continued without letting the voice on the other end respond, "I was wondering if you could tell me where this place is and how to get there. It sounds like my kind of club." Skip stopped for a breath.

"Who is this?" the voice on the other end questioned him.

"Parker, Brian Parker," Skip answered. "I don't think we've met. I'm a friend of Ben Ralston. You know him, insurance agent over in Ames. He gave me your number."

"Well," the voice said after a moment's hesitation. "It is kind of an exclusive place. You gotta apply for membership. Only members get in."

Skip took his own moment of hesitation, winked at Max and Monica, then continued. "Any chance I could meet you and buy you a cup of coffee somewhere, and then tonight or tomorrow night you take me as a guest? Ben said that you might be willing to do that."

Again there was the hesitation on the other end of the phone. "Well, they don't really allow anyone to bring guests. I think that you got to apply for membership first, and they have to do a background check on you before they allow you to join."

"No shit?" Ship exclaimed. "That is exclusive. They won't even let you come in and at least get a sample of what you're gonna get before you sign on the line?"

"Nope," the man answered. "They give you the rules right up front. Very exclusive and very discreet."

"What the fuck?" Skip exclaimed. "I mean, what they got up there? All this bullshit for some penny ante poker games?"

"Oh, no," the voice answered, a little more forthcoming. "They got some high stakes poker going on there. In the other room they got a craps table. Big buffet line all night long, and drinks."

"Shit," Skip said. "I didn't know that they was that big of a concern. It sounds like a friggin casino!"

"It is like a casino," the man replied.

"Well shit," Skip said. "Why all the background checks and shit? I mean, if I want a craps table and a buffet, I just go to Meskwaki."

The voice at the other end of the phone laughed. "The fact that the place is discreet. Meaning you aren't going to run into anyone who you might not want to run into, like you might run into at Meskwaki. Plus, they got amenities," he added.

"What kind of amenities?" Skip asked.

"Well, first off," the man said. "They'll give you a line of credit if you're coming up a little short. You can pay it back later. Second, they got some women there." The man waited for a reply.

"Women?" Skip asked.

"Yeah, women," the man said, bragging now. "And if you need a little break you can go up and relax with one of the women, if you know what I mean. A hundred bucks. But if you're losing a lot, well, sometimes they give 'em to you as a consolation prize, kind of sweeten the empty pot for you. Otherwise it is a hundred dollars a shot. James treats everyone pretty good there."

"James, the guy in charge?" Skip asked.

"Yeah, James," the man replied. "Nice guy, as long as you stay on the right side of him. He doesn't put up with a lot of shenanigans."

"Okay," said Skip. "Where is this place and how do I get an application? This sounds like my kind of place."

"Got something to write on?" the man on the other side of the call asked.

Skip quickly made a writing motion toward Max, who in turn opened the glove box, coming up with a road map and a pen. He handed it to Skip.

"Shoot," Skip said into the phone and started writing down a number a few seconds later.

"Call that number," the man on the other end instructed. "James will get you set up."

"What about these girls?" Skip asked. "Nice? I mean they ain't scags, are they?"

"They're all prime," the man answered.

"Where is this place?" Skip asked. "I wanna drive by it and take a look."

The voice on the other end was silent. "Just call James," he finally answered.

Skip felt Monica tapping his shoulder and he turned around. He saw a deputy sheriff's patrol car through the back window, pulling into the lane behind his car.

"Hey, gotta go," Skip said into the phone. "Do I need a reference or something? Can I use your name?"

"Red," said the voice. "Just tell James that Red gave you his number."

"You got a last name, Red?" Skip asked, watching the door of the patrol car open through his rearview mirror.

"Just Red," the voice on the phone replied, and ended the call.

Skip put down his phone and watched Duffy walk up to his car.

Skip rolled down the window as he got to it.

"What are you guys doing out here in the woods?" Duffy asked in a friendly tone.

"Hunting mushrooms," Max joked across the car.

"Two old guys out here with this very young and beautiful lady in the back, and you're telling me you're out here hunting mushrooms, Max? I'd think that a guy with your past experiences would come up with something better than that," Duffy joked back.

"Monica, Duffy; Duffy, Monica," Skip introduced. "Monica is our receptionist-slash-secretary-slash-bookkeeper."

"Slash-detective," Monica interrupted him.

"Slash-detective," Skip repeated.

"I think that Ms. Benson and I have met before," Duffy said. "How's Milton these days?"

"Fine," Monica replied.

"We just pulled off to make a phone call," Skip told Duffy. "Hard to talk on the phone and drive these winding roads at the same time."

"So how's the case going?" Duffy casually asked.

"Slow," Skip replied. "Hey, Duffy," he continued, "there's a place right up the road here. Big two-story house, set back a ways from the road, four car garage, a couple of out buildings, big iron gate with an intercom box. Who does that belong to?"

"Galen Butrow," Duffy answered without hesitation.

"So what's his deal?" Skip asked. "Nice digs."

"You thinking that's the gentleman's club that everyone is talking about?" Duffy asked.

Skip didn't answer.

"Owns several farm implement dealerships. Got one in Boone, one in Madrid and another in Ogden. Big bucks. I don't think he's into late night illegal gambling, though," Duffy replied.

"Nice place," Skip observed.

"Yep, it is," Duffy said lightheartedly. "Okay," he slapped the open window frame in the door. "I got some patrolling to do, so I'll let you and your two compatriots here go mushroom hunting, or whatever you're doing, and I'll get going."

"We're right behind you," Skip said.

Skip backed out behind Duffy, who turned north. Skip went the other direction toward Boone.

"Keep 'em peeled," Skip said as they drove. "Maybe that's not the place after all. Maybe we'll see that pickup truck in one of these other places along here."

Monica and Max kept looking while Skip drove.

"Monica," Skip called back. "Get on your phone and see if you can find anything on Galen Butrow."

Monica dug her phone out of her purse and started swiping the screen. "How do you think that they spell Butrow?"

"No idea," Skip replied.

The two detectives were quiet while Monica sat in the back seat searching on her phone. They all three had been convinced that Butrow's place was the place that they were looking for. They had felt so close. Now they were all three at a loss again.

"Let's go back to the agency and regroup," Max suggested. "Driving around Boone County is getting us nowhere, and I gotta go."

Skip drove through Boone to get to Highway 30, then turned toward Ames and the agency.

"I can't find any Galen Butrow," Monica said. "When we get back to the office I'll look on my computer. It'll be easier."

Halfway back to Ames, Max asked about the phone call.

"Guy's name is Red. There is a gentleman's club somewhere," Skip said. "And it sounds like it has a lot of action going on. Poker, craps tables, a buffet, and they definitely have some prostitution. Red said that they charge a hundred bucks a pop for the girls, but that some people get a complimentary freebie. Evidently the hookers, and a good line of credit, is what entices customers."

"Plus, you probably aren't going to run into anyone unexpected who might tell your wife that you're not at the office working late," Max suggested. "So it sounded like you have to apply for a membership?"

"Yep, exactly what Red said, it is discreet. Red wouldn't take me as his guest," Skip replied. "Evidently bringing guests is not an option."

The two didn't speak for a mile or two.

"I just didn't see anywhere other than Butrow's place that even looked like it could house all that action," Max stated.

"I don't know what to tell you, Max," Skip said. "It doesn't have to be on that road, could be anywhere."

"Just saying," Max replied.

"I'm just saying, too," Skip answered, a bit irritated. "I don't know what you want me to say, other than I don't know, either."

"Why are you pissy?" Max asked.

"Because I'm trying to think and you won't let me," Skip replied.

Monica had quit searching and was sitting quietly watching the two bicker. She didn't know how men could do that, and then five minutes later carry on like nothing happened.

"We don't even know that the place we're looking for is on the river," Max said. "We don't know where the hell it is. It could be anywhere. Who even said that it was on the river?"

Skip didn't answer him. They continued to the agency in silence.

When they arrived at the agency, Skip parked next to Monica's car. Monica unlocked the agency door and held it open for her two employers. Skip sat down on one of the chairs in the waiting area and pulled out his phone.

"I'm gonna get myself a membership to this gentleman's club," he announced. "Will this thing still hide my number if I make a call?" He held up his phone so that Monica could see it.

"It should," Monica said.

Skip took the road map and punched in the number that he had written on it. The phone rang three times before a deep male voice picked up.

"Hello."

"I'm looking for James. My name is Brian Parker," Skip said in a low voice. "I'm a friend of Red's, and I would like to apply for membership."

Monica gave him the look that she had before when he used the name of her ex.

"Mr. Parker," James said. "So you say you are a friend of Red's? He gave you this number, I presume?"

"Yes, he did," Skip replied.

"Mr. Parker," James addressed him again. "I'll need to get some information from you and do a background check before we grant you membership. There is a fee for the background check. It is the only fee that you will be charged for membership if you are accepted. I'll need a credit card number."

Skip stopped in his tracks.

"A credit card number?" he asked, stalling for some time to think.

"Yes, Mr. Parker," James replied. "A credit card in your name, sir. Your card will be charged one hundred dollars for the background check, and you understand that this is the only financial requirement for membership?"

Skip was looking frantically at Max and Monica.

"Just a moment," Skip said into the phone. He held his hands up to Monica as if he expected her to produce a credit card in her ex-boyfriend's name and give it to him. When she gave him the same gesture back, he put the phone back up to his face.

"I'm sorry, but I actually do not have a credit card on me at this moment. I mean, I do have a credit card, but not one that I would want to charge something on of this delicate nature," Skip said into the phone. "Is there any other way?"

"I understand completely, Mr. Parker," James said. "When you get a credit card number that you do feel comfortable using in a delicate matter such as this, give me a call back and we'll get things rolling."

"Sorry about that," Skip replied. "I guess Red didn't tell me about this part of the application. If there is any other way…" he trailed off, letting his voice rise in a question.

"No problem," James replied. "It happens all the time. I look forward to talking to you again soon."

James ended the call.

"Fuck," Skip said out loud. "They charge you for a background check. A hundred bucks. You gotta give them a credit card number."

"Actually, that's pretty clever," Max observed.

Skip shook his head back and forth. "Dang, it is," he remarked. "I never even thought about that." He looked up at Max.

"Screw it," Max said. "I'll just call up and use my own name and my own credit card number."

"Max," Monica replied. "Max Mosbey, Powerball winner, former cop, current private investigator? I'm sure all that is going to slip right past a Google search."

"You're right," said Max. "That probably isn't going to work. I wasn't thinking."

Monica had been searching on her computer while Skip made his phone call. She did not go back to it after Max had spoken. Instead she said, "Thing is, speaking of Google searches, there isn't any Galen Butrow anywhere on the internet. There aren't any farm implement dealerships that are common to Boone, Ogden and Madrid, and that house that Duffy says belongs to our non-existent Galen Butrow is listed on the Boone County assessor's office site as belonging to an LLC called Buzzard Bend Properties." She looked up at the two. "Even if Mr. Butrow is somehow under the radar so far that even LinkedIn hasn't ever heard of him, and LinkedIn knows who even I am by the way, what Boone County businessman with three farm implement dealerships has an LLC called Buzzard Bend Properties? That just doesn't make any sense."

Both Max and Skip stood up and walked around behind Monica where they could look at her computer screen over her shoulders. She was on the assessor's page. There was a picture of the house. It looked even grander in the picture than it did from the road.

"Why in the hell would Duffy feed us shit like that?" Max asked. "Something is going on here, and I'm wondering what's with Duffy. He would have to know that we would check him out. This is too easy."

"Agreed," Skip said quietly while he read the assessor's page. "Widen the search on this Buzzard Bend Properties," he instructed Monica.

Chapter 22

Thursday

James hung up the phone after he had spoken to Parker. It wasn't unusual for someone to balk when he asked for a credit card number in their name. In fact, most of them balked. If Parker was the real thing, he would call back with a card number. Some card that his wife didn't even know he had. It could take him some time to find one that would work. James wasn't worried. Red was a good customer and a happy loser. If Parker was anything like Red… Well, he would be a good customer, too.

James typed "Brian Parker" into his computer and came up with pages and pages of Brian Parkers. Brian Parker was a common name. There were ten of them alone on LinkedIn. James typed in "Brian Parker Iowa." He got more than a dozen listings in the white pages. He looked through them, but found nothing exceptional about any of them, none local.

James was going to give it up and wait for Parker to call back with a credit card number, but his curiosity got the best of him. He pulled up Iowa Courts Online and typed "Brian Parker" into it. Two Brian Parkers came up immediately. "Here we go," James thought to himself. "I think I found Mr. Brian Parker of Ames, Iowa." There was nothing recent, which was good. It meant that Parker had learned how to keep himself out of trouble. But he hadn't always been such a good boy. James checked his date of birth and made a mental calculation to determine how old he was. James was not real good at adding and subtracting in his head, but his rough estimate put Brian Parker a lot younger than the voice on the phone had sounded. It could be a different Brian Parker, he thought.

James sat back and looked at the screen. It didn't make any difference. He had some questions that helped him do a more thorough background check when the prospective customers called back, but James couldn't see anything from his brief search that should make him suspicious. Just the same, James was always suspicious. It was what kept him from showing up on Iowa Courts Online himself.

Duffy was pulling up to his house. He looked at the clock on his dashboard. He had ten minutes before he went off duty. He sat in the car listening to the radio traffic. It had been a routine day. He had not gotten anything other than minor calls, which was not a bad thing. It gave him time to keep an eye on those two damned detectives who were snooping around. He wished that they would just take a long weekend off. Wishful thinking, he knew. But still, it would be nice. They weren't doing it for the money, he was sure of that. The girl was pretty. He had only seen her a few times with Jackson when he and Carlisle had run into them out on the town. Carlisle said that she used to be a stripper, but Duffy had never seen her in action. Carlisle had also told him that Jackson was a little touchy about it, so it was best not to say anything. Anyway, as far as he could see, she had the equipment for it. He wondered how an ex-stripper ended up working for Mosbey and Murray, and getting engaged to Jackson. That was weird.

Duffy was restless. He looked at the clock again. He wished that he hadn't made up that story about the owner of the house. He couldn't even remember what name he had given them. Gaylord something. Gaylord Buford, he thought. That didn't sound right. And how did he come up with the idea that the guy owned a bunch of farm implement dealerships? None of that story was going to hold water. He knew it the moment that it came out of his mouth. He wondered if he should call Joe. He had already talked to Joe twice today. Duffy didn't want to explain to him and Hammer why he told those guys what he did. He would just let it go. It could take its own course. Then he started wondering if he should call Kind and tell him everything that had happened. He looked at the clock. Two more minutes. He decided that he would talk to Kind in the morning. That could take its own course, too. He wouldn't worry about it now.

Duffy watched the clock roll over on the hour. He picked up his mic and called himself out of service. Screw 'em all, he was off duty. Duffy got out of his car, made sure all of the doors were locked and went into his house. He could hear his kids in the back yard raising a ruckus. He was glad that they were being raised in the country where they could run around all they wanted and learn about the outdoors. He wished that he could have grown up that way, and not in Boone, like he had. He hated growing up in town. It wasn't easy and it wasn't cheap living out in the country, but it was worth it.

"What now?" Max asked. "Duffy's bullshit is making me think that he's got some interest in this and that we were eyeballing the right place all along. Why would he want to throw us off?"

Skip thought for a moment. "Well, Kind has not been particularly happy about us working our case there, in his jurisdiction. Maybe he has Duffy watching us. Maybe Duffy just told us that bullshit about Butrow to confuse the issue. Maybe Duffy doesn't like us working his part of the county, either. Maybe Duffy knows exactly who owns the house, but was just fucking with us for the fun of it. Remember when you were redirecting traffic that one day and you kept telling people there had been an airplane crash? Same thing."

"Lots of maybes there," Max remarked.

"That's all I got, is lot of maybes," Skip agreed. "I'm pretty sure that there is something going on, but I'm not sure what it is. I mean, Duffy knows that we are looking for Angie. He knows who Angie is. I actually can't see him screwing around with us like that if there was any chance that she is actually in that house. Think about it: you're a cop, and if someone was legitimately looking for someone else who is missing, would you play games with them like that just for fun?"

"Probably not," Max replied.

"I have no doubt that Duffy was jerking us around, but I just can't believe that he is purposely throwing us off track. That just doesn't make sense."

"Unless?" Max said.

"Not ready to think that yet," Skip replied.

"Is it possible?" Max answered.

"If you want to think that, then you gotta think that Kind is in on it, too," Skip countered. "And if you want to think Kind is in on it, too, then you have to be willing to consider that other people in the sheriff's department are involved. I'm not willing to think that the whole department has something to do with Angie being missing."

Max shrugged his shoulders. "So you think that Duffy was just messing with us?"

"That's what I think," Skip said.

"Here's Milton," Monica said jumping out of her chair excitedly, breaking the focus of the conversation.

"You get all gaga because you haven't seen him for six hours?" Max teased.

Monica ignored Max while Milton walked in. He was driving his own car, but still in uniform. He came through the door and gave Monica a kiss before he took a seat in one of the easy chairs. Monica sat back down.

"That's my chair," Max told him.

Milton did not get up. Max and Skip were still standing behind Monica's desk watching her search for information on Buzzard Bend Properties, LLC.

"Question," Skip asked him. "How much do you really know about Duffy?"

"Him and Carlisle are casual friends," Milton said. "Not like real tight, but they used to go out on the town sometimes. Monica and I ran into them a few times."

"We did?" Monica asked.

"Yeah, last summer, downtown, I think a couple of Friday nights. They were trying to impress some women." Milton was trying to help her remember. "They didn't really want to talk to us a lot, thinking we might say something that would cramp their style. Like, you know, talk shop?"

"Okay," she responded, not convincingly.

"I'm just going to put it out there," Skip said. "Any chance that Duffy might be rubbing shoulders with the other side?"

"What?" Milton exclaimed. "Why would you think Duffy would be tight with the other side?"

"Just that we were checking out a place up in Boone County, he shows up at the most inopportune time, and then when we ask him about it, he feeds us a big line of bullshit to throw us off," Max answered.

"I don't know Duffy that well," Milton said. "But I don't think Carlisle would be hanging out with him if he wasn't legit. Besides, the guy has a wife and two kids. He's Mr. Typical American Family Guy."

"Typical American Family Guy out hustling women in a bar with Carlisle?" Skip remarked.

"Yeah," Milton said. "Like that is the crime of the century?"

"Oh," Monica exclaimed. "So that's how you think typical family men act? That's a good thing to know before I decide to say 'I do.'"

"That's not what I'm saying," Milton shot back defensively. "I'm not saying that he's cheating on his wife, I'm just saying that him and Carlisle go out on the town once in a while and, you know, he flirts around a little. He's the wingman."

"I think that you better quit digging," Max advised him.

Milton stopped talking. Monica was glaring at him. "I just shouldn't talk," Milton said.

Monica was still glaring at him.

"I don't think that Duffy is a bad cop," Milton said to Max.

"But do you think that he would dick with us?" Skip asked. "You think that he would feed us false information to throw us off an investigation for fun, like being the wingman for his buddy in the bar?"

"Yes to the first question, no to the second. I mean, no, I don't think that he would purposely throw you off of your case." Milton replied. "That's all I have to say about it."

"So what now?" Monica asked, giving Milton a break. "Should we go up there and stake out that place?"

Skip and Max thought about it.

"First of all," Skip said. "There's no place up there to park and still see who's coming and going. Closest place to pull off and sit is that drive where we pulled off to make the call. That's at least a quarter mile down the road."

"Second," Max chimed in. "We still don't know if that is the place we're looking for."

Monica sat in silence for a moment.

"So another night where we don't do anything?" she replied. "Another night where Angie is missing and we all just go home?"

Skip had been on edge all day. "How about we go up and sit in that bar in Pilot Mound and see if she comes in for a drink tonight?" he suggested. "How about we sit outside Duffy's place and follow him around in case he has her stashed away on the side in the Heart Break Hotel over in Boone?"

Monica was taken aback and a little hurt. "What's this all about?"

Skip sighed. "You are absolutely right," he answered. "It has been four days. I'm as frustrated as you are. I want to solve this case for you. I want to help you find your friend. But I don't know what to do. I've been a cop my entire adult life, and I don't know how to find Angie right now."

Everyone was silent. It was as much emotion as Max had ever seen Skip show.

"We all need to calm down," Max said. "This case has us all at each other's throats. That's not going to get us any closer to finding Angie. We all have to take a deep breath and understand that everyone here wants to find her."

They all sat in silence a little longer.

Finally, Milton stood up. He looked at Monica. "I'm going to go home and change, then I'll come over to your place," he said. "Or you can come over to my place. I think that it would be good if you and I just sit down and talk about it. You can bounce it all off of me, and we'll take a look at everything from a different angle. You guys have all been cooped up together way too much lately."

Monica didn't respond. Milton walked out the door and got into his Jeep. As soon as he backed out, Monica turned off her computer and got up. She took her purse, walked past Max, and went out the door without a word. The two detectives watched her get into her car and back out of her parking place.

Max looked at Skip. "I'm going home," he said.

"Me, too," Skip replied, his shoulders sagging in resignation.

Max stuck out his hand. Skip took it.

"We'll figure it out," Max said as they shook. "We always do."

Skip let go of Max's hand and slapped him on the back as Max turned to go out the door.

"I'm going back to the office for a little while, then I'm leaving too," Skip said. "First thing tomorrow?"

"See you first thing tomorrow," Max replied.

Chapter 23

Thursday

Monica's mother had already picked up Essie from daycare by the time she got home. Essie was glad to see her and demonstrated it by throwing her stuffed bunny Oscar across the room and then running after it, looking over her shoulder to make sure that her mother was watching. Essie's antics amused Monica and put her in a better mood.

Monica sat down on her easy chair and turned on the early news. She absently played catch with Essie and Oscar, tossing the bunny to Essie, who threw it back at her. Shawna was preparing supper. Monica's phone rang. She picked it up and saw that it was Milton.

"Hey," she answered.

"Monica," Milton said, "can Shawna watch Essie for a while tonight?"

"I don't know," Monica replied. "I don't feel like going out again tonight. We just went out last night."

"I was thinking about driving up there to Boone County and taking a look around," Milton replied. "I know that is what you want to do, and I'm up for it. Let's just go up there and nose around a little, you and me."

Monica took the phone away from her mouth and called out to the kitchen. "Mom, can you watch Essie for a little while tonight? Milton and I are going for a drive after supper."

"You were out last night," Shawna called back.

"I know, Mom," Monica yelled. "I won't be out late. We're just going to go for a drive."

"Okay," Shawna replied. "I guess so."

Essie was standing between Monica's knees, resting a forearm on each. "Can I go?" she asked.

"No, honey," Monica said to her in a gentle voice. "Milton and I are just going to go for a little drive."

"I wanna go with Milton, too," she replied.

"No, honey," Monica said. "Milton and mommy are going for a ride alone. You need to go to bed and be ready for school tomorrow. We will take you for a ride some other time."

"When?" Essie asked.

"This weekend," Monica replied.

Essie pushed off of Monica's knees and walked away, obviously not satisfied with her mother's answers. Monica was caught between her desire the keep looking and her need to spend time with Essie. She put the phone to her mouth and spoke.

"After supper, I'll text you," she said.

"I'll see you then," Milton said. "I love you," he added.

"Love you too," Monica replied, then ended the call.

Milton picked her up an hour later. Monica climbed into his Jeep Wrangler and settled in. It was already dark.

"Where to?" he asked.

"Just take Highway 30 past that main drag there at Boone, and there's a road that goes north, just this side of the river," she instructed.

Milton pulled out of the parking lot of her townhouse and made his way to Highway 30.

"Look," Milton said after they were westbound. "I'm not saying that Duffy going out bar hopping with Carlisle is a good thing. I'm not saying that at all. I'm just saying that I'm not going to judge him when I don't even know the circumstances. It isn't any of my business."

"Is that what you're going to do after we get married?" Monica asked. "After a while, when I have another kid or two, are you going to get bored and go out with your single friends and bar hop?"

"Come on, Monica," Milton replied. "I didn't even go bar hopping when I was single, before I met you. You know me, I stay home and drink beer and watch TV with you. Why would that ever change?"

Monica pondered his answer. "Things change," she said. "Guys get bored, I've seen them."

"I don't think that is completely fair," Milton shot back.

"What's not fair?" Monica asked.

"I feel like you just compared me to the guys who used to frequent the bars that you used to dance in," Milton replied. "I don't go comparing you to the women that I've run into dancing in those bars."

Milton's words stung a little.

"I'm not talking about bars that I danced in, I'm talking in general," she replied defensively. "I think it is unfair that you just automatically go there with your thinking."

"I don't just automatically go there," Milton replied. "Where else have you been that you have this insight on how pathetic the male species is? Is it something that you've been studying in school?"

"I don't want to talk about it," Monica replied.

Milton drove quietly for a while. He reached the four-way stop at Highway 30 and Story Street in Boone.

"Keep going straight," Monica told him.

"I am," Milton replied.

A mile later Monica pointed out the turn to Milton. Milton did not reply to her directions. He made the turn north and followed the county blacktop that followed the river. After ten minutes of silence, Monica spoke up.

"Up ahead here," she said, her voice just above a whisper. "That's the house that we were talking about on your left. It sits way down. Big house. There's a gate at the lane. You'll see it. That's the place that we think is the gentleman's club."

Milton spotted it as they drove by. It was well lit up, and he could see several cars parked below.

"What do you think?" Monica asked.

"I think it's a big house with a lot of cars parked by it," he replied.

"Does it look suspicious to you?" Monica asked.

"Not particularly."

"Turn around and drive back by it so that I can get another look," Monica said.

Milton drove a quarter of a mile up the road before he found a drive that he could pull into and turn around. He drove back past the house and Monica almost pressed her forehead on the window trying to look down at it.

"Seems like a lot of cars down there," Monica observed.

"Tupperware party," Milton answered her.

In the dim light of the dashboard reflected off of her face, Milton could see that Monica was giving him a look that said she was not in the mood.

"Think about it," Milton said. "It isn't that late. Who comes to a gentleman's club and starts gambling this early? Sure, some, maybe, but I'm just saying that a Tupperware party works in my head more than a high stakes gambling den. I'm just trying to keep my thinking unbiased."

"Pull in that drive," Monica instructed him.

Milton spotted the reflectors on the two gate posts ahead. He slowly turned in, looking carefully for a chain or cable strung between them. He drove in and stopped.

"Now what?"

"Can you turn around?" Monica said.

Milton maneuvered the Wrangler back and forth until he was turned around, facing the blacktop. He turned off his headlights.

"Well this could be fun," he said.

Monica leaned over and kissed his cheek, running her hand up and down his thigh.

"I don't want to fight anymore," she said.

"Are we going to get it on right here?" Milton asked hopefully. "'Cause I'm up for that."

"No, I don't think so," Monica said teasingly. "We're going to keep our eyes open and see what traffic comes up the road here."

"I was afraid that was what you had in mind," Milton said with a sigh.

The two sat quietly listening to the radio and watching the occasional car come by. Monica would make a brief comment on each one, which began, "Where do you think they're going?" Milton had given up guessing after the third car. They spent almost an hour watching cars go by. Monica thought that the traffic was picking up. Milton was skeptical, but did not say anything.

"Follow him," Monica said as a late model Buick went by northbound. Milton flipped on the headlights and pulled onto the blacktop. He could not see the taillights of the car ahead because of the curve in the road. As they came in sight of the gate for the large house, they both saw in the beam of the Wrangler's headlights that the car was pulled up to the intercom box and a man was leaning out the window talking into it.

"What did I tell you?" Monica whispered as they drove by.

"To follow that car?" Milton answered.

"Yeah, and look where he's going," Monica replied. "He doesn't look like the kind of guy that goes to a Tupperware party."

Milton slowed a bit as he drove past the car, but not enough to draw attention to himself as they passed by. The driver didn't look up from the intercom.

"Turn around and go by again," Monica said.

Milton found the drive that he had turned around in earlier and repeated the process. As they passed the house, the car was gone. Monica surveyed the property below.

"I think that I see that car down there," Monica announced while Milton drove on. "Turn around."

Milton got to the gate into the woods where they had parked earlier and pulled in enough to back out and go the other direction. He looked below as he passed the house and thought that he could see the Buick parked down there as well.

"Turn around," Monica said.

"You're sure?" Milton asked. "I mean, I will if you want, but what are we looking for? What are we accomplishing by driving back and forth by that house?"

"Keep going straight," Monica said.

"Where we going?" Milton asked.

"Let's go up to Pilot Mound," Monica replied. "There is a bar up there. I just want to check it out and see who is up there."

Milton continued north into Pilot Mound. Monica directed him to the bar. Milton had to admit to himself that he would have driven right past it if Monica hadn't pointed it out. Milton pulled into an open parking space and shut the ignition off.

"Let's go," Monica said.

"So you know this place?" Milton asked.

"We've eaten lunch here the last two days," Monica answered. "This is the place where the guys shoot pool with the bikers and I try to get the bartender to talk to me."

Milton got out of the Wrangler. Monica was already making her way to the door while he hit the lock button on his key fob. Milton followed her in and gave the place a quick scan, as he always did when entering someplace unfamiliar. There was one pool table to the left where two older men were shooting a game of eight ball. The jukebox by the door was playing country. Four people were sitting at the bar together, chatting. Milton couldn't decide if they looked like two couples or just friends. The bartender was watching them cross the room. She was a middle-aged woman.

"What'll ya have?" the bartender asked as the two perched themselves on their stools.

"Miller Lites," Monica answered.

The bartender turned toward the back of the bar and took two glasses. She filled them at the tap and placed them in front of Milton and Monica.

"Hey," Monica said easily. "We're from Ames, and we were just out for a drive tonight. I used to have some classes at ISU with a gal named Angie Williamson who said she lived up here somewhere. Kind of a party girl. I was just wondering if you knew her."

"I know an Angie Williamson," the bartender replied. "But I doubt that she ever went to college."

"Have you seen her around?" Monica asked.

"Not for a while," the bartender answered. "The Angie Williamson I know is a stripper. She hangs with the Hell Fighters. You say you met her at ISU?" The bartender looked Monica up and down, assessing her story.

"Yeah," Monica replied. "She took a Psychology 101 and 102 class with me."

"I don't think so," replied the bartender.

"Say," said Milton, getting the bartender's attention, giving her a wink and a smile. "When we were coming up here we saw this huge mansion type place three or four miles south of here. All lit up. You could see the lights in the sky two miles away. What's up with that place?"

The bartender was sizing up Milton as well. "I don't know what place you're talking about," she answered.

"Big place," Milton explained. "Honestly, it surprised me. I was thinking that maybe some bigshot from Des Moines must have built it on the river. That's all."

"Need anything else?" the bartender asked, walking away before either could answer.

"Okay," said Milton in a low voice. "From her reaction, I'm guessing that there might be a reason she doesn't know what I'm talking about."

"See?" said Monica.

Milton downed his beer while Monica sipped hers and looked around. There wasn't much to see. The bar was quiet, except for the country music coming from the jukebox. Monica thought that even the balls colliding into each other on the pool table sounded muted.

"Ready?" Milton asked.

"I guess," Monica answered.

Milton called the bartender over and paid the bill. He gave her a four dollar tip. "Buying a little happy to see you again," Milton said to Monica as they turned from the bar. "Just in case we want to come back."

"Just in case of what?" Monica asked. "You planning to come back with your buddies?"

"Cut it out," Milton teased as he poked her in the side walking out the door.

The two got back into the Wrangler and Milton backed out.

"Where to?" he asked. "I mean, you tell me."

"Back the way we came," Monica said. "I don't know what we can do up here tonight," she sighed.

Milton drove back south. He slowed a bit as they passed the house. It looked like there were a few more cars parked down by the house, but it was hard to tell from their vantage point. He sped up when he got past.

"Pull in up here," Monica instructed him as they approached the gate where they had sat earlier. Milton turned the Wrangler into the drive and maneuvered it back and forth until he got it turned around again.

"Okay," Milton asked. "What now?"

Monica put her hand on his thigh and leaned across the console. "I guess we get it on," she whispered in his ear, pulling her bottom up over the console and between the seats and sliding herself into the back.

Chapter 24

Friday

The sheriff heard Duffy's footsteps down the hall and was watching when he came to the door.

Duffy laughed. "Well, it isn't good news," he said. "Yesterday afternoon while I was on the way home I found those three detectives parked off the road not more than a quarter of a mile from James's place, having a confab. I stopped to see if they needed any assistance moving on down the road. They took the opportunity to ask some pretty specific questions, like who does the place belong to."

"So what did you tell them?" the sheriff asked.

"I made up some bullshit that ain't gonna hold water when they follow up on it, which I'm betting that they've done already," Duffy said.

"I'm getting so tired of this," Kind sighed. "I'm starting to think it isn't worth it."

"What do you want me to do?" Duffy asked. "Like I said, I'm guessing that my credibility is pretty much shit right now."

The sheriff didn't respond.

"Anyway, I had to tell them something," Duffy defended himself. "I either lied to them or I told them truth, it isn't like I had any other options. You think I should call up and let those other two know that those detectives have all but figured it out?"

"No," the sheriff said after a moment of thought. "Fuck 'em. Let it go. I can't just go out there and stop someone from looking around and asking questions, if that's what they want me to do. If it goes down, I'm not going to be in the middle of it. If the shit hits the fan, we just say that we were busy doing what we're supposed to be doing, protecting the citizens of Boone County. They can fend for themselves."

Duffy gave a sigh of relief. "Sounds good to me," he said. "It is getting harder and harder to cover for them."

"Keep an eye on it, but don't get involved at this point," the sheriff instructed. "Let it take its own course. We'll deal with it when we have to."

Duffy nodded and left the office. He felt a big weight had come off his shoulders. He had not been happy being stuck in the middle of it. He smiled. It might even be entertaining to watch it all go down, and Duffy was pretty sure that it was going down.

Hammer sat in his Ford F-150 parked in the parking lot at the Des Moines Area Community College Boone Campus. He threw the temporary parking sticker up on the dash. He listened to the morning news while he waited for Joe to come by and pick him up. He looked around at the campus. It was nice. The buildings looked almost brand new. Hammer watched Joe come off the street and pull up alongside the F-150. The Harley was no longer in the back of the pickup. He got out of his own truck and locked the door.

"Where's the Harley?" he asked as he climbed into Joe's truck.

"I put it in my garage," Joe answered. "I didn't like it back there. Makes it hard to see if those detectives are tailing us. We don't have any use for it right now, anyway."

"Yeah," Hammer replied. "I never thought about it before, but it was in the way yesterday." Hammer turned and looked out the rear window as he spoke. "Much better."

"It's got a flat tire. It was a pisser getting it out of there," Joe said off-handedly.

"Could have called me," Hammer replied.

"I got the next-door neighbor to come over and help."

"What do you think of those guys?" Hammer asked. "What are we going to do about them?"

"I'm hoping that Kind and Duffy are doing something about them," Joe remarked. "That's what they're supposed to do. What can we do?"

"I don't know," Hammer said. "We could have a little two-on-two with them, sort of explain in no uncertain terms that they need to go somewhere else to play detective."

"I don't think that's going to work. They're looking for that girl." Joe replied. "I'm leaving it up to Duffy and Kind. They can have a talk with them if they think it will do any good. Besides, the girl is gone after tonight. Hopefully that will get them out of our hair, if she's not there."

Joe pulled into the Dairy Queen drive up. "I'm gonna get something to eat here in Boone. I'm just afraid that if we go up to the bar for lunch, those two will be up there waiting for us. I mean, two days in a row, and I'm pretty sure they tried to tail us yesterday."

"You're probably right," Hammer agreed. "But we got a lot of time to kill if we grab and go."

"I might turn the table on those two," Joe thought out loud. "I might follow them around for a while today." He pulled a business card from his pocket and handed it to

Hammer. "Got it from the bartender," he said with a satisfied voice.

"G&B Detective Agency," Hammer read out loud. "Even got an address here."

"What do you want?" Joe asked as he pulled up to the drive-up speaker.

"Fish sandwich and fries," Hammer replied.

Monica got to the office a little later than she had all week. It was unseasonably warm. For a moment she wished that she could have done something fun for spring break. It was easy for Milton to get time off during spring break, when all of the college kids were out of town. She thought about Angie and felt guilty for wishing that she was on vacation. The reality of it was that had she gone on vacation, she wouldn't have been here to help Angie when she called. It had been five days, Monica thought. Five days, and they hadn't been able to do a single thing to help.

Skip's car was already there. Monica parked, got out of her car and walked to the door. She could see Max's bicycle leaning on her desk.

"Been waiting for you," Max called out from his office as soon as she came through the door.

"Would you come up here and remove your bicycle from my desk?" she yelled back at him.

"Yeah, just a minute," Max shouted. "I'm looking at something."

Monica put her purse on the floor behind her desk. She took Max's bicycle by the handlebars and started walking it down the hall to the back room. When she got to Max's office, she saw him and Skip pulled up on their office chairs side by side, looking at Max's computer screen.

"Widening our search area," Max explained when she stopped at his door. "I would have gotten that," he nodded toward his bicycle.

"I'm sure you would have," she replied. "Like, when you were ready to go home."

Monica rolled the bicycle into the back room, leaned it on the wall and came back to Max's office.

"So you don't think that house yesterday is the one?" she asked.

"Yes," Max replied. "I do think it is the one. I think it is the gentleman's club, the gambling den, whatever you want to call it."

"What about Duffy?" she asked. "What do you think about that?"

"That he gave us the runaround," Max replied. "I don't know what else to think. We discussed that yesterday."

"So if that's the gentleman's club that Red's talking about, and Angie made the call from Red's phone, then Angie is there," Monica said. "Why can't we just go up there, hit the button on the intercom at the gate, and say that we are looking for Angie? It seems simple to me."

"I guess that is an option," Max replied. "We could do that."

"And if that place isn't the gentleman's club, what do we lose?" Monica asked. "They just say that we got the wrong house."

Skip thought for a moment. "She called you and asked for us to help her," he said, thinking out loud. "I think she wouldn't call you out of the blue and ask for help unless she is in some kind of real trouble."

Skip looked up at the other two to see if they agreed. Both were nodding their heads.

"So if we drive up there and ask for Angie, and she's there," Skip continued, "do they say, 'sure, we'll open up the gate for you, come on in'? I don't think so. I think they say that they've never heard of any Angie, and Angie is in even more trouble than she was when she called Monica."

"What about Duffy?" Monica asked. "We could tell Duffy that we have proof that she is there."

"We don't have proof that she's there," Skip replied. "And I don't trust Duffy anymore."

"Go over his head," Max suggested. "Call Kind."

"And tell Kind that we don't trust Duffy, because Duffy was jerking us around about this house that we are absolutely sure is a gentleman's club, that we know is engaged in illegal gambling and prostitution, and that they could be very well be holding a woman against her will in there, right under his nose? And we want him to make them let us go in to take a look around?" Skip asked. "I don't think that is going to go over well with Kind. I don't see him jumping right up on that and helping us. And honestly, we aren't absolutely sure that is the place. If we were, we wouldn't still be looking at other places."

Monica let her shoulders fall in resignation. "Milton and I went up there last night," she told them. "We drove up and down past that place five or six times. Drove up to the bar and talked to a different bartender, spent a couple hours accomplishing nothing. Well, we accomplished something, but we got nothing."

"So you two are back together?" Max asked.

"We were never apart," Monica pointed out.

"Well, you two were on the outs when he left yesterday," Max replied.

"We weren't on the outs. How have you stayed married so long?"

"His wife is dedicating her life to suffering in the hopes that there will be a reward in the afterlife," Skip observed.

"Well, we're not on the outs," Monica replied. "We had a very nice drive last night, even though we didn't come up with anything new in the investigation."

Max was swiping his computer screen back and forth, up and down, stopping to zoom in on other likely places for a gentleman's club, even though he had no idea what it might look like.

"I want to go up to Pilot Mound again," Skip finally said. "I want to follow those bikers. The bartender told us that they work for a gentleman's club. They're in that bar every time we've been up there. Let's go up there, and instead of going inside this time, we stake them out. If they're not there, we wait until they are. Then we follow them wherever they go. They're Hell Fighters, and I think that wherever Angie is, she is with Hell Fighters. Let's just see where they go. That will settle it. Then we figure out how we are going to get to Angie."

"Why not? In broad daylight on a Friday afternoon? That shouldn't be too difficult," Max replied, getting up and walking past Skip and Monica, who were still seated. "We don't have any coffee, so I'm going over to get us some coffee," he said as he walked to the breakroom to find their mugs.

Monica got up and wheeled her chair back into Skip's office. He followed with his own chair. He placed the one that he was pushing behind his desk. He moved the other one to the same spot it had been when Monica went in to get it. Between Max's bike and Monica just shoving everything wherever, it was hard for Skip to keep his office tidy.

Joe drove past the strip of offices on the ground floor of the building that housed the G&B Detective Agency. He drove around the block and came by again, pulling into the parking lot of the coffee shop across the street. Joe parked away from the street, where he wouldn't draw attention. Hammer ran in to get them each a cup of coffee while Joe watched. The Audi that had been parked next to them at the bar in Pilot Mound was parked in front of the agency. Joe got out his binoculars and tried to look across the street without being too conspicuous. He could see a bicycle through the window, sitting just inside the door. Suddenly, a maroon Nissan Sentra came into his view and parked directly in front of the agency. Joe recognized the woman who had been with the two detectives both days previously as she got out of the car and went through the front door. She put her bag behind a desk and wheeled the bicycle somewhere out of his vision.

Hammer got back into the truck and gave Joe his coffee.

"What do you see?" he asked.

"That Audi, someone's bicycle just inside the front door, and the black chick just showed up," he answered, taking a sip of the scalding hot coffee and putting the binoculars up to his eyes again.

The two sat for close to a half hour watching the agency, taking turns with the binoculars. Finally, they saw one of the detectives come out of the office and walk directly toward them from across the street. They both slid down in their seats, trying to hide. They recognized the man as he walked by, holding what looked like three travel mugs in his hand. He came by just three cars away and entered the coffee shop. They watched him closely through the windows, afraid to move for fear of drawing attention to themselves. The man was in no hurry, and they could see him through the window exchanging pleasantries with the barista. After a while, he came back out with the three mugs nestled in a cardboard carrier. The man walked past them again on the way back toward the agency with the coffee. Hammer was almost laying on the floorboard of the truck. Joe just peered through the window. The man crossed the street and went back into the agency.

A few minutes later, the two detectives and the woman came out, got into the Audi and backed out. Joe started his engine and waited for them to pull onto the street before backing out himself. It was a nice, bright day. He pulled out of the parking lot behind them on a loose tail, hanging a long way back, just keeping them in sight up ahead.

The Audi went straight out to Highway 30 and westbound. It was easy for Joe to follow behind when they got on the four-lane. There was not a lot of traffic, but enough to make it not obvious that they were following. When they reached Boone, stopped for the stop sign at 30 and Story Street, then continued west, Joe was confident that he knew their next move. He held back a bit more and lost sight of them. That was alright; he didn't want them to see him making the turn behind them when they went north. As soon as he made the turn himself, he sped up to the speed limit. Hammer was a little nervous that Joe was letting them get so far ahead, but Joe kept a steady speed for a half dozen miles. Two miles before James's place, Joe accelerated to catch the Audi. He was curious what they would do when they got to that point, but he was not able to catch them in time. He blew past James's place at sixty-five, hitting the curves twenty miles an hour faster than they were posted.

"Where are they?" Hammer asked.

"I don't know," Joe said. "I would have thought that we'd have caught up to them by now."

Joe kept his foot in it until they approached the Pilot Mound city limits, straining ahead to see if they could spot the Audi parked at the bar.

"Here they come," Hammer exclaimed.

Joe looked up. "Shit, shit, shit," he said as he met them coming toward him from the other direction. He tried not to look directly at them as they passed.

"What you going to do now?" Hammer asked. "Did they recognize us?"

Joe pulled off the road and parked in front of the bar.

"Got us right where they want us," Hammer observed.

"Fuck," shouted Joe. "Get out and go in. Act like we didn't see them."

Hammer did as Joe told him. Joe switched off the engine and followed Hammer into the bar.

Once inside, Hammer asked, "What now?"

"Same thing," Joe said. "Set 'em up and look like we're just doing what we always do."

The two went to the bar and ordered beers. Hammer got some quarters for the pool table and went to rack the balls while Joe waited for their beers. They both watched the door, waiting for the detectives to come in.

Chapter 25

Friday

Skip didn't slow down when they passed the place that they believed was the gentleman's club on their way to Pilot Mound. They had been by it enough times that they didn't have to look at it again. He did slow down when they got close to the Pilot Mound city limits.

"Look for a good place to set up," he instructed his passengers.

Max pointed out a side street two blocks from the bar. Skip gave it a quick glance before focusing his eyes on the front of the bar, looking to see if the red pickup with the motorcycle in the bed was parked there. He could see that it wasn't.

"They'll come right past there on the way in and on the way out," Skip observed. "Good chance of getting spotted. Let's see if there is a better vantage point up the street."

Max didn't respond.

Skip drove up the street a few blocks without spotting a better place where they could sit unobserved but still in sight of the front of the bar. He made a dog leg turn and drove back the way that they had come. As they neared the bar from the north they all three saw the red pickup coming toward them.

"Shit," Skip blurted out the moment he saw the truck.

"There they are," Max said at the same time.

Monica just gasped.

"Duck down, Monica," Skip said.

Monica laid sideways in the back seat. Skip and Max stared straight ahead as they met the truck. When they had passed, Skip watched through the rearview mirror as the pickup parked and the two occupants got out. Skip kept driving, out of town and out of sight. When he was sure that they would not be observed, he made a U turn, drove back to the side street that Max had pointed out earlier and parked. He was as far back as he could get and still see the pickup parked in front of the bar.

"That was awkward," Max noted. "Did they recognize us?"

"I don't know how they couldn't have," Skip remarked.

Monica was sitting up again, leaning forward between the seats where she could see the truck, too.

"Now what?" she asked.

"We sit," Max replied.

"They might see us here," she remarked.

"We already broke the rule of first viable option, and got caught," Skip replied. "You don't get caught sitting near as fast as you get caught moving. We should have taken this spot in the first place."

"They saw us," Max said. "They saw us, and they're sitting in there looking out the window right now to see what we're up to."

"Probably," Skip agreed. "So let the games begin."

Monica leaned forward a little more to get a better look.

"They took the motorcycle out," she commented.

Joe came back from the window drinking his beer. Hammer was shooting pool by himself.

"They're parked a few blocks down there behind a building," Joe told Hammer.

"They got us right where they want us," Hammer observed again.

"Maybe so, but I got an idea," Joe replied. "We walk out of here like we do every day. We don't even look in their direction. We get in the truck and we just head north. Take 'em the wrong direction. Drive 'til they give up. Whatever it takes. We can drive 'til dark if we have to."

"They're down there waiting for us to make the next move," Hammer remarked. "Good a plan as any."

Skip was the first one to comment when Joe and Hammer came out of the bar.

"Heads up," was all he said.

The three watched the two bikers get into the truck and start to back out. Monica leaned back and hunched down. Skip considered backing up a bit and waiting for them to pass, but decided that would attract more attention than just sitting still. There probably weren't a lot of late model Audis around town, but his was a nondescript color and would probably go unnoticed to a casual observer. The thing was, though, those two bikers probably were not causal observers.

"Duck down," Skip told his passengers.

He was taken by surprise as he began to slide down in the seat, anticipating that the pickup would drive past them, when instead, the pickup turned north.

"Where they going?" Max asked.

Skip sat up and gave the bikers time to get farther up the street. When he thought that they were far enough, he pulled out to follow them. The truck kept the speed limit, only accelerating when it hit the city limits and the fifty-five mile an hour speed limit sign.

Skip kept his distance. For almost an hour, he followed the truck steadily northbound through two small towns. They followed in silence, except for Max. Three times Max asked where they were going, and three times no one answered him. The fourth time Skip replied.

"No idea," he said. "We've been following them for an hour."

"You think they know that we're back here?" Max asked.

"The motorcycle is gone," Skip replied. "They got a clear view. It is broad daylight and there isn't any traffic. They'd have to be blind not to know."

No one commented.

"What do you want to do?" Skip asked Max.

Max thought for a moment. "Go back," he replied. "They're leading us away from where we should be looking around."

Skip slowed down, pulled into a drive, and turned around.

Up ahead Joe and Hammer had been driving in silence, playing the waiting game. Joe kept one eye on the road and the other on his rearview mirror.

"They gave up," he finally said, not slowing down.

"We going to turn around?" Hammer asked.

"It might be a trick," Joe replied. "Might be they figured out what we're up to. They'll pull up somewhere and wait for us to turn around and come back. Get the map and figure out how we can circle around."

Hammer fished the road map out of the pocket on the side of the passenger door and opened it up. "I don't even know where the fuck we are."

Skip found a place to pull off the side of the road. He parked the car.

"What's up?" Max asked.

"Just gonna wait here for a while," Skip answered. "See if they spotted us and decided to turn around and back-tail us."

Max moved his head until he could see up the road through the passenger side mirror and waited.

"I think we should go hunt down Grubber," he said thoughtfully. "We haven't talked to him since we started on this."

"Might be a good idea," Skip replied. "I'm sure that he didn't just forget us. He might have come across something that would help us out since we last talked to him. We'd just have to pry it out of him. That shouldn't be too hard."

"Check the bars?" Max suggested. "That's where we found him last time."

"Well, he lives in Ogden," Skip remarked. "We could go down there and ask around. He seemed to be acquainted with that bartender down there at Temple's."

"We could check his place if we knew where he lived," Monica suggested.

"Could," Max replied. "Maybe we could convince the bartender down there to tell us, if he knows."

"One-thirty-five Sycamore Drive, number twenty-two," Monica said. "That's his address."

"How do you know that?" Skip asked, surprised that she knew Grubber's address off the top of her head.

"I just looked it up on my phone," Monica explained. "I can't find any Galen Butrow anywhere on the internet, but Byron Grubber from Ogden comes up in the white pages first thing." She stopped for a moment.

"Duffy made that name up," Max said.

"Let's check out Grubber's place," Skip said.

The other two agreed wholeheartedly. Skip pulled back onto the road and they drove south toward Ogden.

An hour and a half later, Skip drove into the mobile home park at 135 Sycamore. Max started reading off mobile home numbers as they drove past them. When they got to number 22 they stopped. Max thought that the place looked well-kept for somewhere Grubber would live. He expected a dump, but it was just the opposite. He noticed an older brown pickup parked in the drive. Skip put the car in park and left it on the street, turning off the ignition. The three got out and walked up the paved parking pad. Skip walked to the driver's side of the truck and looked through the window. Max was standing behind it. Monica was still standing in the street, staying back and not knowing what to expect. Skip tried the door handle. The door was unlocked and it came open.

"Fayette County plates," Max called to Skip, who was looking inside the truck. Monica took a couple of steps closer.

Suddenly the door of the trailer slammed open and a man in his mid-thirties, close to six feet tall with a stocky build was standing on the deck outside the door of the trailer.

"Get your fucking paws off," the man shouted.

"Billy the fucking Kid," Max shouted back at him. "Just the guy we been looking for. We wanna talk to you."

"Well, I don't have anything to say to you." The man moved closer to the steps that led to the ground.

Within the blink of an eye, Max exploded toward the stairs without another word. Monica was surprised by how fast he moved. Skip was right behind him. Monica ran after them both. At first Billy looked like he was going to stand his ground, but then he turned to the open door of the trailer and made a lunge for it. Max got a hand on the back of his collar and Billy pulled Max into the trailer behind him. Once inside, Billy slammed against the wall on the other side of the room and tried to wriggle free, but Max had an iron grip on his shirt and used it as leverage to pull himself closer, wrapping his left arm around Billy's neck, positioning Billy's chin in the crook of his arm. The hold had been called the Funky Chicken early in Max and Skip's career, before it was outlawed. Max took just a moment too long getting into the position that would allow him to put pressure on both sides of Billy's neck and slow the blood flow to his brain and eventually render him unconscious. Billy placed his palm under Max's elbow and tucked his chin. He was able to squat down and squeeze his way out of the hold. In the process, he got himself turned around with his back against the wall. Billy placed his open hand on Max's chest to shove him away and get some room to maneuver. Max deftly reached across with his right hand, grasped Billy's thumb and twisted it back. Billy turned, lost his balance and fell backward. As he fell, Max reached in with his other hand, grabbed Billy's hand from the other side, bent the wrist and locked the elbow, then twisted the opposite direction. Billy flopped over on his stomach, his face planted in the carpet. He felt his hair pull as his head was turned away from his attacker, then he felt the pressure of a knee on the side of his face, pinning his head. He tried to kick out of the hold, but Max torqued his locked wrist and elbow enough to make Billy realize that any attempt to move would be rewarded with agonizing pain.

"Just lay still," Skip quietly said to him.

"Fuck you, bastard," Billy's tirade was cut short by another torque to his wrist. He let out a gasp and a whimper. He could hear a woman whimper in sympathy to the pain that shot through his shoulder and elbow.

"Billy," he heard Skip's voice in his ear again. "We aren't here to hurt you, but you need to cooperate with us.

If you don't, my partner here is going to have to dislocate your shoulder, and he will do that. Don't think that he won't."

Max gave the wrist another slight twist.

"I give up," Billy gasped.

"If we let you up, can you act like an adult?" Skip asked him. "Because we'll let you up if you can control yourself and not be an asshole."

"I give up," Billy said, this time without the whimper. "I give up."

Skip took his knee off of Billy's head and stood up. Max reached down to Billy's elbow, let up on the pressure, and in a fluid motion, wrist still bent, Max pulled him to his feet and twisted his arm behind his back into an armlock. Billy was helpless in Max's grip.

Max propelled Billy to the couch and didn't let up on the armlock until he was forced to sit down. When he did release it, Billy sat cradling his injured arm with his other.

"You guys tracers?" he asked.

Max and Skip looked surprised that Billy thought that they were looking for him to serve the warrant for probation violations.

"No," Max replied. "We're private investigators. We're looking for Angie Williamson. We heard that she might be with you. We just want to locate her and talk to her."

Billy recognized the surprise in Max's voice. He relaxed a little. "I ain't seen her in a while," he responded.

"She was living with you in Oelwein," Max said, hoping that Billy would think that he knew more than he did.

"Yeah, she was living with me, but she run off with another guy," Billy explained.

"Who did she run off with?" Max asked.

"Some druggie," Billy answered. "I didn't go looking for her. She's just another meth whore."

"She wasn't just a meth whore," Monica spoke up.

"Yeah, she was," Billy shot back.

Max got Billy's attention again. "So you got no idea where she might be now?"

"Nope," Billy replied smugly.

Max stood a moment contemplating what his next move would be. He was half tempted to give Billy a hip pointer, just a little shot of pain to jog his memory, but decided against it. He didn't think that Billy was going to give up anything just because he got a knee in the hip.

"Call Duffy," Max said.

Skip pulled out his phone and found Duffy's number.

"Who's Duffy?" Billy asked.

"Boone County deputy," Max replied.

"You turnin' me in?" Billy started to stand up but Max hit him in the middle of his chest with the palm of his hand. Billy fell back against the cushion. He could hardly breathe.

"Don't fucking move," Max instructed him.

Skip was on the phone, talking to Duffy.

"He'll be here in ten," Skip said to Max, taking his phone from his face.

Max and Skip questioned Billy until the moment Duffy walked through the door, but got nothing from him except that Angie had run off with someone else. Billy wasn't going to change his story.

When Duffy came in, he surveyed the room. Some furniture was tipped over and there was a hole in the far wall. Max, Skip and Monica were standing over Billy, who was sitting quietly on the couch with his hands on his lap. The four looked up at Duffy.

"This is Billy Bonney," Skip said. "I believe there is a warrant out on Mr. Bonney for probation violation in Fayette County. We thought that you might like to take him in."

"Yeah, I checked on the way over," Duffy said. "They said that they would come get him."

Duffy was getting Billy to his feet and cuffing his hands behind his back.

"I was almost home when you called," Duffy said, a little miffed. "You could have called dispatch and they would have sent someone else. You didn't need to call me on my private phone."

"We just wanted to see you," Skip replied.

"Whose place is this?" Duffy asked.

"I think it belongs to a guy named Galen Butrow," Max replied.

"Who?" Duffy asked again.

"Galen Butrow. You know him."

Duffy feigned confusion. "I have no idea what you're talking about."

"The same guy that owns that place south of Pilot Mound," Max replied.

"Glen Burrows," Duffy said. "I don't know where you got that other name."

"You said Galen Butrow yesterday," Max answered back.

Duffy was already taking Billy out the door. "I don't know what you're talking about," he repeated over his shoulder.

Max and Skip followed Duffy and his prisoner down the steps.

"What's Buzzard Bend Properties, LLC?" Skip asked.

"Got no idea what you're talking about," Duffy said while Max and Skip watched him put Billy in the back of his patrol car. "Right now I'm off duty, and I don't have time to chit-chat. And you can go ahead and lose that phone number you have for me. You all have a nice day."

The three watched Duffy walk around to the driver's door of his patrol car and leave.

"What now?" Monica asked.

"Make ourselves comfortable and wait for Grubber," Skip suggested. "See what else he isn't telling us."

Chapter 26

Friday

Hammer directed Joe to the east, and then five miles later, back south. Neither realized exactly how far they had journeyed the wrong direction before Max and Skip had decided to quit following them. Still, they harbored no illusion that the two had given up. They stayed alert, expecting to see the Audi in their rearview mirror at any time.

"What is motivating those guys?" Joe mused. "These guys don't give a shit about the gambling and the bootlegging. It isn't even about the whores, it seems to be about one specific whore."

"Which one, though?" Hammer asked. "He's got a bunch of whores."

"I'm guessing the one that James is taking out of there tonight," Joe answered after a moment of thought. "If my hunch is right, he's gotten wind that those three are looking for her and that makes him nervous. Makes me nervous. Because if James has gotten wind that those detectives are zeroing in, who knows what else he's gotten wind of?"

"I don't know," Hammer replied, ending Joe's speculation. "But what about the whores in general?" Hammer asked. "Like I said, there's more than one. I hardly ever see them. I don't even know how many there are, three maybe, and that Jean, is she one of them?"

"You know, we been concentrating so damn much on bugging the place, recording and taping chit-chat," Joe replied. "When's the last time you let the boss know what's going on?"

"A week ago," Hammer replied.

"Did he say anything?" Joe asked.

"Said to keep digging, said that he would let us know when he has enough to make a move," Hammer replied.

"That's it?" Joe asked. "No direction?"

"That's it," Hammer answered, shrugging his shoulders. "We're just the hired help."

"I think that we need to get closer to the action so that we can get a better handle on this thing," Joe said. "We're too focused. I think that we need to get to know the whores better. James has him a big operation going on here. I'm not sure the boss realizes how big it is."

"Okay," Hammer said. "But that's gonna be a trick."

"Yep," Joe mused. "James likes to keep a close eye on his whores."

"James keeps a close eye on everything," Hammer agreed. "I don't think I've ever seen anyone so paranoid."

"I think maybe he's doing coke," Joe observed. "I think he sees a cop behind every tree, and an undercover agent in every customer who comes through the door."

"Well, so far," Hammer replied, "he's done a pretty damned good job keeping us up in that room over the garage unless he needs us. Sometimes I feel like we're prisoners."

"I'm gonna try to talk to Jean today," Joe said.

"Be careful. Anything you say to Jean is going right back to James," Hammer warned. "Just watch what you say."

Joe didn't answer. He pulled up to the gate and hit the opener tucked up over the visor of the truck. The gate rolled to one side of the wall that protected the entire property from the road. He drove down the lane, glancing at the gate closing in his rearview mirror. He parked behind the shed and noticed that the ground had dried quite a bit since the day before. The two got out and went into the garage, walked past James's Escalade and then up the stairs to their surveillance equipment. Joe clicked the spacebar on the computer keyboard that sat on the table against the wall and brought up the camera to the gate.

"Keep an eye on this," he instructed Hammer. "I wanna know if those detectives come by scoping us out."

Hammer pulled up a chair and propped his feet on the table where he could watch the monitor, while Joe unlocked a box on the floor full of equipment and pulled out a GPS tracker. Joe bent over the keyboard again and keyed in a command that brought up a feed on an adjacent screen from a camera that was directed down the hall from the door that led from the house to the garage.

"I'm going downstairs for a minute. Whistle if you see anyone come down the hall," Joe said, walking out the door and down the stairs. Hammer kept his eye trained on the screen that covered the hallway. He knew that Joe was down there putting the GPS tracker on James's Escalade, and he knew that Joe most assuredly did not want to get caught doing it.

In a few minutes he heard Joe coming back up the steps. There had been no movement at all in the hall while Joe was down there, but as soon as he came through the door, Hammer saw Jean coming down the hall with a tray of food.

"Close," Hammer remarked. "Here comes Jean."

"Timing is everything," Joe huffed.

Jean came through the garage and up the stairs.

"James said that you guys are late," she said as she put the tray of food on the table. "He said to bring you guys up a bite to eat because you have something to do for him later on."

She pulled the cover off the tray and revealed two plates heaped with roast beef sandwiches, mashed potatoes and gravy.

"Looks good," Hammer said, walking over and scooping up one of the plates. Jean brought them supper every night, but usually later, around eight o'clock.

"I guess we're serving roast to the guests tonight?" he asked.

"Put one in the crock pot this morning," she replied.

"Sit down." Joe pushed a chair out for her while he grabbed the other plate. "Keep us company while we eat," he said in a friendly manner. "You never stay and talk. What, you don't like us?"

Jean smiled and took the seat that Joe offered her.

"I can stay a while," she replied.

"How long you been working for James?" Joe asked casually.

"A couple years," she answered him.

"He's been here a couple of years?" Joe exclaimed.

"No," Jean laughed. "We've been here two months. He had a place just like this over in eastern Iowa on the Missouri river for a while, and before that he had a place outside Lincoln."

"Why come here?" Joe asked.

"I don't know," Jean said thoughtfully.

Joe took a couple of bites out of his roast beef sandwich. He smiled at Jean.

"This is delicious. You could open up your own place with cooking like this."

Jean blushed a bit.

"I see you all the time, but what's the deal with the other women here? What do they do?" Joe asked.

"They entertain the customers," Jean replied.

"I watch the camera every night, but I don't see them on the floor much," Joe said.

"They come down once in a while," she replied. "They rotate down on the floor. Usually they stay upstairs, though. They entertain privately." She smiled.

"I've just never met them," Joe said. "How many are there? I've only seen two."

"Why are you questioning me?" Jean asked suddenly.

"Just curious," Joe acted surprised by her comment. "We're supposed to be security here, but we don't even know half the people who work here. Just trying to determine who all belongs and what they do, is all."

Jean stood up. "I think I need to get back to work."

"Thanks for the sandwiches," Hammer said as she started for the door. "Best part of working here is eating your cooking."

Jean smiled at him and went out the door.

"What do you bet we get a visit from James?" Hammer asked when he could no longer hear Jean's footsteps.

Joe nodded. "Evidently he's keeping an eye on us. He knew that we came in late."

The two busied themselves with their equipment, keeping their eyes on the two cameras that Joe had brought up on the monitor. Not more than fifteen minutes after Jean had left, Joe spotted James coming down the hall with a manila envelope in his hand. He went to the keyboard and turned off the monitor that covered the hallway.

"What's up?" he asked as James came in the room.

"How you guys getting along up here?" James asked.

"Fine," Joe replied. "Every day we get things tweaked a little better. We get a little better understanding of what to watch for. I think that it is going well."

"Good," said James. "I happened to see that you guys got in a little later than you usually do," he commented.

"Yeah, well, we got some info from some of our people that there's been a couple of guys snooping around and asking questions the last couple of days, and we tried to track them down today and see what their problem is," Joe explained.

"What kind of questions?" James asked.

"Just questions about who owns what property around here, what everybody does, who is who, just a lot of questions like that," Joe answered.

"Lots of people have questions," James remarked.

"Yeah, probably nothing, but then we like to stay on top of things," Joe said, looking up and smiling at James. "I mean, that's what you hired us for, to stay on top of things. Anyway, like I say, probably nothing, but we had to check it out."

"Did you find them?" James asked.

"We did," Joe answered.

"Did you talk to them?" James asked.

"We tailed them for a while," Joe answered. "We tailed them around and they seemed to be looking at a lot of properties with for sale signs. I think they are just looking for something to buy. New neighbors, maybe."

"That what you think?" James asked.

"Yep," Joe replied.

James stood leaning against the door jamb, staring at Joe. Joe stared back with a smile. He knew that James was trying to intimidate him. The two stood, locked.

"Anything else you're concerned with that you think we need to check out?" Joe broke the silence. "If there is, let us know. That's what we're here for."

"You know what you're doing tonight, right?" James asked.

"Going down to talk to Billy," Joe replied.

"You good with that?" James asked.

"We're just gonna have a talk with him. It's up to him which direction it goes," Joe answered. "Totally up to him. But there will be an understanding before we leave. I promise you that."

James tossed the envelope on the table in front of Joe. "That's all I want," he replied. "Take your time, make sure he comes to that understanding before you leave him. I don't want to see or hear from him again, ever."

"For sure," Joe smiled.

James left the room and started down the stairs. Joe opened the envelope and pulled out a stack of hundred dollar bills. He held them up for Hammer to see, then put them back into the envelope. When they heard James leave the garage and enter the house, Joe spoke up. "He likes to play games."

"I'm looking forward to seeing the look on his face when he realizes he's no longer in charge here," Hammer remarked.

"Might happen sooner than we think," Joe replied.

Joe continued to fiddle with the equipment.

"I can't get that mic on the back patio to come on," he said. "I can get video, but I can't get audio. Can you go out there and talk to yourself for a little while?"

"What about the detectives?" Hammer asked.

Joe shrugged his shoulders. "If they haven't passed by now, they probably didn't find us again and follow us. We can't watch it all day."

Hammer got up and sauntered toward the door.

"Today would be nice," Joe remarked.

Hammer hustled down the stairs as fast as he could, almost falling on the way down. He looked up to see if Joe was watching, and was disappointed that his antics had no audience. He sauntered again through the door and down the hall, not looking up at the camera that he knew Joe was watching.

James walked into the kitchen where Jean was cleaning up. "Ready for tonight?" he asked.

"I will be," she said.

"You talk to Angie?" he asked.

"She wanted to know where you were taking her. I didn't know what you wanted me to tell her."

"I'm taking her back to Billy," James replied, pulling the explanation off the top of his head, but thinking that it was a good one. "He paid up what he owed and he can have her back."

Jean looked up in surprise. "You want me to go up and tell her that?"

"I will," James said. "I was just talking to Joe and Hammer. I think that you don't need to stay up there and talk to them anymore, if you know what I'm saying? They got work to do."

"I'm sorry," she said.

"No big deal. I'm just over careful, you know that," James told her.

"I'm really sorry," she said again.

"Hey, you want to make it up to me?" James asked. "I need someone to take up the slack for Angie. Just this weekend. Is that something you would do for me?"

Jean hesitated.

"Just the slack," James said again. "I'm not going to run 'em through one after another, just the slack. Maybe, if it's slow, you don't have to do it for me at all."

"I guess," Jean relented. "Just the slack."

"Look," James said. "You're in charge of things while I'm out delivering Angie to Billy, so you just keep things going. Then, when I get back, we'll see how busy we are. We just go from there. Tomorrow night, only if I can't get someone else in."

Jean nodded her head.

"I'll make it worth your while," James reassured her. "There's a bonus in it for you. You don't need to do anything weird. Just slam, bam, thank you ma'am. That's all. I won't even put you upstairs if I don't absolutely need you."

"I said I would do it," Jean said with a bit more of a pushback than James was used to.

"Good," he replied.

James went out of the kitchen and worked his way upstairs. The house was huge, and it extended four levels. When he found himself at Angie's door he knocked, something that he usually didn't do.

"Come in," he heard Angie's voice.

James opened the door and went into the room. Angie was sitting by the window reading a book. James sat on the bed.

"Where did you get the book?" James asked in a friendly tone.

"Jean got it from one of the other girls. She asked me if I wanted to read it."

"Is it good?" James asked.

Angie shrugged her shoulders but didn't reply.

"How would you like to go back and be with Billy?" James asked.

"I would like that," Angie replied. "I got a nice view here, but I would like to go back to Billy." She did not display any emotion. She sat waiting for James.

"Billy took care of things, and he wants you back. I told him that he could have you back as long as that was what you wanted to do. But I knew that you would want to go back to him," James said. "It is hard, what we ask you to do here," he commiserated. "I know that."

Again, Angie did not respond.

"I'm coming back up here for you at six-thirty," James said in a gentle tone. "You need to be packed up and ready to go. Make sure you get everything. I don't want you leaving anything behind. We'll go meet Billy."

"I'll be ready," she assured him.

James got up and went to the door. "Six-thirty," he repeated.

Chapter 27

Friday

Max and Skip were sitting on the couch, watching the evening news on Grubber's television. Monica was in the corner, texting Milton on her phone. It was evident that Grubber kept the place pretty clean. Most of the clutter seemed to have been generated by Billy, who had obviously been sitting around the mobile home all day while Grubber was off working.

When Byron pulled up to his place, he saw that the lights were on, Billy's truck was in the drive and an Audi that he recognized was parked on the street in front, parked where he had been parking his Saturn since Billy had taken over the drive. Byron almost drove by to find somewhere else to spend his evening to avoid whatever it was that was going on inside his home, but he didn't. Resigning himself to the inevitable he turned around, came back and parked on the other side of the street. He sat in his car for ten minutes trying to decide exactly what his next move would be. Finally, Byron got out of his car, walked across the street, up the drive and through his front door, which was unlocked.

"What are you guys doing here?" he asked, surveying the room. "Hey," he said to Monica, recognizing her from when she danced at the Ladybug with his brother's woman, the one everyone was looking for.

"Hey," Monica responded.

Byron walked to the hallway and looked down toward the bedrooms, then turned back to the living room where everyone was sitting and watching him.

"If you are looking for your roommate, he got arrested," Skip told him.

Byron looked at the hole in his wall in his living room, near the hallway.

"Billy done that," Skip said. "He didn't want to sit down and talk like a civilized person, so we had to get him to understand that was all we wanted, for him to sit down and talk like a civilized person. He ran into the walls several times and fell on the floor a lot."

Byron came back into the living room. Max got up from the couch and motioned for Byron to sit down.

"Have a seat," Max said. "We've been waiting to have a little civilized talk with you. We are hoping it won't be like the one we had to have with Billy, if you know what I mean."

Byron hesitated.

"I insist," Max said, motioning to the couch.

Byron sat down next to Skip. He was very uncomfortable. Monica sat in her chair, legs crossed, looking at him as if she was about to witness something ominous from afar that she had no intention of stopping. Her stare unnerved him more than Skip's and Max's combined.

Before Byron could say anything, Max walked over, put his hands on both of Byron's knees and leaned in.

"Here's the thing," he said with no emotion in his voice. "We talked to Billy before we called the sheriff's office to come pick him up. We've talked to James, and we got a pretty damned good idea where the hell he is, and a pretty damned good idea that whatever it is that he is doing up there, Angie is there too. And we have a pretty good idea that you know a lot more than you have been letting on. So I got one question and you're going to answer it, because if we don't think that you are being up front with us, there will be hell to pay. Do you want the next moments of your life to turn into a living hell?"

Byron shook his head negatively.

"Does James live in that big house on the river just below Pilot Mound, the one with the big gate, on the west side of the road? Is that where he has his gentleman's club? Is that where he's doing business?"

Byron did not know what to say. He could not think. He just sat there staring into Max's face.

"Byron," Max said, seeing that Byron was trying to think. "Don't try to think up some bullshit to tell me so that I'll leave here. That game has played out and you lose."

Byron gulped and started to protest, but Max held up his palm to stop him.

"Don't even try," Max said. "I will do whatever I have to do to get what I want out of you, and no one will stop me."

"Yes," Byron answered him. "That is where James lives."

"You know where I'm talking about, right? And it's a gentleman's club?" Max asked him to clarify.

"Yes," Byron replied.

"Keep going," Max told him.

"He has a place, the one you're talking about, and it is an exclusive men's club. I don't know what all they do there. I honestly don't. I hear that they do a lot of gambling there and that he takes sports bets. That is all I know, honestly."

"What's your connection?" Max asked.

"I don't have any connection," Byron said.

"Bullshit," Max said. "What is your connection?"

Byron resigned himself. "I keep my ears and eyes open, and if I see or hear something that I think that James might like to know, or if I find anyone snooping around, I call him up. He pays me a little bit once in a while for the info."

"How long has this been going on?" Max asked.

"Just a couple months," Byron said. "He hasn't been in business that long."

"Did you tell him about us?" Max asked, pushing Byron down into the cushion of the couch.

Byron gulped. "Yeah, I did."

"You shithole," Max said. "I ought to just beat the shit out of you right now."

Byron lowered his head as if he expected Max to make true his words.

"Is Angie there?" Max interrupted his thoughts.

Byron looked back up at Max and shrugged his shoulders. "I don't think so," he said with as much honesty in his voice as he could muster. "I asked Billy where Angie was, and he told me that he gave her to someone to pay off some debts he owed."

"He *gave her* to someone?" Monica said harshly from the corner. Her appearance in the conversation unnerved him. He began to think of terrible things that Monica could do to him if Max and Skip held him down and let her. She was not on her feet, but she was leaning forward in her chair. "How the fuck does that work?" she barked at him.

"When a woman comes into the Hell Fighters, she belongs to the club," Byron explained. "The club members can do what they want with her. If someone doesn't want her anymore, or if someone dies, she gets passed on to someone else. Billy owed debts, he used her to pay them. That's all I know."

Monica was standing up. There was fury in her eyes.

"It's not me," Byron pleaded directly to Monica. "I'm just telling you. It's not me. I don't have anything to do with it. I'm telling you what Billy told me. That's all."

"Let's go," Skip said suddenly. "Billy gave her to James."

Max looked at Skip and knew that Skip's revelation was right. Skip was already walking toward the door.

"You breathe a word of this before we get there, you make a single call and fuck this up, I'll come back here and kill you," Max threatened. Then he stood up and ran after Skip.

It took Monica a moment to process what was going on. Grubber was still sitting on the couch looking at her, not moving a muscle, looking like he feared Monica would attack him without the two detectives to stop her. Max and Skip had just run out the door. Monica gave Byron one last look and bolted after them. As she came out the door and across the deck she jumped, clearing the four steps that led to the ground. She fell and scraped her knee and put a rip in her jeans, but she got right up and sprinted for Skip's car. It was already started, and Max had reached back to open the door for her. She dived through the open door into the back seat. Skip put the accelerator to the floor before she could close the door. It slammed shut on its own with the momentum. She sat up and looked over the seat to see that Skip was at sixty and climbing.

"Got a plan?" Max asked casually, much too casually for Monica to process. Her heart rate was going through the roof. She looked out the window as the fifty-five mile an hour sign that marked the city limits flashed by.

"Yep," Skip replied.

"Gonna share it, or is it going to be a surprise?"

"I'm going to crash through that gate, kick in the door and search that place until I find her," Skip said in a very matter-of-fact tone.

"Sounds like a good plan to me," Max replied, settling back in the seat. "Can I kick in a couple of doors?"

"Be my guest," Skip replied.

Skip continued northbound with purpose. When he reached the Des Moines River bottom, where the road curved in unison with the river, the Audi fought for traction as Skip hit each curve with no caution whatsoever. Max was calmly watching the scenery out his window. Monica had put on her seatbelt and was pulling it tighter with every curve.

"Whoa! Whoa! Whoa!" Max shouted as Skip swerved back into his own lane to keep from running head-on into a vehicle in the oncoming lane. Skip slowed a bit, but kept going. He was two miles from James's place, and he was already prepared to hit the gate at speed. "Turn around," Max interrupted his concentration. "Black Escalade with tinted windows, southbound. You just almost hit him."

Skip slowed a bit more.

"Black Escalade with tinted windows," Max explained. "The gal at the Boone PD told you that an officer stopped a black Escalade with tinted windows, and Angie was in it."

Skip hesitated a moment more, then slammed on the brakes to make the U turn in the middle of the curve. He trusted Max's gut, he always had, and he was going with it now. Skip came out of the turn and put the accelerator to the floor.

"This Audi has a lot of kick," Max observed. "Handles well, too."

"It does," Skip said calmly.

"Nothing like the old 'Stang though," Max remarked. "I mean the kick. I don't think I've ever driven anything as quick as that 'Stang."

"How about the Camaro?" Skip asked. "How does it compare to my Audi?"

"I think it might be a toss-up," Max replied.

"Turbo chargers," Skip replied. "Gotta love 'em."

"No shit," Max replied. "You know, that little go-cart of Gloria's puts out two-hundred-sixty horsepower. I mean, it is a four cylinder engine. Dual turbos. Can you believe it?"

"Could you two pay attention?" Monica shouted from the back seat.

As Skip came around a curve, he caught sight of taillights. He slowed to the speed limit. At the next curve he caught sight of them again as the Escalade went around the next bend.

"Got him," Skip said.

Max had caught sight of the taillights as well, and was concentrating on the road ahead in an attempt to see them again.

"Wonder where we're going." Max remarked.

"No idea," Skip answered him. "You're the one who used to hang out up here."

"When I was sixteen years old," Max replied.

They drove in silence for a mile, catching sight of the Escalade's taillights with each curve.

"Fraser," Max announced.

"Even if that is James, what makes you think that Angie's in there with him?" Monica asked.

"I don't know if it is James, and I don't know if she's in there with him," Max replied.

"What are we doing, then?" Monica asked, exasperated.

"Just go with it," Skip replied. "Half the time he's right, the other half of the time he's not."

Monica didn't know what to say to Skip's logic.

"Look, if she is in the car and we don't follow, we lose her and never find her again," Max explained. "If we follow him, he stops somewhere, and if she isn't with him, then Skip gets to turn around, go back, ram the gate with his Audi and kick in doors. The only thing we lose in that case is a little time."

Monica realized that he was absolutely right. She never ceased to be amazed by those two.

As the Escalade reached the Fraser town limits, it slowed down. Skip caught up to it and held back. He put on his turn signal, pulled into a driveway and gave it a slow ten count. He turned back onto the street and sped up to catch the Escalade again, knowing that Fraser wasn't that big of a town, and that in the seconds that he had stopped so that he wouldn't draw attention to the fact that he was following, the Escalade would be out of town and accelerating to fifty-five.

Skip glanced down at his speedometer. He was up to fifty-five long before he hit the city limits. He did not want to stay out of touch any longer than he had to in order to confuse the driver of the Escalade.

"Where the hell is he?" Max said, straining his eyes for the taillights ahead.

Skip checked the odometer as he had when he left the town limits of Fraser. He had gone more than three miles with no sign of the Escalade.

"He has to have pulled off," he said to Max.

"Tilly's Hole," Max replied. "Old fishing hole back there about a mile. There's a turnoff, and a dirt road goes back into the woods along the river."

"You think that he's going fishing?" Skip asked.

"I don't know what he's doing," Max replied. "But I agree that he turned off and that is the only place that I know."

Skip turned around and went back the way they had come. "You know where it is in the dark?"

"I haven't been there for thirty years," Max replied.

Skip was just about to comment on Max's poor memory when Max spoke up.

"And there it is, on the right," Max said casually.

Skip found the drive and turned in. He turned off his headlights and used his parking lights to guide him. Even though it wasn't a full moon night, there was enough moonlight that Skip could make out the two-wheel path into the woods and follow it. After close to a quarter mile, he spotted a glint of moonlight off the Escalade fifty yards ahead. He switched off his parking lights and stopped.

"Holy shit," Skip exclaimed. "I can't believe it. Your mojo is working tonight."

Skip and Max looked out the side windows in both directions.

"You know your way around here?" Skip asked Max.

"If they went down to the river, I know the way," Max replied.

"Okay," Skip said. "Max and I go on foot down to the river. Monica, you stay put."

"I don't want to stay here," Monica replied as soon as Skip's words came out of his mouth.

"You stay here," Skip said again. "Max and I will go stealth. You watch the Escalade, and if anyone comes back and gets into it, you hit the horn and don't get off it until you see us coming. That should cause enough confusion to give us time to get back here. Everybody has a job, and your job is to watch the Escalade. This is not the time to argue about it, Monica."

Monica resigned herself. Skip reached across in front of Max and opened the glove compartment, where he pulled out a flashlight.

"You packing?" he asked Max.

"Yep," Max answered. "Are you?"

"Yes, I am," Skip replied. "Let's go. I want to check out that Escalade first."

It took just a moment for Monica's eyes to adjust from the dome light to the moonlight again after Max and Skip opened the doors and got out of the car. She watched their silhouettes as they crept up to the Escalade and peered into the windows. After a moment, Skip's flashlight came on for a few seconds as he looked inside, then it abruptly went off. The two shadows passed the Escalade, and she lost sight of them. Monica looked around. It was quiet. Skip had left the keys for her. She slipped between the seats so that she would not turn on the dome light by opening the door and got up front, behind the wheel. She switched the key to accessory and opened both windows. She listened. She could hear a strange sound that she finally decided was the river flowing somewhere in the woods. It seemed to be coming from every direction. She settled back and strained her eyes to see the Escalade. Monica was tempted to get out and look around, but she trusted Skip's experience in these kinds of situations. She sat quietly, waiting.

Chapter 28

Friday

James stood in the window of his office, where he could see Joe's truck parked behind the shed. He was lost in thought while he waited for Joe and Hammer to leave on the mission that he had given them. James liked Joe and Hammer. He had faith in their ability to do what he hired them to do. He did not trust them at all. They were Hell Fighters, and Hell Fighters were known for muscling their way into other people's businesses. If you kept them around long enough, they would get something on you and try to take over. James wondered how long it would take Joe to propose a deal.

The thing was, James wasn't afraid of Hell Fighters. That made him different from most of the dumbasses out there. He knew that most Hell Fighters—most bikers everywhere—were a lot of show and no go. They were brave when it was five-on-one. But one-on-one, a Hell Fighter's technique was to stall until more Hell Fighters showed up. James was sure that he could handle Joe and Hammer. He knew how they worked, and knowing that gave him a leg up, a sense of security. But one thing about bikers, they didn't talk to the authorities, and that is what James liked about using them. Especially for security. You couldn't trust them for anything else, but you could trust them to keep their mouths shut.

James's vigil was rewarded after a while when he saw the two bikers wearing their colors and walking toward Joe's pickup. It was just getting dark, but they were clearly visible by the lights that surrounded the grounds. Joe had the envelope in his hand. They got into the truck, backed around and drove toward the gate. James walked to the window on the other wall of his office, where he had a clear view of the gate. James loved the setup. He could keep an eye in every direction from his office. He watched the pickup's taillights go through the gate and turn south. Step one of his plan had come and gone without a hitch. Now was step two, taking Angie to Tilly's Hole.

James had met Billy the Kid in Nebraska. Billy had been just a Hell Fighter running home-cooked meth from Oelwein, Iowa, to Lincoln, Nebraska. James had hired some other Hell Fighters to work security at his place in Lincoln, and they had brought James a proposal, one that would have him peddling Hell Fighter meth to his customers. James decided to expand his business and went into a partnership with the Hell Fighter from Oelwein. But Billy was a loose cannon who got himself into a bind. James bailed him out and kept the tab open on Billy until he thought it was the right time to call it in. That time came when James needed to relocate. He called on Billy, who said he knew just the place: Boone County, Iowa. A mixture of middle class, hard-working people from Webster City and Fort Dodge, and high rolling farmers with nothing to do nine months out of the year. Close enough to Des Moines to attract the professional crowd, and just a short drive from academia at Iowa State University, with its smart, tenured professors who pulled down big wages, had job security, and who were not as smart as they thought they were when it came to betting. Pretty much the same clientele that he had in Lincoln. But the one factor that was most important was friends and family. Iowa was small town judgmental, and being seen in the wrong places got around quickly. That was what made a gentleman's club so popular. The customer's wife wasn't going to come by and spot their car parked at the gentleman's club. The neighbor's wife wasn't going to gossip it around town. A night at the club could be a night at the office, and no one was the wiser. What happened at the gentleman's club stayed there. Everyone there was in the same boat. It was a perfect playground for discreet indiscretions.

Billy had gone with James to show him around Boone County the first time. James could see the potential as soon as he got there. Boone County was a whole different animal from the counties surrounding it. Boone County was a mind-your-own-business county. James liked it.

One warm fall day while he and Billy were driving around, Billy wanted to show James where there was a good fishing spot on the river near Fraser. He called it Tilly's Hole. James wasn't much for fishing but he thought that the drive might be relaxing, so Billy took him to Tilly's Hole, just to look around. It was back in the woods, a half mile or more from the road. One could drive half that distance down a road that was dirt. The rest of the way you had to walk. After they had looked at the eddy in the river that marked Tilly's Hole, Billy took James the long way back along the river, which took them to within a hundred yards from where they had parked. James had asked why people didn't just go straight to the river and fish, instead of hiking a quarter mile down the path to go fishing in the same river. Billy told him that the fish congregated at Tilly's Hole. James didn't press the conversation; he didn't intend to go fishing in the river anyway. But he was glad that he had gone with Billy to check it out, because Tilly's Hole was where he was taking Angie, and he needed to get going.

James walked into Angie's room and saw her sitting on her bed. Her suitcase was standing on the floor next to the door. James looked around to make sure that she had not left anything personal that could connect her to his place later if anyone came snooping around. The room looked empty.

"Ready?" he asked in a lighthearted tone.

"I guess I am," Angie said, standing up and walking toward her suitcase.

"I got it for you," James said, pulling up the handle and wheeling it behind him, leading the way. Angie followed to the garage, where James put her suitcase in the back cargo area while Angie got in the passenger side door of the Escalade.

"Let me throw your purse in here," James called to her.

"It's okay," she replied. "I can hold it."

"Let's put it back here," James said forcefully.

Angie got out of the Escalade and walked back to give her purse to James. Then she turned around and went back to the passenger door and got in.

James got in on the driver's side and pushed the door opener before he started the ignition. When the door was completely open, he backed out of the garage, shut the garage door and started for the road. Going up the drive, he had to pull as far to the right as he could to let a car pass that was coming down the drive toward the house. It was a customer. James wondered who had let him in. Joe and Hammer were gone; it had to be Jean. James went through the gate and turned right, toward Fraser.

They drove in silence. Angie was not used to talking unless spoken to, and James was nervous about what he was going to do. He didn't want to get any closer to Angie during the ride to Tilly's Hole. It was going to be hard enough as it was.

As soon as he got on the road, he barely avoided a head-on collision with a car that was speeding in the other direction. The car swerved to get back into its own lane. James watched its taillights in his rearview mirror for a few seconds until it went around the curve and out of sight. A few minutes later he noticed that there was a car behind him. He kept an eye on it. It seemed there was a lot of traffic on the road. James was just naturally suspicious, even though his logic was telling him nothing was wrong. Just the same, James kept his eye on the car behind him to make sure that no one was tailing him. As he passed through Fraser, the car behind pulled into a driveway, and he did not see anyone behind him after that. Angie seemed content to watch out the passenger's side window and ride in silence. James wondered if she was thinking about Billy.

When James pulled into the drive that led into the woods toward Tilly's Hole, Angie became agitated.

"Where are we going?" she asked.

"We're going to meet Billy," he answered.

"Here?"

James did not answer. He continued to drive until he reached the end of the lane. He stopped the Escalade, turned off the engine and watched his rearview mirror for a minute to make sure no one was pulling in behind him. He rolled down his window. Angie was talking, but he wasn't listening.

"Angie, shut up," James commanded her. "I'm trying to listen."

"Listen for what?" Angie asked.

"I told you to shut up," James replied.

James listened. He could only hear the current of the river, off to the right. James intended to take Angie in that direction. If he took her to Tilly's Hole, she might stay caught in the eddy there. The current was stronger off to the right, and it was closer.

"Stay in the car," James told her. "Don't open the door."

James didn't want her to climb out and get any ideas to bolt into the woods. He removed his keys from the ignition, reached into the back seat and felt around the floorboards for the battery powered Coleman lantern that he had put back there earlier. He got out and walked around the front of the Escalade to the passenger's side door, where he opened it for Angie and helped her out. Taking her arm, he shut the door, locked it and proceeded into the woods, the lantern lighting the way. The going was rough. The ground was still wet in low places and the mud was like molasses, sticking to their shoes. As they got close to the river, they had to climb over a deadfall, then another one. Angie fell getting over the second one, and James helped her up.

"Why are you taking me out here?" Angie asked.

"Don't worry about it," was all that James replied.

"I am worried about it," Angie said. "I don't know why you are bringing me here. I don't think that Billy is here."

Angie started walking faster. She got in front of James. He was listening to the water, trying to keep an eye on Angie in the light of the lantern and look for the river at the same time. All of a sudden, James got the urge to finish it. He reached forward and grabbed the hair on the back of Angie's head, jerking her back to him. He put one arm around the top of her head and the other hand on her chin, then twisted quickly with all his might, hoping to snap her neck. Instead, his hand slipped off of her chin and he managed nothing more than to turn her head to one side.

Taking advantage of her disorientation, he took a tighter grip and tried it again. This time she turned with him and he found her facing him almost as if they were in an embrace. He could make out her face just six inches from his, looking up at him. The lantern was laying on the ground casting its light upward, forming macabre shadows in her face. It scared him. He almost kissed her for some reason, but then wrapped both his hands around her throat and squeezed. Angie started to gurgle and James squeezed tighter. She tried to remove his hands but she did not have the strength. In the light, James could see her wide open eyes flutter and then close. She fell, limp, and he squeezed tighter, holding her off of her knees by the sheer tightness of his hold on her throat. He finally let her drop.

James was shaking. He picked up the lantern and walked a few paces to the dead tree that they had just climbed over, placed the lantern on it and sat down. He stared at the motionless body of Angie on the forest floor. He watched her for a long time, it seemed, and then he saw her head move. She turned it and looked toward the light. She got her arms under her and started to sit up.

James was freaking out. He pulled his Colt model 1911 pistol from his waistband, racked the slide and pointed it toward her. He put pressure on the trigger, but could not bring himself to pull it.

"Lay still," he commanded her. "Do not get up."

Monica thought that she heard something in the woods to her right. She looked out the open window. She was sure that she had seen a glint of light. She almost hit the horn to summon Max and Skip. She stopped and watched again. She could clearly see a light a long way off in the woods toward the river. She took out her phone and brought up Max's number. She tried to call, but nothing happened. She looked at the top of the screen and saw that she had no reception. Monica opened the door of the car and got out. She held her phone in the air, but she still had no reception. She started walking quietly and carefully toward the light, checking her phone as she went.

Slowly, Monica worked her way closer and closer to the light. She could hear a man's voice giving orders of some kind. Monica tried to stay as quiet as she could, staying on her tiptoes and feeling the ground carefully so that she would not snap a twig and reveal her presence, like they did on TV. Little did she know that Mother Nature was already protecting her from detection by turning everything into a water-soaked world that would bend but not break. Monica crept up to a fallen tree and peered over it. She could see a man sitting on another log across a small clearing, facing her direction, with a gun pointed at a woman who had her back to Monica. Even though she could not see the woman's face, she knew that it was Angie. The man stood up and walked close. Angie turned away from him and was now looking into the dark woods where Monica was hiding. The man was swearing. "Fuckin' do it," she heard him say. The man put the gun up toward Angie's head, but then let it drop again. Monica was frozen. She didn't know what to do. "Fuck," the man shouted. Then he raised the gun again.

Monica could not wait any longer. She decided that she had to make a move. Just as she got ready to stand, she felt a hand on her shoulder that pushed her back down, and a large man in green trousers and a tan shirt stepped over the tree, using Monica's shoulder for support, a pistol in his other hand. He took four steps toward the other man before the man even saw him. He stopped. Monica could see now in the light of the lantern that the man who had walked past her was wearing a uniform. He produced a small LED flashlight from his pocket with his left hand and held it backhand in front of him, so the beam of the flashlight illuminated the other man's face. He placed his gun hand over the top, resting it on the hand with the flashlight, and sighted down the beam of light.

"You need to drop the gun," Sheriff Kind instructed.

James did not move.

"It's all over now, James."

"I'll kill her," James threatened.

"You were gonna kill her, but you didn't," Kind replied to the threat. "You haven't killed anyone. Put the gun down while you're ahead."

"Get up, Angie," James instructed her. "We're walking out of here."

"That's not one of the options on the table," Kind replied. "You're not leaving with her, for sure. So if you want to talk about what's going to happen in the next few minutes, the conversation needs to take a different direction."

James didn't answer. His gun did not waiver from Angie's head, his finger was tight on the trigger. There was a ruckus to his right as two figures appeared in the lantern light. James did not look away from Angie, but he could see the two men out of the corner of his eye.

Kind took his eyes off of his sights and looked to see Max and Skip show up with guns in hand.

"Put 'em down, gentlemen," Kind instructed them. "When this goes to shit, me and James here are going to be throwing enough bullets around without your help. We wouldn't want to accidently shoot your junior secret agent back there, now, would we? "

The two stood, saying and doing nothing for a moment.

"Where's Monica?" Max asked.

"Right behind me," Kind said.

Max and Skip glanced in the direction behind Kind and could barely make out the top of Monica's head and her eyes reflecting at the edge of the light. Even from a distance, Max and Skip could see that she was scared.

"Lower the weapons and holster 'em," Kind instructed again.

The two detectives did as they were told.

"Okay, your turn," Kind told James.

James did not move.

They all heard another ruckus to the left, and presently Joe and Hammer arrived in the light, guns in hand.

"Christ," Kind said. "Fucking unbelievable. Who else is running around out here? Put the gun down now, James," he ordered.

"I think we got company." James replied. "Looks to me like we had an even fight 'til you made your boys put their guns away. Now it looks like we got you covered. Maybe you need to drop your gun."

James could see that Hammer was slowly walking toward him from his right, his gun in hand. A tactical move, James thought. He looked over at Joe to see that he was pointing his gun directly toward him, instead of Kind. Hammer was carefully advancing, while staying out of the line of Joe's fire. Hammer walked up until he was almost on top of James, towering over him. Hammer reached down slowly and wrapped his gigantic hand around both James's hand and his gun, positioning the web between his thumb and his finger between the hammer of the Colt and the firing pin, rendering the gun inoperable. He squeezed tight and gently removed the pistol from James's hand. Then he stepped back toward Joe with it. Kind came forward, took James by the shoulder and turned him around, placing his hands behind his back and cuffing them.

"You are under arrest for attempted murder. To start with, anyway." Kind told him. "You have the right to remain silent. Anything you say can be used against you in a court of law. You have the right to have an attorney present before questioning. If you cannot afford an attorney, one will be appointed for you. Do you understand your rights?"

James did not reply. He had not taken his eyes off the two bikers since Hammer had taken his gun from him. Monica had run up and was helping a sobbing Angie to her feet. Joe was there with her.

"We'll take her with us," Joe told Monica.

Monica gave him a doubtful look.

"It's okay, ma'am," Joe said, putting a hand gently on her arm. We're state agents. We're going to take her down to the law enforcement center in Boone to fill out a statement. You can come down there, too, and wait for her if you want."

Monica nodded her head. Max and Skip just stood, watching. It seemed that Kind and the agents had everything under control.

Chapter 29

Saturday

Max, Skip and Monica were sitting in the office at the agency waiting for Duffy. On the way out of the Boone County Law Enforcement Center the night before, Kind had told them that he would send Duffy over at nine in the morning to explain everything to them. It was nine-thirty, and no Duffy. Milton had gotten an earful the night before from Monica, and was on the phone again now, telling Monica that he was on his way to a call and would come to the agency when he got through with it. Carlisle had come by, and was chatting with Max and Skip.

A plain Buick Riviera pulled up in front of the agency. Duffy got out of the driver's side, Hammer unfolded himself from the passenger's side and Joe got out of the back. The three sauntered up to the door and walked into the crowded room. They stopped and surveyed the people looking at them expectantly.

"Let's go into the conference room," Skip suggested.

Everyone followed Skip. There were six chairs around the table.

Skip went to the bar across the hall, wheeled in another chair and took a seat.

"We all here and ready?" Duffy asked.

"Yep," said Max.

"Should I start?" Duffy asked the two agents. They nodded, so he began.

"I'll try to make it short, then you can ask your questions if you want because I know you're going to have some. First, let me introduce Agents Joe Fisher and Mike Hammer from the Iowa DCI."

"I'm a trooper," Hammer said.

"Mike Hammer?" Skip asked with humor in his voice.

"Trooper Hammer," Duffy corrected himself, not responding to Skip. "Three weeks ago, Trooper Hammer pulled over a pickup truck on I-80 for driving erratically, with two Hell Fighters and a shitload of meth and marijuana in it. Trooper Hammer sniffed out the drugs, placed the bikers under arrest, read them their rights, and on the way to the pokey in Atlantic, they spilled their guts. They said that they were on their way to Boone County to work security for one James Burnett at an illegal gambling establishment that he had set up here. A check on Mr. Burnett revealed that he was suspected in Nebraska of running a syndicate that dealt in illegal gambling, illegal distribution of alcohol, prostitution and he was probably heavy into drugs, considering the amount that those two bikers had with them."

Duffy stopped to see if there were any questions. No one said anything.

Duffy continued. "The bikers got a court appointed attorney, who advised them to make a plea deal. Two days later, Trooper Hammer, by virtue of his arrest, and Agent Fisher, by virtue of the fact that he is the top undercover vice agent with the DCI, took over for the two bikers and ended up in the employ of James Burnett, sans drugs, which never even came up. No one had any evidence except what the two bikers had said and supposition in regards to Burnett, so Agent Fisher and Trooper Hammer were supposed to get themselves settled in and determine exactly what of that smorgasbord of illegal activities he was actually engaged in, and how deeply. They were to wire the place up, gather intelligence, get names and numbers, and turn it all over to the state attorney general. When the AG got enough for an indictment, he was going to come down on Burnett. They were just starting to get some good intel logged when you guys came along. They did not have enough yet, though, for the AG to build a case. They were just getting started."

"So you were the liaison between them and the Boone County Sheriff's Department," Max remarked. "And when we got to snooping around, you decided to throw us off the trail and give them time to make a case?"

"In my defense," Duffy replied. "You never told me that you suspected that the woman you were looking for was a victim of a sex trafficking ring. We thought that even if she was there, she was there of her own accord. A lot of times, missing persons are missing because they want to be. You know that. You've been around. We all assumed that was the case. We wrongly assumed that was the case. No one knew that she was in danger. But yes, I started throwing whatever I could in your way to give them time."

"And Kind was in on it, too?" Max asked.

"Of course," Duffy answered. "But he was still pissed because you came over to our county and didn't even have the professional courtesy to check in with us."

"I'll shoulder that one," Max replied. "That was my fault, and I wasn't thinking. I should have checked in."

"So," Duffy continued. "While everyone was just assuming that your missing person was not really missing, and even though no one ever mentioned to us the phone call to Monica asking for help, agents Fisher and Hammer got a bad feeling yesterday. They got a gut feeling that James was trying to get them out of the way for a couple of hours, that he was up to something and that he didn't want witnesses. Not even Hell Fighter witnesses. Add to that, they were aware that you guys were trying to locate a missing person and that you were getting very, very close. They got suspicious that something wasn't right, put two and two together, placed a tracker on James's Escalade and decided to put a loose tail on him just to see what he was up to."

Duffy stopped again.

"How in the hell does Kind figure into last night?" asked Skip.

"I called Kind as soon as I got to the station with Billy," Duffy said. "Kind is just one hell of a cop. He worked his way up. He figured that there was no stopping you guys. He knew you were close, he knew that you had no idea what you were getting into, and he just decided to tail you guys and make sure you didn't get yourselves in over your heads. So he went over and staked you out at Grubber's place. When Grubber came home and you all came flying out of there, Kind was right behind you. But when you two got out and hightailed it down toward Tilly's Hole, Kind decided that he should keep an eye on Monica, because she was there alone. When she got out of the car and took off through the woods, Kind was right behind her. He said that she was making enough noise to wake the dead. He was surprised that James didn't start taking shots in the dark. When she was hiding behind the fallen tree and getting ready to stand up. Kind was so close he could smell her shampoo."

That statement unnerved Monica, who had been listening to every word.

"So," Duffy continued. "You guys were following James, and Fisher and Hammer were following James, too. Kind was following everybody. It was a regular parade. So that's it. You know the rest. Any questions?"

No one said anything for a moment.

"You guys almost got Angie killed," Max suggested.

Joe spoke up. "No, actually you guys almost got her killed."

He paused for a moment for his words to sink in.

"First of all, James is very paranoid. Super paranoid," Joe continued. "So when he found out that some private detectives were looking for Angie, his first inclination was to get rid of the evidence. That has been his M.O. He is obsessed with leaving no trail. That is how he has operated this long and stayed under the radar. But this is the first time he has had to get rid of a person as a piece of evidence. He didn't know what do. But he convinced himself that she was just something that had to be gotten rid of. Evidence that, if you guys got ahold of it, would lead the authorities to him.

Joe paused for a moment. "But here's the thing: Angie actually planted the seed of paranoia. When she called Ms. Benson on Sunday night, the phone she used belonged to a client who was in the shower. When you called her back, the client figured it out and was not happy about her using his phone. He mentioned it to James, and then it all just snowballed downhill from there."

Joe paused again, collecting his thoughts.

"If I might say something, at this juncture," Duffy took the opportunity to speak up. "What we had here was one of those jurisdictional fubar situations where everyone wants to get everything they can from everyone else and not give anything up themselves. That's what almost got Angie killed. I think that if people would be a little more forthcoming and trusting, things would have not gotten to that point."

No one said anything for a moment. Joe broke the silence.

"The thing that saved Angie was, first of all, James had to work up the courage to finish the job, and we all, all of us, followed the same gut feeling and showed up in time to stop him before he did. So nobody almost got her killed. Circumstances almost got her killed, and circumstances saved her."

"Where's Angie now?" Carlisle asked.

"She's at my place," Monica replied. "Just until she gets herself together."

Everyone sat in silence while they thought about what had gone down.

"Why did you guys key my car?" Skip suddenly asked, looking directly at Fisher and Hammer.

"We didn't key your car," Fisher answered. "When was your car keyed?"

"That first day that we played pool with you guys," Skip answered.

"It wasn't us," Fisher replied.

"Who was it, then?" Skip asked.

"How the hell should we know?" Fisher replied. "It sounds to me like you got another case to investigate."

Skip looked at Duffy.

"I didn't do it," he said.

"I want to file a vandalism report," Skip told him. "I think that you have a case to investigate."

Duffy laughed.

"I'm not kidding," Skip said.

Duffy gave Skip a condescending look. "I'll go right out and get a vandalism form and you can fill it out." He got up and left the conference room.

Carlisle was not happy that Duffy had misled him as well, when he had relayed the information that he had gotten about the gentleman's club. It seemed that Duffy didn't subscribe to the professional courtesies, either, and

Carlisle had thought that Duffy's little speech about sharing info was a bit hypocritical.

Monica went out to her desk and thought about her conversation with Milton the night before about her adventures. Milton was not particularly happy about what had gone down, but he had kept it to himself.

Max turned to Skip. "I'm going to Filo's," he said.

"I'll come over when I get done with the report," Skip replied, slouching in his chair.

Max went past Monica and out the door. The two agents were standing by the car waiting for Duffy. They did not pay any attention to his leaving. Max enjoyed the warmth from the spring morning sunlight as he crossed the street. He was eager to hear Skip's take on the whole thing without everyone else listening in.

Carlisle put an envelope on Monica's desk.

"What's that?" she asked.

"Coupons for tuxes and limos. I've been picking them up all over the county. It's getting close to prom and everyone has a deal. I thought that if we book now, maybe we could get in on them," Carlisle said.

"Thanks." Monica picked up the envelope and put it back down without looking into it.

"I hear you got a wedding shower coming up," Carlisle said.

"That female officer, Sarah, is putting it on," Monica said. "Milton and I think it is going to be a good opportunity for me to meet some of the women that work at the PD and some of the wives."

"I'm sure it will," Carlisle said.

"That Sarah, though," Monica continued. "I just get the feeling that she doesn't like me. I'm wondering if she thinks..." Monica didn't finish.

"She doesn't think anything," Carlisle piped up. "It's probably just a little awkward for her, considering that she and Milton dated for a while."

"They did?" Monica remarked. "Milton failed to mention that."

"It was a long time ago," Carlisle said. "Besides, I'll bet that you don't go telling Milton about every guy you ever went out with before you met him."

"What happened?" Monica asked.

"They weren't compatible," Carlisle replied. "Sarah's a little domineering."

"You mean she's like a dominatrix?" Monica asked, raising her eyebrows.

"Well," Carlisle smiled. "Maybe not quite that domineering, but close."

"I think that you're teasing, now," Monica said. "I heard that you're going out with her."

"We go out once in a while," Carlisle replied. "Friends. Someone to hang out with. Only consensual and non-binding domination going on between us."

"You're a shit," Monica laughed.

"I'm leaving, I've said too much," Carlisle replied. "Don't go piling on Milton about Sarah, because he'll come back and blame me for it."

"I'll keep our little secret," Monica called to Carlisle as he went out the door.

Chapter 30

Monday

Max was sitting in Filo's Coffee Shop watching the world go by from the window. Across the street he could see the offices of G&B Detective Agency and Skip's Audi parked in front. While he sat sipping his coffee and downing the blueberry muffin in front of him, Monica pulled up in front of Filo's and parked her car in the one parking space that blocked his view of the street and the offices beyond. Max was a bit put out by it, in the way that a father might be put off by his daughter parking her car behind his own and having to move hers before he could go somewhere.

Monica got out of her car and came into Filo's. Max watched her order a latte, and then come toward his table. He looked out the window again and was surprised to see Skip walking across the parking lot. Monica sat down opposite Max.

"How's your Monday?" she asked.

"Back to normal, thank God," Max replied.

Skip came through the door and walked directly to the table, looking over at the barista who was already preparing his latte. Skip took a chair next to Monica and looked out the window.

"Nice view," he commented, nodding his head toward the grill of Monica's Nissan.

The jab was not lost on her. "You want me to go out and move it?"

"We're fine," Max said.

The barista brought both lattes and asked Max if he wanted a refill. Max sent him off with his mug.

"So how is Angie?" Max asked.

"Okay, I guess," Monica answered. "She left yesterday."

"Where did she go?" Max asked.

"She went back to Billy."

"What the hell?" Skip exclaimed.

"I know." Monica shook her head. "I did everything but tackle her, but she left. Billy came by and picked her up."

"I thought Billy was in jail," Skip exclaimed again.

"Got out on his own recog Sunday morning," Monica exclaimed. "He's on double probation now. He's supposed to head straight back to Fayette County and check in with his PO today. He stopped by and picked her up on his way out of town."

"And Angie went with him?" Max said incredulously.

"That surprises you?" Skip asked him.

"No," Max replied. "So now what? I mean, are they going back to Oelwein, or what? Is she going to be around to testify when James goes to court?"

"No idea," Monica replied. "She just told me that she had been talking to Billy and that he wanted her to come back to him. So she gave him my address, and the next thing I know, he's standing at the door. I didn't even know that she had been talking to him. I mean, she was with me less than forty-eight hours. We didn't even hardly have time to talk. Boom! She's gone."

The three sat in silence.

"Maybe it is for the good," Skip said. "I mean, you got a lot on your plate right now. You got Shawna, Essie,

Milton, a wedding coming up, classes." Skip paused for a moment.

"You got us to take care of," Max added.

"Sometimes you have to step back and ask yourself how much you want to invest," Skip continued. "The rescuer can become the victim."

"What's that mean?" Monica asked.

"Sometimes you just can't save someone," Skip explained. "Sometimes you just gotta let them go. If you don't, you end up being victimized by their dysfunction. I think that is the case here: I don't think you can save Angie. I don't think Angie wants to be saved."

Monica thought about it for a moment. "Maybe you're right," she said.

"What's up with Milton?" Max asked, wondering what Milton's reaction was to Monica's adventures the previous week.

"He's not happy," Monica replied with a bit of a mischievous smile. "But he's not saying much. He likes to be in control of things, and he can't control everything. He knows that, and he works at it, but it still bothers him that I was out there 'in harm's way,' as he puts it, and he wasn't there to keep me all protected and stuff."

"Honestly," Skip said. "I wasn't too happy about you being 'in harm's way,' myself."

They sat again, looking out the window at Monica's car.

"Let's not do this again," Skip said after a while.

"You mean another case?" asked Max.

"Exactly," Skip replied.

Monica got up and gathered her purse. She was about to leave when she turned back to Max and Skip. "What made you think that I was worth saving?" she asked.

"What made you think that I wouldn't just make you the victims of my dysfunction?"

Max looked up at her and smiled. "We just needed a receptionist, that's all," he said.

"You weren't saving me?" she asked.

"Nope," said Skip. "We figured that if you were half the receptionist that you were a dancer, everyone would come out ahead from the arrangement."

Monica stood for a moment looking down at her friends seated at the table. She loved those two guys.

"I'm going to class," she announced.

"Good, your car is in the way. I can't see anything," Max replied.

Three weeks later

Monica walked back toward Skip's office with some papers in her hand. She knocked on the doorframe, causing him to look up.

"Will you sign these papers so I can take them down to First National Bank?" she asked, walking in and placing them on his desk in front of him.

"I was going to come up and do that," Skip said while he signed.

"You said that you were going to do that two hours ago," Monica replied, emphasizing the "said."

Skip handed the papers back, looking expectantly for her to say something.

"I'm out of here for the day," she said as she took the papers.

"Hey," Skip said before she could leave. "Hope you have fun at the wedding shower tonight."

"I'm sure it will be great," she said in a not-so-convinced manner.

"It will be fine," Skip said.

Monica went back to her desk and picked up the two checks that sat there, then left the office and locked the door behind her. Skip didn't like people walking in when he was there alone. She got into her car and drove out of the lot. She went north and took a back street across town, going a mile out of her way to avoid traffic on Lincolnway. The guys were rubbing off on her, she thought. She arrived at the bank and went inside.

As soon as she entered the bank she went straight to the glass front office where Max and Skip's personal banker sat at her desk.

"I got those papers signed, Leslie," Monica said, handing them to Leslie.

"Thanks," Leslie smiled. "What else you got there?" she nodded toward the checks in Monica's hand.

"I have to deposit these," Monica said.

"I can do that for you," Leslie said, reaching out to her.

Monica handed Leslie the checks and she took a quick look at them, frowning a little as she did.

"You wrote G&B Detective Agency a two-hundred dollar check and they turned around and wrote you a two-hundred dollar check?" she asked.

Monica rolled her eyes. "I sort of hired them to do a case for me, so I wrote them a check for services and expenses. Two hundred bucks. And then they turned around and gave me a bonus for helping them with my case," she explained. "It is dumb. They think it is hilarious. They laughed about it for two days. And then they gave me a raise." Monica was wishing that she hadn't brought up the raise.

"I'm in the wrong business," Leslie laughed.

"Trust me, it's like child care." Monica said. "It isn't easy."

"I'm sure that you earn every cent with those two," Leslie remarked. "Sit down and I'll be back."

While Leslie was gone, Monica texted Milton that she would meet him in the parking lot of the bank, across the street from City Hall and the police station, in a few minutes. She had timed it that way so that she could drive him home to his place. He texted back that he would be waiting.

When she finished her business and went out into the parking lot, she found Milton leaning against the driver's side door of her car. She fished her keys out of her purse and tossed them to him as she walked around to the passenger side. Milton caught them and unlocked the car.

"How was your day?" Monica asked as they drove out of the parking lot onto 6th Street and past the police station.

"Fine," Milton said. "Slow day." He paused a moment. "There's a detective opening, and I went over to HR and put in the paperwork to take the test."

"I thought that you are patrol through and through!" Monica questioned him. "Didn't you say that investigations are too boring for you?"

"I'm rethinking that," Milton replied. "I'm thinking that eight-to-five, Monday through Friday, is sounding better."

"And on call one week every month," Monica added.

"That's as good as it gets with police work," Milton said. "They hardly ever get called out."

"Are you doing this because you think that you would like to be a detective," Monica asked, "or are you doing it for me?"

"I'm doing it for us," Milton said. "You, me and Essie."

Monica didn't say anything.

"What about the big wedding shower tonight?" Milton asked, changing the subject. "I think that Essie and I are going to go out to eat. Someplace really nice, white tablecloths, expensive wine, fancy waiters."

"Yeah, right," Monica said. "Meanwhile, Shawna and I will be sitting there with all of the women connected with the PD, none of whom we know, sizing us up to see if we are worthy."

"Gloria and Marjorie are going to be there," Milton said.

"I didn't know that they were invited," Monica replied.

"I'll bet they give you something nice," Milton remarked.

"Great," Monica said sarcastically. "My bosses' wives, a bunch of lady cops, me, and my opinionated mother who thinks all the police are corrupt thugs. What could go wrong?"

Milton thought for a moment. "Not all cops," he finally said. "I think that she likes me."

Made in the USA
Las Vegas, NV
28 February 2023

68277552R00194